D1024459

PRAISE FOR

Lord's charming new mystery is so full of love for books... readers will eat it up. Full of homespun characters and curious goings-on, Lord's mystery is a love letter to both Dickens and to the small town amateur detectives who've kept the peace in hamlets from River Heights to Cabot Cove.

—Chelsea Cain, *New York Times* best-selling thriller writer

Christopher Lord has all but immortalized Charles Dickens—his characters, his enthralling sense of story, his entire fictional universe. From the opening pages, *The Christmas Carol Murders* is an enjoyable contemporary spin on the lush psychological environs of Dickens's own territory. With this story of a small town bookseller turned gumshoe, Lord emerges as a bright new voice in mystery.

—Evan P. Schneider, author of
A Simple Machine, Like the Lever

THE CHRISTMAS CAROL MURDERS

A delicious romp through the world of Dickens wonderfully imagined in the twenty-first century by Christopher Lord. *The Christmas Carol Murders* has it all: mystery, eccentric characters galore and a touch of frivolity. You don't have to be a Dickens fan to fall in love with this novel.

—Margaret Coel, author of *Buffalo Bill's Dead Now*

The Christmas Carol Murders is a smart, satisfying and contemporary twist on the literary landscape of Charles Dickens. It features a likeably urbane amateur detective, an unforgettable cast of supporting characters, and a juicy mystery that puts the trappings of Christmas Past, Present, and Future to new and grisly uses. Whether you've read Charles Dickens or not, *The Christmas Carol Murders* will delight and surprise you.

—Pamela Smith Hill, award-winning
author of *Laura Ingalls Wilder: A Writer's Life*

THE CHRISTMAS CAROL MURDERS

BEING THE FIRST DICKENS JUNCTION MYSTERY

by

CHRISTOPHER LORD

The Christmas Carol Murders

Harrison Thurman Books, Portland 97210

Illustrations by Tina Granzo.
Book design by Alan Dubinsky.
Editing and production by Indigo Editing & Publications.

Printed in the United States of America.
21 20 19 18 17 16 15 14 13 12   1 2 3 4 5

ISBN: 978-0-9853236-0-8

Library of Congress Control Number: 2012935363

For Stephen

My earliest "reading" memory: when I was six, my eleven-year-old brother took me to a summer children's event at the Astoria Public Library. During a contest where thirty children competed for prizes by shouting out answers to book-related questions, he whispered, "Say 'Tiny Tim.'"

He raised my hand for me, and I shouted out those two words.

The answer was, indeed, Tiny Tim. The prize: this memory.

I miss you.

But I am sure I have always thought of Christmas...as a good time: a kind, forgiving, charitable, pleasant time: the only time I know of, in the long calendar of the year, when men and women seem by one consent to open their shut-up hearts freely, and to think of people below them as if they really were fellow-passengers to the grave, and not another race of creatures bound on other journeys. And therefore...though it has never put a scrap of gold or silver in my pocket, I believe that it has *done me good, and* will *do me good; and I say, God bless it!*

—From *A Christmas Carol,* by Charles Dickens

I came here to say that I do not recognize anyone's right to one minute of my life. Nor to any part of my energy. Nor to any achievement of mine. No matter who makes the claim, how large their number or how great their need. I wished to come here and say that I am a man who does not exist for others.

—From *The Fountainhead,* by Ayn Rand

There never was such a goose.

—Charles Dickens

THE CHRISTMAS CAROL MURDERS

BEING THE FIRST DICKENS JUNCTION MYSTERY

by

CHRISTOPHER LORD

MAPS & ILLUSTRATIONS
by
TINA GRANZO

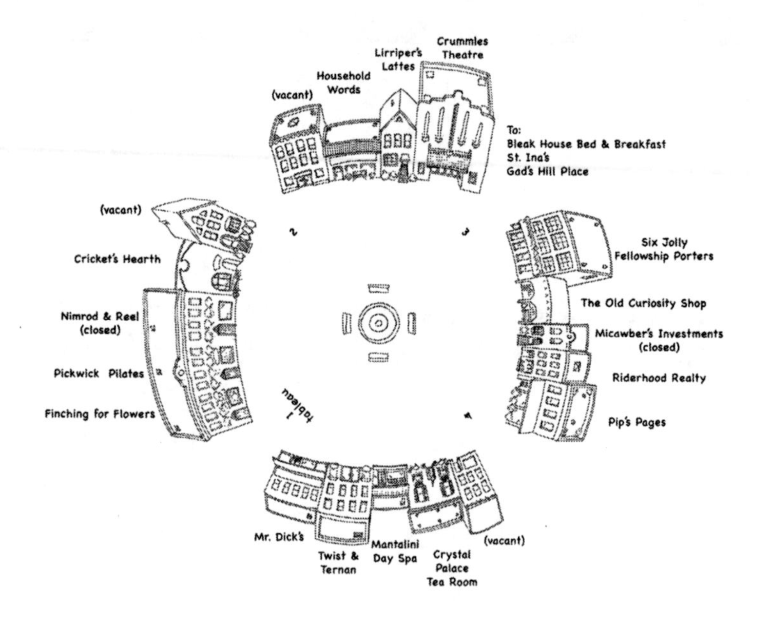

Zach's Map of Dickens Junction, Business District

Detective Boggs's List of Suspects

Simon Alastair, owner, Pip's Pages

Grace Beddoes, owner, Cricket's Hearth Cards and Gifts

Zach Benjamin, reporter, *Rainbows*, a travel magazine

Dagny Clack, CEO, Marley Enterprises

Solomon Dick, mayor, Dickens Junction; owner, Mr. Dick's Sandwich Shop

Father Blaise Gilmore, rector, St. Ina's Episcopal Church

Viola Mintun, owner, the Crystal Palace Tearoom

Ariadne Neff, principal broker, Riderhood Realty

Duncan Neff, investments advisor, formerly of Micawber Investments (closed)

Brock Spurlock, Simon's assistant at Pip's Pages and personal trainer

Mavis Spurlock, owner/innkeeper, Bleak House Bed and Breakfast

Bradford Sturgess, publisher/editor-in-chief of *Household Words*, a weekly newspaper

Charity Wilkinson, high school English teacher

Other Junxonians/Visitors

George Bascomb, artist, Simon's oldest friend

Josephine Boggs, detective, Clatsop County Sheriff's Office

Lowell Brundish, owner, Nimrod and Reel Tackle Shop (closed)

Joelle Creevy, owner, the Six Jolly Fellowship Porters, a restaurant and pub

Ladasha Creevy, chef de cuisine, Bleak House

Bethany Cruse, Simon's housekeeper/chef, Gad's Hill Place

Elmer Cuttle, Dickens Junction resident

Allegra Dick, the mayor's wife

Mervin Roark, acquisitions, Marley Enterprises

Miss Lucretia Tox, Simon's Devon rex

Mimsie Tricket, Dickens Junction resident

Sebastian Venable, amanuensis to Dagny Clack

STAVE 1

MARLEY'S GHOST

No one was dead: to begin with.

Simon Alastair stood behind the counter at Pip's Pages, looking through the plate-glass windows that faced Dickens Square. Ten days before Christmas. Things should be busier. Only a few customers had been in all day, so Simon had given his young assistant, Brock Spurlock, the afternoon off with pay to help set up tonight's tableaux. There was Brock now, across the square, his wide shoulders stretching the fabric of his gray hoodie; he was hoisting one of the backdrops that would stand behind the actors portraying Scrooge being visited by Marley's Ghost.

As Simon moved toward the back room to get his sport coat and leave for lunch, he heard the shop bell. Along with a rush of chilly air came a small man wearing a well-tailored black heather wool topcoat. *Not from around here,* Simon thought—no Junxonian wore such a coat in this wet climate, even on a dry day like today.

"I'm looking for a book," the man said. He had an accent Simon couldn't quite place—Boston? Tulsa? Not the flat notes of an Oregonian. The five-foot-five stranger was half a head shorter than Simon, with close-cropped hair and rimless glasses framing pale brown eyes. He pulled a slip of paper from a black leather briefcase. "*Atlas Shrugged*," he said. "By Ayn Rand." He pronounced it correctly; Rand's one-syllable first name rhymed with *mine.* Simon was impressed by that at least, if not by the stranger's cologne. Too much musk.

Simon gestured that the man should follow him. "In the young adult section, just over here."

"It's a children's book?" he asked, following Simon across the store. "I didn't think…"

Simon stood in front of the Nancy Drew and Dana Girls shelves, one hand gesturing toward the adjacent racks. "People should read Ms. Rand early, and get her out of their systems, so they can move on to other authors," he said, handing the stranger a paperback copy of *Atlas Shrugged.*

"It's big," the stranger said, taking the book from Simon.

"Yes, but the ideas in it are small." Realizing that he was being rude, Simon stepped away and returned to the register nearby. "You're not familiar with Rand?"

The stranger read the back cover. He looked up at Simon. "I'm new—" He stopped, then began again. "I mean, I'm curious about her." He bent his head and examined the shelves, first other Rand titles, then books throughout the store. "You have a lopsided inventory," he said. "All of this Capote, but no Tom Clancy? A whole shelf of Faulkner, but nothing by Ken Follett?"

Simon smiled. "I only stock books that I have read," he said. "I want to give my customers the best recommendations possible, if they ask."

"Hard to make a living that way, I'd think."

Simon looked down. The stranger sported hand-stitched cap-toe brogues. Barely scuffed soles. Money and taste. Clean fingernails; no ring. Maybe forty-six or so, Simon's age. But hardly Simon's type. Especially his reading tastes.

"Fortunately," said Simon, "my livelihood does not depend solely on bookstore sales."

"That must be nice," the stranger said. Simon didn't care for the sinister note in his voice.

The stranger reached toward a display of seasonal titles. He grabbed a trade paperback of Dickens's *Christmas Books* and brought the two volumes to the counter.

"An excellent choice," said Simon. He rang up the purchases and put the books into a small shopping bag. "Particularly today. Are you staying for the tableaux?"

"It depends," the stranger said, handing Simon his credit card.

Mervin Roark. A hard name, not very fluid. Simon processed the card and handed Roark the slip to sign. "Thank you, Mr. Roark."

"Thank you, Mr. Alastair." Roark smiled. Beautiful veneers, maybe too large for his face. Roark had missed shaving a small patch of brown stubble under his chin.

"You know my name?"

Roark looked at Simon as he placed the books in his briefcase. "Everyone I visited today talked about your connection to this town." His voice had deepened. He pulled open his winter coat and suit jacket enough to reveal an aubergine herringbone tie above a cream-colored, custom-tailored dress shirt with thick mother-of-pearl buttons. He placed a deep-purple-edged card on the glass counter, turned so that Simon could read it.

Simon picked up the card. Old-fashioned card stock. Engraved. The logo was a large ornate dollar sign.

"I've never heard of your company," said Simon.

"You have now," Roark said, flashing the oyster-white teeth. "Perhaps you'll see me later," he added. Roark gave Simon an enigmatic smile—smirk?—as he exited the bookstore.

Puzzled but still hungry, Simon decided that he had time to dash over to the Crystal Palace Tearoom and pick up something to go. He set the hands of the Be Back Soon clock for one and locked the door behind him.

Dickens Square, designed in 1950 by Simon's grandfather as the central civic attraction of the then newly incorporated city of Dickens Junction, was a pedestrian area lined with shops. A central fountain drew the visitor's gaze to its towering monument. The statue was to have been of Charles Dickens, the Inimitable Boz himself, but after Ebenezer Dickens Jr. commissioned it, he learned that Dickens disdained memorials, wanting to be remembered solely by his work. So the statue, already cast, was modified to accommodate interchangeable screw-on bronze heads that could be attached at different times of the year. The current head was Ebenezer Scrooge's, a face too gaunt for the well-fed torso of the mature Boz that rested beneath it. After New Year's Day, the egg-shaped head of Wilkins Micawber would replace it, a genial visage more suited to the body it completed.

Today, bundled-up children and parents sat on the benches around the monument, feeding birds and squirrels, taking advantage of the dry, crisp weather. Some watched Brock and other able-bodied volunteers wrestle with the painted plywood backdrops and props that would accompany the four *Christmas Carol* scenes to be staged that evening.

From the other end of the square, the purple tunic-and-tights-clad figure of Simon's friend Grace Beddoes emerged from Mr. Dick's Sandwich Shop and walked with a brown lunch sack toward her own business, Cricket's Hearth Cards and Gifts. She clutched her wool cap in the breeze, and apparently didn't see Simon's wave.

Simon supposed he should also frequent his relative's business, but didn't want to eat the inexpensive but less-than-savory fare Solomon Dick served up as a flimsy cover for the video poker machines that were the moneymaking arm of the business. Although they were both great-grandsons of the two Dick brothers who had arrived in Clatsop County years earlier, Simon and Solomon weren't particularly close. Simon had voted for Mavis Spurlock in the last mayoral election, and suspected that his cousin knew it.

Mayor Dick and the aldermen had acquired new holiday decorations for each of the four blocks of buildings that faced Dickens Square. The heavy, natural-looking garlands swung from the building corners as Simon walked past the vacant storefront next to Pip's Pages and into the Crystal Palace. A warm breath of spiced air greeted him as he entered.

The Crystal Palace Tearoom had been owned and operated for the last fifteen years by Viola Mintun, a full-figured handsome woman of fifty-five, who greeted Simon at the door. The Victorian tearoom was an explosion of lace and ruffles, tassels and filigree, starched linens, Spode and pale blue Wedgwood china, and heavy flatware. In addition to serving traditional high tea, complete with cucumber and watercress sandwiches and scones with Devonshire cream, the restaurant also offered contemporary fare.

"A chicken Caesar salad to go," said Simon, after he had pulled away from Viola's warm hug. "I should be at the store—in case holiday shoppers suddenly descend in droves." He gave Viola a pained smile. Half of the tearoom's twelve tables were unoccupied.

"We should all be so lucky," Viola said. She entered his order on the laptop in front of her. Viola was dressed in tailored, navy wool pants and a pale-green shell that complemented her light freckled complexion and spiked short red hair.

A few minutes later, while Simon and Viola chatted, a young woman dressed in a black-and-white parlormaid uniform brought out a crisp paper bag and handed it to Simon.

"Thank you, Caitlin," said Simon. The young woman curtsied and went to help other customers.

As Viola made change, Simon noticed on the counter, next to a pristine scratch-off lottery ticket, the same purple-edged card he had been given moments earlier. "You were visited by Marley Enterprises, too, I see?"

Viola picked up the card and examined it. "Someone left this with Caitlin. Said he would stop by later to see me."

"He visited me, too," said Simon. He looked above the front window's lace curtain. "There he is now."

Mervin Roark was leaving Lirriper's Lattes and striding toward Riderhood Realty.

Viola peered out along with Simon. "What did he want?"

"From me? Just a book."

Viola handed Simon his change. "Not from around here, is he?"

Simon shook his head as he opened the tearoom door. "Please let me know what he wants as soon as you've seen him."

When Simon returned to Pip's Pages, a customer was standing in front of the holiday window display. A black leather bomber jacket accented the man's muscular back and narrow waist. As Simon unlocked the door, the man turned to face him.

"Are you Pip?" the man asked.

"If you wish." Simon waved his arm through the open door, letting the man precede him into the store. Simon put his salad on the counter and turned.

The stranger extended his large hand. "Zach Benjamin," he said with a smile. His straight white teeth shone like mirrors against olive skin. He was model-handsome, with curly jet hair, a clean-shaven jaw, and piercing blue eyes. Taller than Simon by an inch or two, and several years younger.

Simon shook Zach's hand. "Simon Alastair."

That smile again. "Much better than Pip, I think," Zach said. "More serious—more literary, perhaps."

A dark, rich baritone. Simon was intrigued. "What can I do for you, Mr. Benjamin?"

"Zach, please," he said. He had a leather messenger bag slung over his shoulder. He reached in and pulled out a recent issue of *Rainbows*, a monthly gay and lesbian travel magazine. He opened to a page in the back and pointed at an ad for Pip's Pages. "This brought me here."

Even better, Simon thought. "The ad has been good for business," he said. "Dickens Junction is a welcoming community. What can I do for you?"

Zach held out the opened magazine to an article titled, "He Sells Seychelles."

"'By Zach Benjamin,'" Simon read. Zach's broad, manicured thumb covered part of a photograph of a vanilla-bean plantation.

Simon was close enough to sense Zach's smell, a combination of cloves and that cold dryness of the outdoors. "The Seychelles are on my list."

Zach put the magazine back in the bag. "I'll keep that—and you—in mind if I'm ever sent back there." He looked around the bookstore. "*Rainbows* wants a story about the charms of this little village." He paused. "Unfortunately, I'm supposed to drive back to Portland tonight and fly to LA in the morning. What can I see in a few hours?"

Simon led Zach to the windows. The Dickens Carolers strolled through the square, two men in black velvet overcoats and trousers and two women with green taffeta skirts over full Victorian capes. One female caroler's hands were tucked into an oversized fur muff. The men sported black beaver hats; the women wore matching wide-brimmed bonnets.

"'The Junction,' as most of the locals call it, has charms all year long," said Simon, "but the holidays are special. You can see the *Christmas Carol* tableaux this evening, but if you leave so soon, you'll miss the village display competition, the Fezziwig Ball, and so much more."

Zach's face was close to Simon's. After a moment, they turned to face each other. Zach's eyes moved up and down. Simon could smell the mint on Zach's breath. "I like what I've seen so far," Zach said.

The guy was assertive. Simon liked that. A lot.

Out of embarrassment at that thought, Simon moved a step away. "I would volunteer to be your guide, but I need to keep the store open until six, and I'll be getting ready for the tableaux at seven. I portray one of the Scrooges, so..."

"No worries," Zach said. "I like to find my own way, at least for a while. But how about a drink when you get done posing?"

A drink would be good. "Sure. Meet me at the Porters here on the square. The tableaux are over at nine—if that's not too late."

"I look forward to it."

Zach exited the shop with a confident step, looked one way, then another, hands in his pockets. Simon continued to watch until Zach disappeared into Lirriper's Lattes.

He didn't see Zach again in the square that afternoon, but more than once he caught sight of Mervin Roark: looking in the window of Twist and Ternan's, as if notions were the most important things in the world; talking earnestly with Viola Mintun as she tried to cross the square; coming out of Cricket's Hearth. He last saw Roark at four fifteen, leaving Mr. Dick's and heading into the neighborhood beyond the square, toward Bleak House Bed and Breakfast, St. Ina's Episcopal Church, and City Hall.

A few minutes after that, mayor Solomon Dick entered the bookstore. A ruddy-faced man of sixty, stout and hearty, Simon's distant cousin reminded him of a Dickens character in modern dress. "Business not so good?" Dick asked, looking around the empty store. He didn't wait for Simon's answer. "I've had to donate half my sandwiches this week."

"Sorry to hear it." Simon asked about the mayor's wife, who was out of town visiting a sister recovering from surgery.

"Allegra will be back for the Fezziwig Ball. Thanks for asking." He rubbed his bulbous nose with his sleeve. "Had a visitor today," he added. He hitched up the waistband of his pants and tucked in the wrinkled white dress shirt, pulling it even tighter across his belly. "Thought I saw him come in here earlier, too. A little man named Roark."

Simon lifted his eyes to the mayor's. "Yes, he was here."

"Did he tell you why he was in the Junction?"

"He did not."

Outside, Brock had finished putting up the tableaux sets and was placing other needed props: Scrooge's tombstone, the Cratchit dining table, the cap for the Ghost of Christmas Past.

"It's turning out to be an interesting holiday season," Dick said. He rocked on the balls of his feet.

Simon tried to remain patient. "What does Roark want?"

"Property," Dick said. "He wants property. Mine, to be specific." In addition to the building that housed his sandwich shop, Dick also owned the two adjoining properties leased to

Twist and Ternan's and the Mantalini Day Spa. Viola Mintun owned the Crystal Palace and the adjacent vacant storefront that completed one block of the square.

"For what purpose?" Simon asked.

The mayor smiled; he had wanted a reaction from Simon—and gotten it—*but why?* "He didn't say. But he's willing to pay a lot of money for it. A. Lot. Of. Money."

Simon tried to act nonchalant. "Are you interested?"

The mayor put his thumbs on his chest, as if tucking them under nonexistent suspenders. "I'm meeting him later at the house," he said. "Before the tableaux. It depends on how much he sweetens the pot."

Simon needed to be careful. "The character of this community is important to me," he said. "We have something to preserve here in the Junction. The square's property owners—"

The mayor's face got red; a vein on the side of his head throbbed. "You don't need to tell me about community. My side of the family has been here as long as yours." As if he regretted this outburst, he paused. "The other owners aren't rich like you—Brundish, for example. You don't like change. But this time you might not be able to prevent it." The mayor checked his watch. "I've got to get back. See you at the tableaux." Dick opened the door and left. A breeze blew in a random scrap of paper. Simon caught it midair. An expired Mirrorball lottery ticket, someone's dashed dream. Simon tossed it in the wastebasket.

The mayor's rebuke stung. Simon believed that his grandfather would be proud of the traditions that he had carried on.

His grandparents had raised him after his parents, Ebenezer III ("Trey") and Sharon, were killed in an automobile collision in 1968. Upon their son's and daughter-in-law's deaths, Grandpa Ebbie and Grandma Melanie had brought three-year-old Simon to Dickens Junction to live. When he finished his graduate studies, as a statement of his independence, Simon legally changed his name, as his grandfather Ebenezer Dick had done before him for the same reason. Simon opened Pip's Pages the following year.

Simon closed the shop a few minutes before six. Since he had sold several titles from the window display during the day, he went outside to determine what he needed to restock in the window. As he stood at the window, Lowell Brundish opened the door of Riderhood Realty next door, almost colliding with him as he tried to move past.

"Excuse me," Simon said diplomatically.

Brundish was in his early sixties, a lumpen sort with unshaven jowls, high forehead, and basset-hound eyes. Although his own business, Nimrod and Reel Tackle Shop, had closed several months ago, an early victim of the economic downturn, Brundish still owned the building it had been in and the adjacent two buildings on the opposite side of the square. Grace Beddoes owned the building housing her store and the other vacant storefront at the end of that block.

"Sorry," Brundish said, his voice hoarse. "I have a few things on my mind." He left the square via the exit next to Mr. Dick's.

Simon restocked the window display and then went to his back-room office to check e-mail on his laptop. One e-mail got his immediate attention.

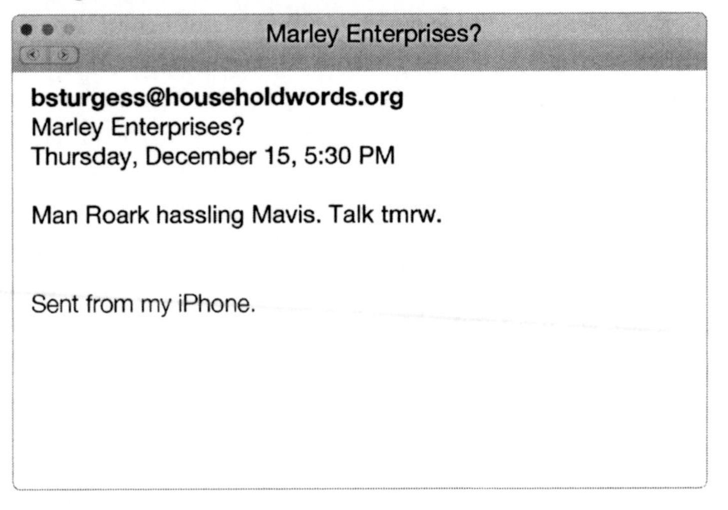

Everyone, it seemed, was walking about with Marley Enterprises on their lips.

Mavis Spurlock, Brock's mother, had been Simon's grandparents' housekeeper and now owned Bleak House, the bed and breakfast just off the square. Why was Roark "hassling" Mavis, and why, instead of calling Simon, would she tell Bradford Sturgess?

Simon started to type *Marley Enterprises* into a search engine, but then checked his watch. *Time to prepare for the tableaux.* He powered down the computer and pushed himself away from the desk.

His costume, a white, full-length, man's heavy muslin nightshirt, hung on the coatrack. After removing his work clothes, he put on a thermal top and bottom, then plunged his arms into the nightshirt sleeves and thrust his head through the neck hole, letting the nightshirt fall.

Simon picked up the wig with its wisps of gray fringe and, holding it by his fingertips, checked himself in the mirror. His real hair, short and graying, was rumpled from contact with the nightshirt. Otherwise a good-looking man with a decent build and flat stomach, now hidden under the stiff muslin. *Good-looking enough to attract someone, say, in his late thirties? Probably not in this outfit.* He pulled the wig onto his head, tucking in his hair, and dabbed spirit gum on the latex flaps that came down to the bridge of his nose and sides of his ears. It wouldn't withstand scrutiny, but he'd be partly in shadow, and every Junxonian already knew him and what role he played.

He reached over and got the kneepads from Brock's high school football gear. He strapped them on and dropped to the ground. Since he would be kneeling for two hours, these were a must. A last touch—the flesh-colored gloves that Brad Sturgess, one of last year's Scrooges, had loaned him. "A godsend," Sturgess had said. "Otherwise your hands will freeze."

Still on his knees in front of the mirror, Simon put his gloved hands in front of his face as the tableau pose required. Simon was practiced at this ritual, one of the many that Grandfather Ebbie had started. A favorite picture, framed on Simon's bedside table, showed his father, Trey, dressed as Bob

Cratchit, posing with two-year-old Simon as Tiny Tim, taken in 1967, the Christmas before Simon's parents were killed.

He had grown up with his grandfather's philanthropy and awareness of the responsibilities that having money gives—should give—to those who have it. Dickens Junction was founded on that principle, laid down by Ebbie Dickens, passed on to his son Trey (who hadn't lived long enough to leave a legacy), and now to Simon himself. Simon loved the Dickens Junction pageantry and pomp—Yarmouth Winter, the Barnaby Rudge Maypole Dance, Bastille Day and the breaking of the wine cask, the changing of the heads in the square, all of the *Christmas Carol* events.

Everything was stable in Dickens Junction. It had been for years. *Maybe the economy has taken a small dip downward,* Simon thought, *but it's bound to bounce back again, and then everything will be as it was before.*

Mervin Roark and Marley Enterprises threatened the future of Dickens Junction, Simon was sure of it, without knowing why. But he was going to find out. Soon. Tomorrow. After the tableaux. Now it was time to go.

STAVE

THE FIRST OF THE BODIES

The Dickens Carolers strolled through the square among the bundled-up crowd, singing "God Rest Ye Merry, Gentlemen." Their breath smoked in the late autumn cold. A large crowd had gathered near Mr. Dick's, the shop closest to the first scene. The Porters had set up a stand for free coffee, tea, and hot cider. An aroma of apples and cinnamon wafted through the air.

Simon got into position at the edge of the foam-board tombstone etched with the name of Ebenezer Scrooge. He was already starting to feel the evening chill under the thermal wear. He was careful to make sure his face was turned so that he wasn't looking directly into the floodlights several feet in front of him. They weren't on yet, but they would be soon.

Next to Simon, Brock was making one final adjustment to the Ghost of Christmas Yet to Come. Using a dummy for the ghost, Simon thought, had been a great idea. It saved using an actor whose face wouldn't be seen anyway under the voluminous cowl of the ghost's floor-length black robe.

"He's heavier than I remember," Brock mumbled. He held the dolly handle that stuck out from a small hole in the back of the ghost's robe. The dummy had been strapped to the dolly and carefully draped with the robe and cowl, everything moving as a single piece. Brock tilted the contraption to position it correctly. The skeletal hand wobbled. "That second trip to the storage shed took me a little longer than I thought," he continued. He wiped a muscular forearm across his brow and short light-brown hair. "Dr. Doom here"—he cocked his head, indicating the dummy—"hadn't been put in the right place after last week's dress rehearsal. I found him in a corner behind an old refrigerator box."

"You'll have to take that up with Duncan Neff," Simon whispered.

"That's another funny thing," Brock said. "When I got to the shed for the second load, Neff was inside, poking around in the near dark."

A small boy was about to step into the tableau, his pudgy outstretched hand ready to grab the ghost's bony claw. Simon started shaking his head and almost stood, but the boy's mother, a sheepish smile on her face, pulled the inquisitive child away.

"He said he was looking for his Bob Cratchit muffler," Brock continued. He positioned the dummy and stood away. The cowl, which covered the dummy's head (an old soccer ball, Simon recalled), draped dramatically forward in a black puddle of cloth. Nothing showed beneath. "I just don't trust the dude," Brock added.

Simon looked across the square. Neff was standing beside the Cratchit home backdrop in the Ghost of Christmas Present scene, winding a long knitted muffler around his neck.

"Well, he found it," said Simon.

Neff, recently unemployed from the collapse of Micawber Investments, wouldn't have been Simon's choice for Bob Cratchit. He lacked the giving spirit that Simon thought Cratchit should have. Nevertheless, he looked passable in the part and, as one of the town's three aldermen, was expected to play a prominent role in Junxonian festivities.

The young boy playing Tiny Tim was standing beside him. Simon didn't blame Neff for not putting the boy on his shoulder one second before he had to—holding a child, as Simon knew from his stint as Scrooge's long-suffering assistant three years ago, was much harder than kneeling for two hours. The boy was pretending that his crutch was a rifle.

The Dickens Carolers had stopped singing. Simon heard the prerecorded music start over the loudspeakers. The floodlights came on, startling him.

"I better scoot. See you, boss," Brock said, vanishing into the dark past Simon's field of vision.

"Psst." Simon squinted to see past the circle of light and caught the gleam of Zach Benjamin's teeth.

"You're not supposed to move," Zach said. He stood closer now, bringing the outline of his body barely out of the shadows.

"Don't make me break character any further, then," said Simon.

"Don't give me a challenge," Zach said. He took Simon's picture with his cell phone. "Looking forward to the drink—or drinks. See you later," he added, and blended back into the dark.

A drink—or two—would be nice—for several reasons. Simon's knees were already beginning to hurt, and a martini with Zach was two long hours away. Simon forced his attention away from the too-thin rubber of the kneepads. Since no one had arrived yet at his scene, he shifted his glance away from the dummy to observe the crowd. There was the handsome father Blaise Gilmore, rector of St. Ina's Episcopal Church, chatting with Charity Wilkinson, another alderman and high school English teacher in nearby Astoria. Viola Mintun, Wilkinson's spouse, stood nearby. Several members of the crowd stepped back so that Father Blaise could be among the first clutch of people moving through the scenes.

The Marley's Ghost Scrooge, one of the many Clatsop Community College students helping with the tableaux, had done a good job using makeup to make himself look older. The elderly Junxonian playing Marley was shackled with yards of

EBENEZE
SCROOGE

cardboard chains, cashboxes, and a safe, all painted pale gray and suspended from wires, giving the chains a lovely drape that helped them sway in the breeze.

Father Blaise moved to the next scene—Scrooge and the Ghost of Christmas Past—and the group was briefly out of Simon's sight. Old Scrooge and the Ghost, this year played by a ten-year-old girl, were caught at the moment in which the young Scrooge's sister, Fan, rushes into his schoolroom to invite him home for the holidays. As the group came back into Simon's view, Charity leaned into Father Blaise and whispered something, making him nod and smile.

Simon watched Ariadne Neff push through the crowd at the third tableau and then wedge herself between Father Blaise and Charity, who moved closer to Viola to give Ariadne access. Mayor Dick, on Viola's other side, also moved a step away. Ariadne was carrying an umbrella and wearing a slick bright yellow raincoat.

In the scene, Ariadne's husband, Duncan, had Tiny Tim hoisted on his shoulder, caught in mid-celebration of the Cratchit family's legendary holiday goose, while Scrooge and the Ghost of Christmas Present, another college student wearing a theatrical beard and hidden eight-inch height extenders under a crimson brocaded robe, looked on. Tiny Tim wiggled his nose at Father Blaise. Simon noticed also that Zach had worked his way into the group. Zach alternated his gaze between Father Blaise and Ariadne Neff. Next to Zach, Grace Beddoes was dressed for warmth in a black tunic, tights, and a down jacket.

Through his fingers, which he was holding still in front of his eyes in character of the terrified Scrooge, Simon watched Father Blaise and the others approach. This close, Simon could hear individual comments, whispers of recognition and delight. The dummy's bone-white skeletal hand pointed down, swaying lightly.

Father Blaise's dark gaze shifted from Simon to the ghost. Then Father Blaise looked down, eyes wide, the whites clear and gleaming in the floodlights. At the same time, the priest's bemused smile flattened into a thin, grim line. In his peripheral vision, Simon saw what the priest must have seen: something moving on the ground, a glint, a dark pool spreading away from the hem of the ghost's robe toward Simon.

Brushing past Grace and Zach, Father Blaise entered the tableau. Simon pressed his palms against the ground and pushed himself to his feet. When he raised his hands, the flesh-colored gloves were moist and stained maroon.

A woman screamed. Someone in the crowd fainted.

Simon and Father Blaise now stood shoulder to shoulder in front of the dummy. Father Blaise pushed back the cowl.

Simon gasped.

The skeletal hand fell to the ground.

Simon didn't immediately recognize the slack, all-too-human cheekbones, the rictus of death exposing the too big, too bright teeth, or the lifeless pale brown eyes. In a jagged slash of light, however, he saw the small unshaved patch at the chin line; beneath that, the loosely knotted purple tie stained with drops of black blood;

and, between those two features, the chiseled point of the narrow spike that had pierced the dead man's neck.

At ten thirty that evening, Simon and Zach sat in a high-backed dark-pine booth at the Six Jolly Fellowship Porters. Zach ate the last bite of his fish and chips. Simon took his fork and nudged a crumble of bleu cheese in his Cobb salad. With help from Brock, Zach had retrieved Simon's street clothes from the bookstore, so Simon was back in chinos and his cotton shirt, now limp with perspiration.

Joelle Creevy, proprietress of the Porters, had established a private interview room in her office; a while earlier, Simon had given his statement to detective sergeant Josephine Boggs of the Clatsop County Sheriff's Department. In another corner of the pub, Father Blaise was comforting witnesses, although, from Simon's perspective, the priest didn't appear his usual calm and reassuring self. Other patrons sat at tables and talked in low voices. Joelle had turned off the big screen televisions. The Porters was quieter than normal, although Simon occasionally heard a muted clang from one of the video gaming machines in another corner of the bar.

Simon pushed away the salad. "Why would someone kill Roark? What was he after, anyway, beyond trying to buy up the mayor's property?" Simon shook his head as the consequences of what he had seen, what had happened, flashed into his head.

"You have a problem," Zach said.

Simon looked at the beautiful man across the table from him. Yes, he had a problem—they all did, now. All Simon wanted was what was best for Dickens Junction, for the people who shared his grandfather's vision of philanthropy, of goodwill.

"This will devastate the Junction," said Simon, nearly choking with emotion. "The economy—and now this? What my grandfather built, what he believed in, could all be destroyed." He paused. "We've never had a murder before. Vandalism, thievery, college hijinks, but nothing like this."

Zach wiped his mouth with his napkin. "You have a problem," he repeated.

He had missed a dab of ketchup below his lower lip; Simon's instinct was to reach over and wipe it away, but he resisted. Instead, he leaned back against the tall hardwood booth and contemplated Zach's face in the dim light. A handsome face. An intelligent face. At the same time, he knew he was resisting the challenge in Zach's words.

"Why do you say this is my problem?" Simon asked. He saw Detective Boggs emerging from Joelle's office with Ariadne Neff, who had been with the detective for some time. Ariadne broke away from the detective and left through the back door near the pool tables. Boggs caught Simon's glance and began walking toward him.

Simon returned his gaze to Zach, a part of him afraid to hear the answer. Zach was poised to leap—at Simon or away from him, Simon wasn't sure—his forearm tendons twitching as he reached forward and put his hand on top of Simon's. "Don't you know this town—these people—better than the police do? You've lived here nearly your whole life, haven't you? You have to investigate and bring the killer to justice."

Simon was conflicted; Zach's words were a challenge, his touch sexy, reassuring. "That sounds melodramatic," said Simon. "I wouldn't know the first thing to do, how to avoid getting in the way of the police, what to ask."

"I could help," Zach said. He squeezed Simon's hand.

"Sorry to bother you, Simon," Detective Boggs said, stopping in front their table. The detective was in her early thirties, with curly auburn hair worn long and full, framing her high, angled cheekbones. She wore a severely tailored navy skirt and blazer over a cream boatneck shell, a Kate Spade bag across one shoulder. She strode confidently on long, lithe, fashion-model legs. Simon had met her several months earlier at an Astoria Chamber of Commerce networking meeting, and knew that she had recently relocated from Los Angeles. She had a California-girl beauty that, combined with a fierce intelligence, made even Simon look at her twice.

Simon eased his hand from under Zach's, immediately missing the weight of Zach's palm. Their hands remained close, almost touching; Simon still felt warmth radiating from Zach's fingertips.

"As a result of the other interviews I've conducted," the detective said, "I have some follow-up questions." She looked toward the two men's hands. "But they can wait until morning. I'll call you tomorrow," she said in a tone that conveyed a change of mind. She turned on her four-inch navy heels and exited the pub.

Simon turned back to Zach. Zach had accomplished one thing—after his last comment, Simon's focus on the murder and the fate of the Junction had been muddled by more personal, intimate feelings. "How could you help? I thought you were going back to Southern California tomorrow."

"Well"—Zach pointed to his cell phone on the table—"I made a few calls while Detective Boggs was taking your statement. I've negotiated a little postponement in my next deadline. So I could stay a few days..."

"But?"

"There are no rooms available anywhere nearby," Zach said. "Mrs. Creevy was kind enough to check for me, but nothing—unless I wish to occupy the dead man's room at Bleak House, and then only after the police complete their search tomorrow."

"I've got plenty of room at Gad's Hill Place," said Simon. "You could stay in the Growlery."

Zach leaned forward. "I'm already intrigued."

Even with so much anxiety in the air, Zach was flirting with him. Simon didn't know whether to be appalled or attracted. "You haven't read much Dickens, have you?"

"Guilty," Zach said. "*Great Expectations* in high school; *Mr. Magoo's A Christmas Carol*, of course, and I was Third Pickpocket from the Left in our high school production of *Oliver!* Do those count?"

"Not for much." Simon smiled for the first time in several hours. "The Growlery is the name for a cozy room in *Bleak House.* A place of retreat. In other words, my main guest room. You should find it comfortable enough."

"If it's not an imposition—"

"Not at all. It will be reassuring not to be alone in the house."

Simon signaled to Joelle Creevy. The diminutive African American behind the bar tore up the check, the pieces drifting away from her slender dark fingers. She smiled. Simon mouthed a silent thanks.

The two men stood to leave. "Growlery." Zach rolled the word around his mouth, his voice half-questioning. "I've never been much for bears."

SIMON'S FEW HOURS OF SLEEP WERE TORTURED BY HALF-formed images of nails, blood, and hands, both alive and skeletal, reaching for him from the darkness. One of the hands was Zach's. When Simon awoke he wondered, *Have I invited a murderer to my house?* At sunrise, he admitted defeat, got out of bed, threw his robe on over his pajama bottoms, and went downstairs.

Even before he reached the kitchen, he smelled and felt the warmth of cooking food. As he found himself doing every morning, Simon silently congratulated himself for hiring a daytime housekeeper and chef, Bethany Cruse.

Zach sat sideways at the butcher-block breakfast table, reading the paper, looking rested and dashing—already showered, shaved, and dressed in a form-flattering olive waffle-weave henley and khakis.

"I see you've met both of the women in my life," Simon said to Zach. His Devon rex tortoiseshell cat sat on Zach's lap, her head tucked underneath a paw, already fast asleep. "Miss Tox tires so easily, giving and giving as she does."

"Yes," Zach said, chucking her under the chin. She didn't move. "She's put in a full day already."

At the stove, Bethany was putting a cast-iron skillet in the oven.

"The frittata smells delicious," said Simon.

Bethany smiled. "I'm not going to let you skip breakfast again today."

If Bethany felt any surprise at finding a strange man in Simon's kitchen in the early morning, she remained steadfastly discreet. She was twenty and beautiful, with short brown hair, hazel eyes, and an athletic build not discernable under the chef whites she wore while in the kitchen. She was studying at the community college.

She moved effortlessly, putting warmed plates on the table in front of Zach and at Simon's usual place, pulling the steaming aromatic frittata from the oven, slicing it, and placing it on a trivet at the table, along with fresh fruit cups, homemade pumpernickel toast, and artisan butter from the Dingley Dell Dairy.

Suddenly Simon was ravenous, and he began eating his bacon and Gruyère frittata slice with gusto. When he did look across the table, he noticed groomed black chest hair above Zach's open shirt button. And, again, that face—a nice face to wake up to.

"The Junction is all over the national news this morning," Bethany said, one hip leaning against the island countertop. She munched on an apple slice. "Radio, television—even CNN."

"National publicity at last," said Simon. "Maybe not the way I've dreamed of."

"Did you know this Roark guy?" Bethany asked.

"I met him just the one time yesterday."

"Looked like a rotter to me," Bethany said. "At least from the picture they ran of him on the *Today* show."

"Not much in the *Oregonian* that we don't already know." Zach pushed the paper toward Simon. "You've taken a better picture, I'm sure." He pointed to a photo of Simon being led away from the tableau by Father Blaise.

Bethany checked her watch and then looked at Simon. "Are you going to Pip's today?"

Zach carefully lifted Miss Tox from his lap and placed her on the floor. She ambled over to the nearby heater vent and curled up on it. Zach pulled a notepad out of his bag, which had been on the floor beside his chair. "You've got work to do," he told Simon. "Can't the sweet young thing handle the store?"

Bethany grinned. "I'm thinking you don't mean me."

"Brock is Bethany's boyfriend," Simon explained to Zach.

"Lucky man," Zach said. "And lucky woman." He turned to Simon. "Let Brock manage the store. You've got to catch the mad fiend who's trying to ruin your city. Where can you start?"

"I could talk to Bradford Sturgess," said Simon. He was trying to sound hesitant, but Zach's excitement was already transferring to him. "About his e-mail. I suppose I should talk with Mavis, too. I usually have coffee with Grace, and I'm supposed to drop in at the high school to check on tomorrow's holiday village display competition, so I might run into Charity and Viola."

"Good start," Zach said. "You need to talk to the detective, too. Find out everything you can about Roark's death—how, when, anything you can get out of her—so we can figure out who had the opportunity to kill Roark dead with a doornail."

"You have a full day outlined for me. What will you do?"

"I'm a stranger—they'll never talk to me. You know the locals, and they'll tell you everything you need to know, unless one of them is the murderer, of course."

"You think someone from town did this?" Bethany looked surprised.

"Could be anybody," Zach said. He ate the last of his toast. "It could be you." He smiled a slightly crooked smile. *He's not totally perfect. Just almost.* "It could be me." Then Zach chuckled.

"I was in Portland at the symphony with three friends," Bethany said, "just for the record." She cleared away the breakfast things. "Just a reminder, Simon—I've got the afternoon off to visit my mom. You'll be on your own for dinner."

"Sure." He put down his fork. The seriousness of what they were discussing had taken away the rest of his appetite. He looked again at the newspaper photo. Not at his own face but at the blurred figure in the background—the body of Mervin

Roark under the ghost's robe. The grim reality of what Simon had experienced was more disturbing than last night's lurid disjointed dreams.

Zach's challenge—that Simon investigate Roark's death—was a concept that Simon, in his shock, had neither fully acknowledged nor agreed to. At least he didn't remember it that way. But somehow, the blurred photo of Roark was more of a threat to Dickens Junction than last night's crystal-clear up-close vision, because this grainy photograph was on thousands of kitchen tables just like Simon's right now, blending the words *murder* and *Dickens Junction* in the minds of the public, both locally and as far as the Internet could reach.

Simon regarded Zach's smile. He hadn't seen an interesting man in a long time, and certainly not one this attractive. Having Zach around would be a pleasant side effect of trying to investigate a crime. Not just a crime—murder. One of the citizens of Dickens Junction could be a murderer. A life—lives—a town—could be ruined.

At first, the discussion, for Simon, had been light, almost banter. But not now. He *could* talk to Sturgess; he *should* talk to Grace.

Could. Should. Conditional.

But now it didn't feel conditional; it felt necessary.

Simon had to know who killed Roark, had to know who was terrorizing the Junction and jeopardizing everything Simon had loved his whole life.

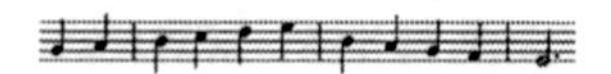

DETECTIVE BOGGS CALLED SIMON AT THE STORE.

"Mr. Alastair—Simon," Boggs said, "you say you saw Mr. Roark in the square as late as four fifteen? Are you positive?"

"I checked my watch. It was just before Mayor Dick came by. Roark was supposed to meet the mayor later, Solomon told me."

"That meeting—if the mayor is telling the truth—never happened. Roark never showed. The coroner's best estimate is that Roark was killed no more than three hours before he was found, and probably no more than two hours."

"The cause of death, Detective?"

Boggs cleared her throat. "I shouldn't reveal anything, but this will be in the paper tomorrow. Multiple wounds from a nail gun. The body was then...attached...to a board, loaded onto the dolly, and dressed for the tableau."

Simon shuddered. "How gruesome."

"Yes," Boggs responded. "In which direction did Roark go when leaving Dickens Square?"

"Toward St. Ina's."

"Or," Detective Boggs offered, "the storage shed at Bleak House, where the tableaux props and backdrops were stored."

So the police thought Roark was killed in the storage shed? That was important. He nodded, at the same time thinking, *Wouldn't someone at Bleak House—Mavis; Ladasha, the breakfast chef; a guest—have seen Roark or his murderer? More people to interview...*

"And, just for the record, Simon, you never left your shop from the time the mayor left you until you stepped into the square dressed as Scrooge a few minutes before seven?"

"Am I a suspect, too, Detective Boggs?"

Simon heard her exhale slowly. "Until we know who did this, everyone is a suspect."

When Detective Boggs ended the conversation, Simon crossed Dickens Square toward the *Household Words* building. Except for the scene of the crime, which was surrounded by police tape, the tableaux had been removed. A clutch of visitors hovered nearby, talking and taking pictures. Someone Simon recognized pointed to him and nodded to the others in her group.

Grace looked out through the window of Cricket's Hearth. Simon waved at her, but she didn't see him. He'd see her at ten anyway for their regular morning coffee break.

Simon stepped into the *Household Words* office. The weekly newspaper, at least these days, contained more ads than copy, and the ads were being threatened, Simon knew, by the Internet. The paper had a lively paid electronic subscription, mainly consisting of amateur and professional Dickensians from the United States and around the world. *But,* Simon wondered as he waited in the lobby for Sturgess to complete a telephone call, *would worldwide interest in Dickens Junction as a tourist attraction stay lively with a murderer on the loose?*

Bradford Sturgess appeared and ushered Simon into his office. One of its glass walls looked inside at his colleagues' offices; another window faced the square.

Sturgess was in his early sixties, six feet tall and slender, and dressed in a rumpled white dress shirt under black braces attached to black slacks. His white hair was frizzed and short;

a pair of reading glasses perched askew on the crown of his head. *The remains of a fine-looking man,* Simon thought. Sturgess affected the look of an old-school newsman, which he was. He had left the pressure of a big daily newspaper in Chicago; his love for Dickens led him to Dickens Junction. Simon's grandfather had spun a rosy picture for Sturgess, and the result was that Sturgess had turned a moribund monthly insert in a grocery-store circular into a thriving stand-alone publication. And the success of that had led him to become a Dickens Junction alderman. Simon had a hard time calling it a newspaper, since it had very little news of note. *Journal* may have been a more accurate word, considering that it was a premier source for Dickens pastiche and carried a new story every week, often by Dickens scholars or renowned authors. The latest edition, a holiday special good for the month of December, featured a reinterpretation of Dickens's last Christmas Book, *The Haunted Man*, by Pulitzer Prize-winning novelist Jane Smiley.

"This is a nasty business," Sturgess said to Simon after he had closed his office door. "I've been on the phone all morning...wire services, bloggers, even *People* magazine."

"I let Brock answer the phone," said Simon. "I didn't want any more questions."

"The mayor was here, too." Sturgess's lip twitched. He had a long-standing lack of respect for the mayor, or at least the business he ran. "He said he's getting pressure to cancel the rest of the festivities."

"He can't do that on his own. That would take full council approval."

"Yes," Sturgess said. "But the mayor is—well, he's a Dick."

Simon never knew whether to defend his cousin or not. Given that he was there for information, he decided to remain silent. "So," he said, changing the subject, "tell me about what happened with Mavis and Roark."

Sturgess looked out on the square. "Mavis said that Roark came by to see her yesterday afternoon, asking questions about various local businesspeople—including you—and offered a snootful of money to buy Bleak House. On behalf of some group named Marley Enterprises."

"He made no such offer to me." Simon watched two young women and an arrestingly handsome young man in the outer office. They were whispering in a huddle around a computer terminal. Journalism students from the college working part-time, likely reading Internet stories about the murder. As so many in Dickens Junction were probably doing at that moment. Simon brought his gaze back to meet Sturgess's. "What time was Roark at Bleak House?"

"Sometime after lunch, Mavis said."

"Where was Mavis between four thirty and five?" Simon's words sounded forced to his own ears, but Sturgess didn't seem to notice. He was chewing on his lip. "Roark might have been nearby...waiting for the murderer. The police believe Roark was killed in the storage shed and then dressed in the dummy's robe. The shed isn't far from the house. Why didn't Mavis see them?"

"I don't know."

"Where were you then?"

"Driving around," Sturgess answered. "I left here around four or so and ended up in Astoria and had dinner. When I got back, everything was a madhouse."

"You sent me the e-mail while you were driving?"

"I wanted to get it off my mind."

"Just driving around?" Simon put weight on each word.

"I thought it would help me get story ideas for the New Year's issue," Sturgess said. "We scored a thought piece by Stephen King on Dickens, New Year's, and *The Chimes*."

"Impressive," said Simon. He plunged on, feeling quite reckless. "Did you get any ideas? Where did you eat?"

Sturgess turned away, then stared hard at Simon. "I ate drive-through at Artful Dodger's." He frowned, seemingly forgetting Simon's questions. "I suppose I should run a story about the murder? It's the Junction's biggest news in years."

"Hard news isn't really in your line anymore, is it?" Simon was surprised at how easily he'd gotten into the swing of Zach's challenge, but he was happier to reassume his role as Good—even First—Citizen of Dickens Junction. "I'm sure it wouldn't suit the overall tone of *Household Words*."

In the outer office, the young people had moved away from the monitor; the handsome man walked toward the microfilm readers. He flashed a toothy grin and bright blue eyes toward the windows. Simon looked away.

Sturgess looked away also. "That reminds me," he said, a small furrow in his brow. "Another thing, maybe connected somehow. Lowell Brundish was here last week, wanting to look through the morgue." *The newspaper archives.* "He asked

Clive"—Sturgess nodded toward the young man—"to help him. He wanted to see recent real-estate sales...commercial properties. Complained that we didn't have our past issues online with search capacity." Sturgess waved his arm. "Does it look as if we have the money for that?"

"That's not a bad idea," Simon answered indirectly. "Let's talk to the Dickens Foundation about a grant—maybe next year."

Simon was about to tell Sturgess about bumping into Brundish, but held back. Something about Sturgess's story didn't hold together. He'd have to think about it, talk it over with Zach. Maybe after he talked to Mavis. And Brundish. And Ariadne Neff.

The list of suspects went on. And on.

GRACE BEDDOES WAS WAITING FOR SIMON AT THEIR USUAL table at the Crystal Palace when he arrived. She rose to hug him.

"It's awful," she said as the two sat. The colonial-styled maple tables were topped with seasonal holiday runners featuring Mr. Pickwick in various imagined Christmas scenes from Dingley Dell. A Pickwick/Sam Weller salt-and-pepper set stood by. "How are you doing with it all, Simon?"

Grace's graying hair was cut in an age-appropriate pageboy, although she otherwise looked younger than her forty-nine years, mostly because of her smooth, creamy skin. She seldom wore makeup other than mascara and barely tinted lip gloss. She had begun to be concerned about her weight; today she wore a rose knit tunic and black tights, with a paisley scarf tied around her neck, ostensibly to cover nascent wrinkles. Her pale-green eyes were inviting and open when she removed her glasses and let them hang from the silver chain around her neck.

Simon and Grace had been meeting at the Crystal Palace at least three times weekly for as long as Simon could remember, starting just after Grace took over ownership of Cricket's Hearth in the mid-1990s. Their common backgrounds had resulted in fast friendship. Like Simon, Grace had been raised by a set of grandparents; upon their deaths, she had used her small inheritance to relocate to Dickens Junction and purchase Cricket's Hearth and the building it housed. Grace's one other tenant, a boutique plant shop called Doctor Marigold's, had folded almost a year ago, an early victim of the economic downturn.

"I'm doing all right, compared with Mervin Roark."

Grace shuddered. "Poor man."

Viola Mintun came over to the table with a pot of tea, cups, and saucers. Like a good hostess, she tried to overhear everything said in the tearoom. "Of course, it's not hard to imagine someone murdering that nasty little man," she said. She put a well-manicured hand to her mouth. "I suppose I shouldn't speak ill of the dead, but—facts is facts."

"He visited you, too, then?" Grace asked.

"Not long after you left yesterday," Viola said to Simon.

"I think I already know the answer," said Simon, "but what did he want from you?"

"My land," Viola said. She turned away to motion to Caitlin. "Miss Havisham's Day-Old Wedding Cake for these two," she said. "My treat," she added.

"I shouldn't." Grace smoothed her tunic around her hips.

"We have to remember the holidays somehow."

Grace smiled. "If you insist."

Simon nodded that he would join Grace and have the cake. Caitlin poured tea for each, covered the pot with a quilted cozy, curtsied, and headed toward the kitchen.

"People are saying he must have been killed just before the tableaux started," Viola said.

"I hadn't heard that," Grace said. "Not that many people came into the shop this morning. I almost let Gloria have the day off."

Simon decided he wouldn't talk too much about the confidences that Detective Boggs had reluctantly shared; if he kept them to himself, he might receive more of them. "At four fifteen he was very much alive and leaving the square," he said instead, blowing gently on his tea before tasting it.

Viola pulled out a chair and sat beside Grace. "He finally caught up with me somewhere around two, after the lunch crowd left"—she looked around; only three other tables were occupied— "such as it was. Caught me outside, as I was coming back from the ATM in Mr. Dick's. He wasn't one for beating about the bush, either." She moved her head closer to the center of the table; Simon and Grace did the same. "He said he wanted to buy my property on behalf of Marley Enterprises, whoever that is."

"He was as subtle as Tiny Tim's crutch," Grace added. She poured cream into her tea from a ceramic cow and stirred it with the silver spoon from her saucer.

"And his offer?" Simon looked at both women.

"More than the market would support," Viola said. "A lot more."

"His offer to me was equally—generous," Grace said. "I'm afraid I actually might have gasped." Grace touched Simon's hand.

"That's the interesting thing." Simon pushed his shoulders back and sat upright; the women did the same. "He never offered to buy my property."

"And you own more than we do combined," Viola said.

"What did you tell him?" Simon looked first at Viola, then Grace.

"I told him that I thought what he was trying to do—whatever it was—would hurt Dickens Junction and our way of life." Viola made a face. "He laughed at me," she added, "almost like one of those cartoon villains. I could have slapped him."

Or worse? Simon wondered.

Viola's bright-blue eyes sparkled. "The Junction's become an incubator for amateur Sherlocks and Nancy Drews," she said, "each of us wondering whodunit. I know what you're thinking. That I might have killed him? Well, I might have, if I'd had the chance." She brushed her hands together in the air as if wiping them clean. "But the last I saw him was when he left the Palace. I was here until a few minutes to four. After that, I was at my Pickwick Pilates class until almost six o'clock, when I went to the Porters to talk business with Joelle Creevy until the tableaux started. As I told Detective Boggs last night, I didn't have time to kill Roark, even if I had the inclination."

Simon felt awkward for a moment, until he remembered Zach and the warmth of his hand last night at the Porters. And the challenge. He had been treating his friends as suspects, grilling them for answers—but it was working. Everything Viola claimed could be checked. If she were telling the truth, she wouldn't have had time to arrive at the storage shed behind Bleak House, attack Mervin Roark with a nail gun, and also see the tableaux with the rest of the spectators. If she were telling the truth. He shuddered briefly at the idea of doubting the word of one of his oldest friends, but he had no choice. Anyone could lie to cover up a murder.

At that point, Caitlin appeared with two dessert plates. She placed one in front of Grace, the other in front of Simon.

Miss Havisham's Day-Old Wedding Cake consisted of three small round tiers of yellow cake covered in smooth white fondant and topped with a tiny silver star—a miniature wedding cake, with lacy cobwebs of spun sugar draped from top to bottom. The tiers were off-center and not quite level, as if the cake had toppled after being abandoned, like Miss Havisham on her wedding day. Each cake sat on its own glass turntable.

Viola pushed her chair back as Caitlin gave each turntable a spin. Caitlin then touched a fireplace match to each cake.

The vanilla vodka that had been sprinkled on the cake moments before in the kitchen ignited in blue flames, and the spun-sugar cobwebs darkened and melted like the lace on Miss Havisham's burning wedding dress that inspired the Palace's signature dessert.

Simon and Grace each leaned forward and blew out the flames.

"I've never actually had this before," Grace said. She picked at the blackened star with her fork. "I've only watched."

"Locals don't order it that often," Viola admitted. "But the tourists love it."

Caitlin curtsied and went back to the kitchen.

Viola stood. "I'll let you two finish your break." Before she turned away, Viola put a hand on Simon's shoulder. "You must do something to save the Junction." She swept her other hand from one end of the tearoom to the other. "I've invested years—not to mention dollars and my heart—in this place. Charity and I expect to grow old—well, older, at least—here. I want to keep things as they are. Don't you?" She looked at Grace.

"Of course," Grace said. "We're in this together." She put a hand on Viola's.

Simon topped their hands with his. "We all do," he said.

Viola went across the tearoom to converse with guests at another table, people Simon recalled having seen at the bookstore earlier in the day.

Grace took a bite of cake. "It's better than I expected," she said. "For such a show." She looked at Simon. "If I had known Roark would be murdered," she said, "I guess I would have found an alibi like Viola's." She smiled. "That's what I told Detective Boggs at the Porters."

"What was your experience with Roark?" Simon asked. If he was going to find out what happened, he had to keep the conversation on the murder.

Grace sipped at her tea. "He came to the shop sometime after two, I'm sure," she said, "because I was alone. Gloria had stepped out to get a bite and, I suspect, buy a Mirror-ball ticket at Mr. Dick's. Roark came in; I knew immediately something was wrong. He just didn't seem the type, you know, to come into Cricket's Hearth."

Simon nodded. The usual clientele for Grace's wares were women of a certain age and income searching for handcrafted soaps, unguents, nards, and knickknacks.

"Just as Viola said, he came right to the point. He wanted to buy my property for Marley Enterprises."

"Did he say why?"

"I asked," Grace said, "especially after he blurted out a price." She named the price to Simon. He felt himself almost freeze as he took in breath. "'I represent a very special group of investors,'" Grace repeated, her voice low and fast, "'who see potential in this quaint little place. Everything would change, of course.'" Simon could almost feel the evil as Grace recreated Roark's voice.

"In what way?" he asked. "And who are these investors?"

Grace returned her voice to normal. "He wouldn't tell me. He just said that if I didn't accept his offer, I would find out too late what a mistake I was making."

"What did you say?"

Grace put down her teacup. "Frankly," she said, pushing away the turntable, now containing only crumbs of cake, "he rattled me. I told him I would think about it and give him an answer in a day or two." She took Roark's card from her purse. Simon took it from her. It was identical to the one Roark had given him.

"Turn it over," Grace said.

There was the price Grace had mentioned. The dollar sign was elaborate and excessively large beside the number, which was itself excessive, almost obscene.

"Of course I wasn't going to accept," Grace said. "I wanted to talk to you first. He frightened me. I don't have as much confidence as Viola," she said, "but I feel the same way she does about the Junction." Her cheeks became red, and she dabbed at the corner of her eyes with her napkin. Simon stood and helped Grace stand. "Silly me," she said.

Simon was still holding Roark's card. "May I keep this?" he said. "I think Detective Boggs might find it interesting."

"Of course," Grace said.

Simon took Grace's arm. "I'll take you back to Cricket's."

After Grace adjusted her scarf and smoothed her tunic, Simon led her diagonally across the square from the tearoom to her shop, passing the place where the Marley's Ghost tableau had been the night before.

Inside Cricket's Hearth, Simon's throat constricted from the intense odors of sandalwood, verbena, frankincense, licorice, rose, and all of the other scents competing for attention in the small store. Shelves of handmade soaps, bath oils and beads, and lavender eye pillows lined one wall of the store. A holiday tree covered with sachet balls took up one corner; next to that stood a table of spice-toned candles resting in a bed of scented faux snowflakes. In the back, Grace stocked more traditional hearth-related items—Victorian fire screens, wicker baskets of fatwood kindling, a few cast iron dogs and cats, some random andirons.

"I know you're not crazy about the aromas in here," Grace said as she straightened up a line of patchouli room fresheners. "I've gotten used to it, I suppose."

Simon smiled at Grace's part-time assistant, Gloria, a wafer-thin high schooler wearing a puffed-sleeve, dotted-Swiss shell over tartan tights and crimson cowgirl boots. Her brunet hair was pulled back with a scrunchie that might have been made from gum wrappers, Simon wasn't sure. "I'll be in the back," Gloria said. "We got our Valentine's Day stock—such as it is—this morning."

After Gloria left, Simon realized that, besides the cacophony of smells, something was different. His usual reaction to the shop was a sense of gentle claustrophobia because of the sheer volume of its contents. Today, however, his second impression was clearer—the shelves and curio cabinets, although seemingly full, were not chockablock with inventory. Several occasional tables, usually near overflowing with beribboned cellophane sacks of bath "jewels," bijoux, and bottles of aromatic linen waters, were not in their usual places—weren't in place at all.

"You must be having an exceptional season," said Simon, fingering a small glass orb containing ylang-ylang balm. "Your inventories are down."

"I've had to cut back," Grace said, her voice softer. "I haven't been replacing stock as often because sales haven't justified it. I'm probably down ten percent or more."

More like twenty-five, Simon guessed.

"This season hasn't been as brisk as I had hoped," she continued. "Viola and I are in the same boat. We're not recession-proof like you, Simon."

Even though her voice had no edge, Simon felt the gentle reproof. Since he didn't need the bookstore to provide him an income to live on, he downplayed the significance of such things as cash flow and quarterly earnings.

"I'm sure the downturn will be over soon," he said, trying to get the conversation back on track. "Let's hope that Roark's murderer is found quickly." Simon picked up a gingerbread-scented teddy bear, then put it back on its table. "So," he continued, "what did you do after Roark left here yesterday?"

Grace fluffed a holiday swag encrusted with faux sugared plums, lemons, and figs. Small bits of the sugary coating fell onto Grace's tunic. She brushed them off. "I intended to find you, but decided I needed to get away and walk off my anger at Roark. So I walked down to the river, watched the ducks for a while, and then went back home and decorated my Christmas tree until it was time to return to the square to see the tableaux. I planned on finishing my tree after I got home, but, well, I was too upset after what happened."

"Of course." Simon pressed on. "Nobody saw you at the river?"

Grace turned back to Simon. "You're such a Hardy Boy, aren't you?" Simon felt himself blush, but Grace's tone was gentle. She was teasing him, and then she indulged him, answering his question. "I don't think anyone saw me—I took the back trail because I wanted to be alone. You can see why I'm nervous about the possibility of Detective Boggs coming round again. Of course, who would believe it's one of us?"

"I'm sure Detective Boggs will find the murderer soon," said Simon.

Grace gave him a full smile. "So, if you're done detecting for a moment, let me do some. Who's the dark and handsome looker who swept you away from the scene of the crime last night? I haven't seen him around before."

Simon gave a brief explanation for Zach's presence in Dickens Junction, and added that he was staying at Gad's Hill Place. If Zach stayed much longer, and Simon hoped he would, the whole town would learn about his lodger soon enough.

"So he's—"

"Yes," said Simon, giving her a gentle *tsk*.

"I was going to say *available*," Grace said.

"We haven't established that yet." Simon felt his face getting warmer again.

Grace moved toward Simon and touched his shoulder. "It's been a long time since David." Simon's last partner had departed five years earlier, citing the irresistible force to be living in a bigger metropolis than Dickens Junction, thus making Simon the immoveable object. "Too long, I think."

"But what about you?" Simon turned the question back on her.

"I'm a confirmed spinster," she replied. "But you, on the other hand..."

"This is hardly the time to talk about relationships," said Simon. "There's a crazed killer on the loose."

Grace tilted her head, acknowledging the need to step back. "Old friends tell old friends their secrets," she said. "Remember that." She turned away, fluffed a crewelwork pillow bearing the inscription, *Because Grandma Says So*, and then turned back to Simon. "What do you think Roark was after?" Grace asked. "Besides property, I mean. What kind of investors would want to buy up land in the Junction?"

Simon twirled the diagonal edges of Roark's card. "I don't know. But I intend to find out."

Back in the square, on his way to talk with Mavis at Bleak House about her encounter with Roark and her curious contact with Sturgess, Simon found his path blocked by two portly gentlemen in their sixties, one with a white handlebar mustache, the other with a silver goatee. Each wore a distressed-leather bomber jacket with various decals and patches. The man with the goatee held a clipboard. Both men were more than six feet tall, intimidating in their collective bulk. They smiled; Mustache had a broken incisor. Simon was sure he had seen them somewhere before.

"Aren't you Simon Alastair?" one asked.

Simon hesitated. "I am," he said.

Goatee gave an ingratiating smile. "We met, I think, a few years back, at the Portland AIDS Walk."

"You were collecting for Bears from Bears," Simon remembered. He reached for his wallet. "Did you want a donation?" The charity was a good one—providing stuffed animals to the Smike Center for Children—and he'd gladly give again.

"We don't do that anymore," said Mustache, almost offended. "We're strictly Objectivist now."

Simon knitted his brow. "No more hospital donations?"

"The parents provide sufficiently for their children," said Goatee.

"And the poor and orphaned?" Simon asked.

Mustache pursed his lips. "The government, I'm afraid, takes care of them. I wish I could say that it didn't."

"Charity," said Goatee, "should begin at home."

"If it begins at all," added Mustache.

Simon attempted to move forward, but the men blocked his way.

"This murder," said Mustache, "is a perfect example of government gone awry. Individual rights and responsibilities must be preserved. We are a nation in crisis." Mustache was no longer smiling. He raised the clipboard toward Simon. "Under the impression that our state and our nation need a new vision, a few of us are endeavoring to gather names and e-mail addresses to raise consciousness and generate a network devoted to a return to individual responsibility. We choose to do this now to take advantage of the heightened sense of fear that last night's crime has created." After making a grand gesture in the direction of the visitors strolling and window-shopping in Dickens Square, Mustache thrust the clipboard at Simon. "May we put you on the list?"

"No," said Simon.

"You wish to be anonymous?" asked Goatee.

"I wish to be left alone," said Simon, now angry. He pushed his way between the men and then turned back around to address them. "Since you ask me what I wish, gentlemen," he said, "that is my answer. I support local government and the administration of our country. Those who need assistance—like ailing children—must look to government and charities for help. Minding your own business is a repugnant form of selfishness that I was taught to shun. I will make a donation to your former charity later today in spite of your ignorance and want of decency. Good afternoon."

SIMON DIDN'T VISIT FATHER BLAISE OFTEN. SEEING A priest was something you did when you had committed a terrible act or were going to get married (his friend George said they amounted to the same thing). But the discussion with the portly gentlemen left Simon feeling shaken and frustrated. He decided to postpone his trip to Bleak House and instead left the square for St. Ina's.

The rectory at St. Ina's was a spacious craftsman house with a deep front porch, clear leaded-glass sidelights, and a dark oak entry with a staircase leading to the private rooms above. On the main floor, a formal dining room with a solid-walnut table and sideboard were visible; the kitchen lay beyond.

Willow Martin, the aged but still spry housekeeper who looked after Father Blaise during the day, let Simon in.

"How good of you to come," she said, her voice like crackled glaze. "I don't usually disturb Father in his study, but he'll want to see you, I'm sure."

She led Simon back toward the study through the parlor, which was decorated in traditional craftsman style, including wide chairs covered in dark leather with flat oak armrests. A reproduction Tiffany lamp graced a side table; Simon knew that its original, an heirloom from Father Blaise's grandparents, rested safely on the staircase's upper landing.

"He's working on a special homily," Willow said. "About the murder." She spoke in a low, conspiratorial voice. "Such a dreadful thing, isn't it?" She knocked on the study door before opening it. "Simon Alastair here to see you, Father."

Father Blaise came out and extended his large, veined hand. "Good to see you, Simon. Please come in. I hope you're feeling better than last evening."

Father Blaise's masculine and efficient study décor reflected the man. Floor-to-ceiling walnut bookcases dominated the two walls behind the solid oak desk and black Aeron chair.

Track lighting was supplemented by two contemporary floor lamps. The computer monitor displayed a majestic view of Mount Hood.

Father Blaise invited Simon to sit in one of a pair of cordovan-leather shell chairs opposite the desk, and sat in the other himself.

Whenever they met, Simon's first reaction was always a moment of disbelief at Father Blaise's physical beauty: the white teeth, close-cropped hair, strong and clean-shaven jaw, aquiline nose, and bright blue eyes. He carried his well-muscled physique with a casual, confident masculinity. Simon's second reaction was always to fall back to earth, remembering that Father Blaise was a priest, even if only Episcopalian. At thirty-eight, he was, as Simon jokingly told him several months ago, coming into his "prime," and hoped it would bring to the priest fewer negative consequences than it had for Miss Jean Brodie. Father Blaise was a well-read man beyond things ecclesiastical ("I have catholic tastes," he liked to joke), and he and Simon often traded barbed *bons mots.* Father Blaise was unmarried, but most said he was just being cautious in choosing his mate. And since so many Junxonian eyes were watching Blaise's every foray into the dating pool, Simon was confident that *cautious* was the word.

"Thank you for seeing me," said Simon. "I can't stop thinking about the murder. I didn't like what little I had seen of Roark, but I didn't wish him dead. Although if I had known what brought him to town—as I do now, in part, at least suspect—I would have had a motive."

"But you didn't kill him," Father Blaise said.

"No. But I don't exactly have an alibi, either. I was alone in the back room at the store much of the time during which the police think he could have been killed. I suppose I could have gotten to Bleak House and back. But I think Detective Boggs is satisfied with what I have told her."

"The detective is doing her work thoroughly," he said, "and handsomely." He paused and smiled; then, as if distracted, returned to his point. "I received a call earlier this morning from Mercy Upton. Detective Boggs had called her to confirm that I was judging the Tiny Tim lookalike contest at Wackford Squeers Grade School from four thirty until a few minutes before seven, when I was due at the tableaux." Father Blaise leaned forward. "Jeremy Upton won the contest. Again."

"It's the crutch," said Simon. "He's lucky that one of his moms is a woodcarver."

Having shared their respective alibis, both men sat back in the chairs. Simon was amazed and delighted that his investigation was going so smoothly. Murder was making everyone jumpy, overeager to share alibis and cast suspicions on others. Simon was glad Zach had goaded him into being a detective—it was even fun, in a macabre sort of way.

Willow came in a moment later with a tray. Simon smelled the Scottish Breakfast tea brewing in the porcelain pot. "Had you heard of or seen Mervin Roark before?" he asked Father Blaise as he leaned forward to pour them each a cup.

"No," he answered. "My first knowledge of Roark was when I...removed the cowl."

"He represented something called Marley Enterprises," said Simon. "I don't know yet what it is, but its 'investors,' as he referred to them when meeting with Grace Beddoes, want to buy up large chunks of land on Dickens Square. And Bleak House, too."

"For what purpose?"

"I don't know yet." Simon sipped his tea, looking over the cup's edge at Father Blaise's wide cheekbones, already at this hour showing traces of dark beard. He'd been asking basic questions of the obvious suspects and witnesses, but now he had an original idea. He felt a spark, and imagined how it would feel different later today when he told everything to Zach. "What do you remember about Objectivism?"

Father Blaise chuckled. "I haven't thought about that since college." He stirred his tea with a rock-candy stirrer, one of the many touches at the rectory that said more about Willow's tastes than the priest's. "Objectivism is the philosophy professed by Ayn Rand and her devotees. I remember reading *The Fountainhead* and *Atlas Shrugged*—yes, both—when I was a sophomore at Meriwether University, to impress this very special blond senior. She was keen on reading—and other mutual interests. But, 'When I became a man, I put away childish things—'" Father Blaise broke off this recollection. "Sorry." He took a long sip of tea, attempting to hide a smile behind his cup. "I sincerely hope, Simon, that you're not thinking of becoming an Objectivist. I would have to reconsider our friendship immediately."

"Roark bought a copy of *Atlas Shrugged* at the store." Simon then told Father Blaise about his encounter with the two portly gentlemen.

"Interesting. A Rand fanatic is the last thing I would expect to find in Dickens Junction," Father Blaise said. "Her self-centered worldview is the antithesis of anything Dickensian."

Simon decided to change the subject. "Willow tells me that your homily this Sunday will be about the murder."

"It pretty much has to be, don't you think? Everyone in town is talking. People are scared."

"I know I am," said Simon.

"Is that why you came to see me?" Father Blaise asked. "I'm always glad to see you, but you don't visit the rectory that often."

After a pause, during which he reflected on just how Dickensian he was, and strived to be, Simon deflected what might have been a gentle rebuke. "I try not to think of the Junction as 'my' town. But I loved my grandfather very much, and I feel a strong—compelling—obligation to keep Dickens Junction as he would have wanted."

"Of course you do," Father Blaise said. "And many expect that of you. I think you know that. But what does that obligation mean in terms of your actions?"

"I'm going to find out what Roark wanted here in the Junction, and who killed him to stop him from getting what he wanted."

"Assuming"—Father Blaise leaned forward—"that he was killed because of his work."

Simon took in a breath. "I hadn't thought of that."

"As your priest," Father Blaise began—an interesting statement because Simon didn't go to church often, and then more from duty than dogma—"I must advise you not to interfere with the police in their investigation. You are not Hercule Poirot," he added with the barest hint of a smile.

"At least you didn't call me Encyclopedia Brown," said Simon, trying to lighten the tone, sensing that Blaise was about to go full-on clerical with him.

On cue, Father Blaise straightened his collar. "Besides, Simon, there's at least one person who doesn't want you to find out what's going on."

"The murderer."

"Exactly," Father Blaise said. "But, as your friend, I'm not surprised that you want to do whatever you can to preserve the Junction and its way of life. I assume," here Father Blaise paused and Simon caught a twinkle in his eye, "that the handsome stranger who's staying with you has something to do with this?" Before Simon could respond beyond blushing yet again, Father Blaise continued, "Everyone in this town, when they're done talking about the murder, is talking about you and Mr. Benjamin. Willow, the soul of discretion outside these walls, is quite the gossip once she closes the rectory door."

"Zach wants to help," was all Simon offered. "He's a journalist, after all. And I just met him yesterday." Simon stood to leave, hoping that his action would not be ascribed to embarrassment. It wasn't, at least not completely. He had other calls to make.

Father Blaise stood also. "Where do your investigations take you next?"

As Simon and Father Blaise exited from the study, they almost bumped into Willow, who was straightening a doily on a side table near the study door.

"To see Mavis," said Simon. "She had a visit from Roark yesterday that upset her."

"Please give her my regards." Father Blaise shook Simon's hand. "I made a brief stop at Bleak House yesterday on my way from the school, to see whether she wanted to accompany me to the tableaux." He stopped, seeming to consider his next statement before he looked at Simon. "But she wasn't in."

BLEAK HOUSE AND DICKENS JUNCTION CITY HALL WERE two blocks away from Dickens Square and about the same distance from St. Ina's. The sandstone structure now called City Hall was originally Dickens House, Simon's grandfather's mansion and the home where Simon had grown up. On his death in 1995, Ebenezer Dickens Jr. donated the building to the city for its offices and sold the adjacent coach house to Mavis Spurlock, his longtime housekeeper, for one dollar. Mavis turned the coach house into Bleak House Bed and Breakfast, and had run it ever since.

Bleak House was a spacious, robin's egg blue Cape Cod with white trim. Large windows with cream-colored curtains were prominent on three sides; the fourth side, to the right of the white solid-oak front door, was a shared wall with Mavis's son's apartment—Mavis had renovated the three-car garage after Brock graduated from high school.

Simon opened Bleak House's front door and entered the foyer. The interior always impressed him—Mavis had rejected the lace curtains and colonial turned-leg furnishings seen everywhere else in town and instead had decorated Bleak House in a contemporary style, with glass and modern upholstery. The wall colors were saturated—the breakfast room to the right of the entrance was ochre, while the sitting room to the left was painted a deep merlot. No faux samplers on the wall; Simon had loaned Mavis several works from his grandfather's art collection, including a Helen Frankenthaler.

"Oh Simon, it's you," Mavis said as she came into the breakfast room from the kitchen. She hugged him; he returned her affection. "It's been the most awful morning. Police everywhere. Come look."

Mavis Spurlock was a trim and fit woman in her early sixties; it was easy to see in her lined but still-beautiful face where Brock got some of his physical gifts. Mavis wore kitten heels and a winter white twin set over tailored fawn slacks, and looked every bit the successful innkeeper that she was. She wore her white hair short with a loose curl. Her makeup was light—foundation, powder, mascara, and lipstick—and expertly applied. Mavis had been Ebbie's and Melanie's housekeeper at Dickens House for years when, at forty, she found herself pregnant and partnerless—the much younger father a commercial fisherman long since gone to Alaska chasing halibut cheeks and Wasilla wahines. There had never been a Mr. Spurlock.

Simon followed Mavis into the kitchen. He greeted Ladasha Creevy, Joelle's daughter, who was rolling out dough on the pastry workstation. She was in her late twenties, with short cornrows and hazel eyes, her ebony skin smooth against her chef whites.

"Quiches for tomorrow," Ladasha explained. A recent culinary-school graduate, Ladasha had returned briefly to Dickens Junction to redesign the Bleak House menu. She was interviewing for *chef de cuisine* positions at various locations both near Astoria and in Portland.

"We're getting raves from the new recipes," Mavis said. "Especially those sun-dried tomato, parmesan, and cracked-pepper quiches. I wish she would never leave, but..." She trailed off as she pulled aside the curtain in the kitchen's largest window. "Just look," she said.

Simon joined her at the window.

The utility shed where Roark was killed stood about twenty feet from the back door of the house. The shed was large enough to store yard implements and the holiday decorations used in the square. The door was crisscrossed with crime-scene tape.

"The police have been through that shed with tweezers, I swear," Mavis said. "I think they're coming back today. At least they're done with the room where Roark was staying. Even though he never slept there, as it turned out."

"Did the police find anything?" Simon looked up, wondering whether Mavis could have seen anyone near the shed from her second-story bedroom.

"Not much," Mavis answered. "Nothing in his room to speak of. A briefcase, an overnight bag. I didn't see them; the police took everything away." She looked out the window with Simon. "In the shed, the place where I keep my nail gun interested them, as well as the original dummy that the murderer replaced with Roark's corpse. They took the dummy away with them."

"Detective Boggs didn't tell me much when I spoke with her this morning," said Simon. "Just that Roark was killed sometime between four thirty and the time that Brock loaded the body to bring it here."

Mavis let the curtain fall back in place. "I don't understand why Roark was even near the shed."

"Meeting the murderer?" Simon suggested. "Too bad you weren't here." Another old friend, yes, but he had to forge ahead.

Mavis squeezed a dollop of sanitizer on her hands and wiped them together. "Considering what was happening out there, I'm rather glad I was shopping and sitting stuck in holiday traffic. I didn't get back until long after the murder had occurred."

"Oh, that reminds me—you forgot the vanilla extract and baking powder." Ladasha laid a round of dough inside one of the two Pyrex pie plates near her.

"I'll pick them up today." Mavis looked at Simon. "I'm surprised I remembered anything I'd gone shopping for. I was so rattled from my conversation with Roark earlier in the day."

"I heard you told Brad Sturgess all about it," said Simon.

Mavis lowered an eyebrow, a slight pause. "Oh, yes," she said. "From my cell, while I was in Astoria. I just had to talk to someone, and I didn't want to bother you, since I knew you'd be getting ready for the tableaux."

"Why Brad? If I wasn't available, why not call Brock? Or Joelle? Even Solomon? I didn't know you and Brad were close."

"We're not," Mavis said, "I mean, I know him—his was the first name that popped into my head." She grabbed the smoked paprika jar from Ladasha's hand. "Not too much," she said. Ladasha looked at Simon and shrugged her shoulders.

Simon chose another tack. "Tell me about what Roark said—tell me everything, if you don't mind."

Mavis took a seat at a small table that contained Bleak House's reservation book, a holder for business cards, a small loose stack of Mirrorball lottery tickets, and a stack of marketing brochures. Simon liked that she'd made the kitchen her business center as well. He sat beside her.

Mavis opened the reservation book. "A man named Venable booked the room here several weeks ago." She was pointing to the words *Marley Enterprises*, which had been penciled in over the faint remnants of a name that had been erased. "When Mr. Venable called I'd just had a cancellation. I remember Venable wasn't interested in any specific day; he just wanted something around the holiday. He didn't care about the *Christmas Carol* events. "But he said that the specific person representing Marley Enterprises wasn't yet certain."

Simon peered at the book, as if it would release secrets that would shed light on the murder. "Did you get contact information from Venable?"

"He said it wouldn't be necessary. He paid in full with a credit card."

"Only one night?"

"Yes," Mavis said. "When Roark checked in, he said he had a lot of business to conduct in a very short time."

"He certainly got around yesterday."

"He returned to Bleak House around four thirty," Mavis said. "He looked confident, I'll say that for him. He said he had the authority to offer me a 'handsome sum' for Bleak House. Mavis named the price that Roark had offered. "Look," she said. Lying on the table was Roark's card; she turned it over. Once again, an exaggerated dollar sign preceded an offer beyond excessive, in the neighborhood of crazy.

"What did you say to him?" Simon asked.

"I wasn't nice," Mavis said. "I felt insulted. That's when he turned nasty, said that his investors would take over the Junction one way or another, so I'd better cooperate." Mavis tapped the edge of Roark's card on the table. "But I had to leave for Astoria, so I basically turned my back on him and left the house." She turned to Ladasha. "Where did he go when I left? You were here."

Ladasha put down the wooden rolling pin. "He said he had another appointment, but that he would be back around five thirty to meet someone." She looked at Simon. "I told him he'd better have his key to let himself in, because I was leaving to go to Astoria myself." She paused. "A night out with the girls. But it was the wrong night."

"Wrong night for what?" Simon asked.

Ladasha looked at Mavis, then back at Simon. "A jazz trio we were going to see at Suomi Hall. But they weren't playing; my friend had gotten the date wrong." She went back to rolling out quiche crust. "When I got back here, everything was crazy."

"Were other guests here when you left?" Simon asked Mavis.

"All out sightseeing—Fort Clatsop, the Peter Iredale, the Astoria Column—at least the ones I talked to. Everyone was having an early dinner in order to be on time for the tableaux."

"So Bleak House was completely empty at five thirty," said Simon. "Do you think the murderer might have known that?"

"I don't see how," Ladasha said. "I had made my plans just a couple days before."

"And I decided earlier in the day to go to Astoria," Mavis said.

"So the murderer was very lucky."

A small buzzer rang above Simon's head; someone had come in the front door.

"A walk-in, I hope," Mavis said, standing up. "We've had two cancellations already today. One woman flat-out said she wouldn't stay here while there was a murderer on the loose. Excuse me, Simon. I'll be back in a few minutes."

"I was just leaving," he said. "I'm right behind you."

"Are you investigating this yourself?" Ladasha asked, after Mavis had left and while Simon's hand was on the butler door.

She lifted the second round of dough into the second pan and smoothed it into place. "You could get in trouble."

"I'll be careful." Simon dropped his hand. "Did anything else interesting happen while Roark was here?"

"Just after Mavis left for Astoria, the house phone rang," Ladasha said. She began crimping the edges of the dough around each pie plate. She rolled the scraps into a small ball, which she wrapped in plastic. "It was Lowell Brundish, wanting to talk to Mavis right away. When I said she wasn't here, he asked for her cell, so I gave him the number. He's never called here before that I know of, and he sounded as if it were urgent."

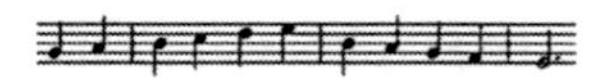

WHEN SIMON RETURNED TO PIP'S PAGES, NO SOONER HAD he opened the door than he was engulfed in a giant bear hug.

"My dear!" a familiar Southern voice drawled. George Bascomb, who could have been Simon's double, except for a few incidentals—height (well over six feet), profession (collage artist), and age (George claimed he was in his early fifties, but he was somewhat more extremely fifty than that). Both men were financially independent and loved the arts, theater, and literature, so when they met years ago at a party in Portland (where George lived), they formed an instant and lasting bond that both men nurtured by frequent visits, telephone calls, and e-mails. "You look simply dreadful," George said, holding Simon at arm's length, "but wonderful just the same. It's been too long."

"As if I couldn't guess," said Simon, "what brings you to the Junction?"

George smiled. "As I was telling Dorian Gray here"—he gestured toward Brock, who, clad in a tight-black club shirt and skinny jeans, looked more like a high-tone rent boy than an aesthete—"I had to come down here and cleave you to the bosom of my protection and support."

"It is a ponderous bosom," said Simon.

"And you know that this is just my favorite place in the whole world." He looked out the front window. "I always expect that, any minute now, Angela Lansbury will come riding by on a bicycle."

"Are you staying awhile?" Simon asked.

"I have already left my steamer trunks in Bethany's capable hands." George removed his glasses, wiped them with a handkerchief, and put them back on. "Although she tells me that you already have a houseguest. A dark and handsome one."

"You can decide how handsome he is for yourself," said Simon. "But no need to stay somewhere else—I have plenty of room."

George took a breath. "Bethany has ensconced me in Boffin's Bower," he said, referring to the guest suite with an attached sunroom that occasionally served as another breakfast room. "The Junction's answer to Hampton Court." He took Simon's hands. "But enough about me. You must tell me everything about this dreadful crime. What's going on? You're all over the Internet, you know." He pulled out his iPhone. "You're on the *Huffington Post*." He held out the screen, but

Simon pushed his hand back, and George put the phone in his jacket pocket. "The hoi polloi will soon be descending in droves."

Simon hugged him again. "I'd love to talk, but I've got a full plate this afternoon."

George's voice dropped to just above a whisper. "Bethany told me that you have taken a personal interest in bringing the fiend to justice."

"I'm doing what I can," said Simon. "So far, all I'm finding are more suspects...people I know well."

Simon looked around the store. Brock was busy with a small group of elderly women who were asking about Louisa May Alcott. Several other customers browsed near the contemporary novels. One man carried a trade edition of *We the Living*. Another Ayn Rand devotee? How many could there be?

"Well, don't worry about me, my dear," George said. "I won't be in your way. Since today is unusually clear, I think I'll drive into Astoria and admire the river from Coxcomb Hill, although it's past the best light of the day." He looked up through the window; a few white clouds dotted an otherwise unusually blue sky. "Who knows," he added, "the colors may inspire me to do something magical with tissue paper and shellac."

Brock waited on the Rand reader, but after the customer left the store with his purchase, Brock approached Simon and George. "You're going to have to order more Ayn Rand," Brock said. "I don't get it. That's the fifth or sixth title of hers I've sold today. What are they—having a convention?"

"That would be unfortunate," George drawled.

"I hope Dickens Junction isn't being taken over by Objectivist pod people," said Simon.

George left and, after confirming that Brock could manage by himself, Simon decided to try for one more interview before going home for dinner and a debrief with Zach—and now George as well. *That should be an interesting combination,* he thought.

He walked to Wackford Squeers Grade School, where the holiday village display competition would be held the next afternoon, with Grace, Mayor Dick, and Simon as judges.

The gym bustled with people setting up their displays of ceramic houses, buildings, figurines, and other diorama elements for the competition. Simon saw one woman working with electric-train tracks. This was one of the fiercest competitive events of the season—of the twenty or more people who usually competed, most would be here until the gym closed at ten, assembling their Dickensian microcosms in the hopes of winning various prizes, including having a full-color photograph of their handiwork in the next edition of *Household Words.*

Simon waved to Charity Wilkinson, who was standing on the other side of the gym. She was watching Elmer Cuttle thread cables into the back of a giant box that had been decorated with wrapping paper and ribbon to resemble a Christmas package, complete with lid and bright red bow. Elmer's display was often the most ambitious, if not the most artistic, and he was determined to win this year after losing to Mimsie Tricket's astounding (if anachronistic) miniature laser-light show that had formed the center of her previous year's display. From the looks of it, Elmer was going to be a tough competitor again.

Charity gave Elmer an okay signal that he had successfully pulled one of the cables all the way into the giant wrapped box, since he couldn't see around it, and then walked over to Simon.

"You shouldn't prejudice yourself," Charity said, leading Simon out of the gym into the hall. "You'll want to see everything fresh tomorrow."

Charity Wilkinson was a tall, soft, doughy woman with dishwater-brown hair going gray. A bobbed cut accentuated the roundness of her face and pale skin dotted with freckles. She had small dark eyes and a pixie mouth that was almost always smiling. Today she was wearing a cream-colored shaker sweater over canvas drawstring pants and scuffed flats. Her passion for teaching was well known; her students had among the highest college-entrance verbal-exam scores in the county.

"After all these years of judging, do you think I'll see anything new?" He thought about the giant wrapped package. "I suspect Elmer has something up his sleeve."

"He does," Charity said, rolling her eyes. "He says he's 'using the big guns.' Apparently he scored some retired piece off eBay at a price just slightly below my monthly salary."

"Everybody has to have a hobby."

"And Mimsie has something all new that she says people will be talking about for years." Charity shifted her weight on one foot. "When will we be invited over to meet the new man in your life?"

Father Blaise was right—everyone was talking. "I met him yesterday," said Simon. "I can't even call him a 'friend' yet. Would you have me married off that quickly?"

"Yes," she said emphatically. "As soon as the law allows." Viola and Charity had been one of the first couples standing in line when the City of Portland briefly accepted same-sex marriage license applications. Before the constitutional amendment outlawing them once again. Both women were fierce community advocates. Charity also served on the board of a human dignity group, the Rural Organizing Project, that focused on raising consciousness about human rights in Oregon's rural communities. Simon supported the organization generously, but Charity gave of her time as well. Which is why she had gently rebuffed Simon's oft-made suggestions that she consider succeeding Solomon Dick as mayor of the Junction.

Charity cocked her head in the direction of the door to the gym. "They can barely keep their minds on setting up their displays. I heard a rumor that *60 Minutes* called the mayor this morning."

"That one I hadn't heard," said Simon.

"I suppose this Roark was a nasty man," Charity said. "At least Viola told me he was. I never saw him…alive, I mean. And when I did see him—last night—he wasn't at his best."

"So you weren't in town at all yesterday?" Simon asked.

"I barely made it in time for the tableaux," she said.

"Wasn't yesterday a half day for the kids?"

Charity put her hands on her full hips. "Are you asking me if I had an alibi for the time Roark was killed?"

Simon could feel his face turning red. "I—yes. I'm trying to find out what happened. In the eyes of Detective Boggs, we're all suspects."

Charity reached up and put a plump hand on Simon's shoulder. "Relax, Miss Marple," she said, a kind smile on her lips. "We all want the same thing—to protect the Junction. Unfortunately for me," she continued, "you're right. School ended at noon and is on break till after the new year. I cleaned up my desk, said good-bye to the janitor, and went home to decorate the house for the holidays. Every year it seems to take longer to put up the decorations, and I don't have anything as elaborate as those people in there." She nodded again toward the gym. "I lost track of time unpacking my snow globes and was barely able to change and get to the square, where I was to meet Father Blaise. I didn't go shopping or anything else, or have someone drop by the house to deliver a package. So I don't have an alibi."

"I had to ask," he said. Even though he knew he didn't. He was back to doubting the wisdom of Zach's challenge.

"I'm not particularly sorry that he's dead," Charity said. "He wasn't very nice to Viola. I'm lucky that I don't own property in my own name, or he would have been after me, too." She paused. "Do you think we've heard the last of Marley Enterprises, whoever or whatever they might be?"

"No," said Simon. "With Roark dead, I'm afraid it may only be the beginning."

SIMON RETURNED TO THE BOOKSTORE, LETTING BROCK have a few hours off to hit the gym. After a decent late afternoon of holiday shoppers, including two more customers wanting Ayn Rand books, Simon closed the store at six, then spent time in the back room placing new orders and checking Brock's work on publisher returns. Before he knew it, it was after seven thirty, and he had forgotten his houseguest. Guests. It had been nice to find something to concentrate on awhile that wasn't directly related to Mervin Roark's murder.

When he got home, he found George and Zach in the kitchen, laughing. He closed the back door quietly, standing in the mudroom. The other two men hadn't noticed him. Zach was at the stove, a metal spatula in one hand, a glass of red wine in the other. George, more than ten years in recovery, was sitting in a club chair at the island, drinking sparkling water.

"I'm not saying that Simon was a prude in those days," George said, his drawl more heavily pronounced, as it always was when he was spinning a tale, "but I should have known that my little plan would be dead on arrival. So this sweet, shirtless young man at the bar—whose IQ was most likely no greater than the circumference of his bee-stung pectoral area—made Simon an offer so…brutally…*proctological* that Simon went white and stormed off. As if the young man had just admitted…that he read Danielle Steel…with a highlighter." Each of George's caesurae was punctuated by a shriek of laughter from Zach, an uncharacteristically tenor descant.

Simon opened and closed the back door again with greater force. "Honey, I'm home," Simon called. He slipped off his loafers and wiggled his stocking feet.

Zach, wearing Simon's *Kiss the Cook* apron over a well-fitted crimson muscle tee, was sautéing shallots and garlic. Salmon fillets, deep brown and crispy with a light sheen of oil, sizzled in a second pan.

As Simon entered the kitchen, he gave George a kiss on the cheek. And while the invitation of the apron was tantalizing, Simon let his natural shyness hold him in check.

"Bethany gave me free rein in the kitchen," Zach said, "before she took off." He checked the doneness of one fillet with his fingertips. "I promised I wouldn't break any of the Waterford." He poured a glass of one of Simon's best Oregon pinot noirs and nudged it toward Simon.

Simon saw Zach's laptop open on the nook table, a stack of loose papers covered with scribbled notes next to it. "I'm glad the two of you have met," said Simon. He took off his coat and sipped his wine.

"We're practically sisters," George said.

"I fear that George has been telling stories about me."

Zach reached forward across the island and offered George a taste of something on a spoon. "Maybe an anecdote or two," Zach said, smiling.

"Well, don't believe ten percent of what he tells you about me," said Simon. "He's the latest in a long line of liars."

"My stories don't have to be *strictly* true," George said, smacking his lips. "They illuminate character."

Simon didn't know how he felt just now, his oldest friend and his newest—what?—so *entre nous* after mere minutes together. But in another moment, he was distracted by the heavenly kitchen odors, as Zach dropped handfuls of chopped kale into the sauté pan and began mixing the leaves in with the shallots and garlic. The kale quickly turned soft in the warm oil and steam; within a minute or so, the meal was on a platter.

"Go," Zach said, shooing George and Simon into the dining room. "I'll be in with everything in just a minute. Then we'll talk about what we all learned today."

Simon followed George into the dining room, which was set with Simon's heirloom china, crystal, and silver. The two men sat; Zach followed a few minutes later, minus the apron, the salmon platter in one hand and a serving bowl of caramelized carrots and Brussels sprouts topped with toasted pine nuts in the other. His biceps were taut, stretching the armbands of the crimson shirt. Simon struggled momentarily with a rush of jumbled thoughts—Zach's breezy familiarity with Simon's home and things, the fact that he was a virtual stranger, the way he filled out that shirt...

"We're going European tonight," Zach said, sitting. "Salad to follow." He sat across from Simon and gave him a wink as he unfolded his napkin and smoothed it across his lap. "Cheers." Zach raised his glass. "To success." Simon and George raised theirs; the three glasses clinked below the Waterford chandelier. "Now, let's eat."

The salmon, kale, and vegetables all were delicious. Simon thought about the last time a man had cooked for him—David, five years earlier. A man could get used to this…good food, a dinner date who was easy on the eyes…

After chewing for a few minutes in silence, Zach blurted out, “Who did you talk to, and who’s got an alibi?”

Simon put down his fork and poured more wine. He didn’t usually have more than two drinks in an evening, but tonight might be worth celebrating for many reasons. He looked over at George, whose gaze shifted from Simon to Zach, then back to Simon.

“Well,” said Simon, “everyone I talked to—Brad Sturgess, Grace Beddoes, Viola Mintun, Father Blaise, Mavis Spurlock, and Charity Wilkinson—had a story about their whereabouts from four thirty until six thirty or so, when Roark was nail-gunned at the storage shed. But of that group, only Viola and Father Blaise have potential corroborators—Viola was at a Pilates class, and Father Blaise was at the Tiny Tim competition.”

“Surely you don’t suspect Father What-a-Waste,” George said.

“Everyone who could have murdered Roark should be considered,” Zach said. “Did you check out their stories?”

“Not yet,” said Simon. “But I suspect that Detective Boggs has. Of the others, Grace and Charity were alone at home. Mavis says she was in Astoria, as was Brad Sturgess, each on some kind of business. Something about Sturgess’s story, though, just doesn’t make sense, and Mavis’s also had interesting wrinkles. Furthermore, both Brad and Ladasha mentioned Lowell Brundish. Sturgess said Brundish had been researching land sales, and Ladasha said Brundish called Mavis just after she left Bleak House."

Zach left the table and returned a minute later with his notes, along with a platter of baby endive salad with—Simon tasted in his first bite—caper and tarragon vinaigrette. Zach had found Simon's pleasure center…at least one of them.

"I've got that name here, somewhere, too," Zach said. "Doesn't he own land on the square?"

Zach held out a hand-drawn map of Dickens Square, showing the buildings and businesses, along with the location of the four tableaux displays.

"Yes." Simon pointed at the map with his fork. "Grace owns this half of this block, and Lowell owns the other half."

"I am transported," George said, skewering a leaf of baby endive. "Food should not taste this good." Simon echoed his sentiments.

"Thank you both," Zach said. "But keep going, Simon. What else did you learn?"

"Those who own property—at least, Mavis, Grace, Viola, and Mayor Dick—all had meetings with Roark sometime during the day. The stories are pretty similar: Roark, on behalf of Marley Enterprises, offered exorbitant sums to buy their properties, and made vague threats about the consequences if they didn't." He took Roark's card that Grace had given him from his wallet. "Here's what he offered Grace."

George whistled when he saw the figure. Zach took the card and held it next to something he had drawn on one of his pages—an oversize dollar sign.

"Yes," Zach said. "I almost expected to see this."

George cleared the table; Zach poured himself another glass of wine. When George returned, Zach picked up the rest of the papers. "I had the toughest assignment," he said. "I had to interview Brock." Zach looked at George. "Gorgeous, but I don't think he'll ever win a Nobel Prize."

"I've known him since he was born," said Simon. "Paid for his education."

"Brock is a certified personal trainer," George told Zach. "And Simon's workout partner. Isn't that convenient."

"Maybe I'll schedule a session with him," Zach said.

"He could hold your feet—" George began.

"Stop right there," said Simon.

Zach smiled. "Anyway, Brock made several trips to the shed to get items for the tableaux. He wasn't watching the clock, but figures he left the shed around four thirty and didn't return again until around six thirty. And that's when he made his last pickup, which included Roark's corpse. So he wasn't at the shed for the two hours during which Roark was killed."

"Unless he killed Roark himself at the shed at the time of his first trip," George said.

Simon pursed his lips. *What an unpleasant thought.* But they were all unpleasant thoughts. Everyone was a suspect. Everyone might be lying. By now, they all knew the estimated time of death, so of course Brock would know to say he wasn't at the shed then. Once again, Simon considered—it was possible, even probable, that he knew the murderer.

"Duncan Neff was at the shed when Brock got there for the last trip," said Simon.

"That's what Brock told me, too," Zach said. "That certainly bears looking into. This Neff—whatever his story is—could have murdered Roark, and Brock nearly caught him in the act. By the way," Zach added, giving Simon an exaggerated scolding look, "you need to give that young man a lighter work schedule. He yawned constantly when I was talking to him. Made him look less than his potential."

"Ah, youth," George said. "I had that once."

Simon pushed his chair away from the table. "What else did you learn, besides how my assistant's mouth looks opened wide?"

George snickered.

"Well," Zach said, after letting his gaze linger on Simon a moment longer than was necessary, "I spent most of my time getting to know Marley Enterprises. And it's aptly named, for it's truly a ghost operation. Very hazy information. Some kind of worldwide interests, a philosophical think tank, maybe even a religious organization. Hard to tell. Its logo is the dollar sign, prominently displayed on the website, which is otherwise almost worthless for determining what it actually does. But other websites show that the CEO of Marley Enterprises is a woman with the improbable name of Dagny Clack."

Zach held up a printed page showing a photograph of a petite woman of indeterminate age walking across an airport tarmac. "Date unknown. Very few photographs of her after high school."

Another photograph showed a startled-looking girl, slightly pretty, but also like tens of thousands of other young women from the 1970s. "Allegedly owns homes in Zurich, London, and New York. Her education record is interesting—she has a PhD in post–World War II American literature. But the local connection is the one I found most interesting."

George and Simon leaned forward.

"Oh, I forgot something," Zach said. George groaned at the delay. Zach returned from the kitchen with his messenger bag. He reached in and pulled out a paperback copy of *Atlas Shrugged.*

It was Simon's turn to groan. "Again?"

"Within the last two years, Ms. Clack attempted to donate a larger-than-life bronze statue of Ayn Rand to Meriwether University in Portland, in honor of a rare visit Miss Rand made there in 1963 to receive an honorary degree."

"Father Blaise's alma mater," said Simon.

"What happened?" George asked.

"Well, according to news stories, the statue was rejected by the board of regents as 'not reflecting the current values of the community.'"

"Thank God for that," said Simon.

"What does that have to do with the Junction?" George asked.

"I don't know," Zach said. "Maybe you should ask Father Blaise to follow up on that." He thumbed the pages. "Ever read this?"

"When I was a callow youth," said Simon.

"Same here," George said. "In my salad days. A near total waste of time. 'Who is John Galt?' A crashing bore." He chuckled. "I do remember, however, having jaw-dropping sex with a bespectacled young freshman crazy for Rand. A gymnast. I said many a prayer kneeling before his iron cross..."

"Well, this big book is one of the top-selling books online," Zach continued, "more than fifty years after publication."

"Only a hundred years less than *David Copperfield*," said Simon. "Or *Middlemarch* or *Moby Dick*."

"I read a few pages today," Zach said, "but if I try to plow through the whole thing, I won't get much other research done."

"Here," George said, "give it to me. It's been forever since I read it, so I guess I could take a bullet for the team and read it again."

Zach handed George the novel. He started to pour more wine into Simon's glass, but Simon put his hand over it. "I shouldn't," said Simon.

"He's the original two-beer screamer," George said.

"These walls look pretty thick," Zach said, nudging Simon's fingers aside. He poured more wine into the glass.

Simon coughed. "So, what's on for tomorrow?" He took a sip of wine. As though Zach could look even more handsome, a pinot blush to his cheeks...or was it Simon's eyes that were wine-dark?

"For you?" Zach asked. "The Neffs, if you have time."

"I've got to judge the holiday village competition, but that's not until late afternoon. I could try." He paused. "The Neffs are no friends of mine. I'm sure they wouldn't talk to you," he said to Zach, "but they might not be willing to talk to me, either."

"But you need to see them tomorrow. And this Brundish, too. I have a feeling he met with Roark. Everyone's a suspect."

"Except me," George said. "I'm a complete innocent."

Simon laughed. "As innocent as Fagin, maybe."

George stood. "On that high compliment, gentlemen, I'll retire for the evening and leave you to your scheming." He put a hand on Simon's. "I can tell when I have nothing further to offer." Simon felt George's hand trail across his shoulders and back and then watched it touch briefly on Zach's shoulder before he headed off to Boffin's Bower.

Zach took a sip of wine. "Alone at last."

Simon let the moment hang in the air before responding. He needed a little time to decompress from all of this talk about the murder. And the third glass of wine was making him very relaxed, even sleepy, a welcome feeling after the previous evening's events. "Tell me a little about yourself," he said, finally.

Zach was quite the talker, especially when the topic was himself. He started with the basics. Thirty-nine, the middle of three children of professional parents. His mother a patent lawyer, his father a psychologist. Raised "a casual Jew," he fell away from Judaism not long after his bar mitzvah. "I tell people now that I have a hint of atheist in me," he said. Close to his two sisters, one a speech pathologist, the other an accountant. "I'm the only one who bounced around from school to school," he said, although he did manage to get a journalism degree before taking a series of writing contracts as a freelance journalist. For relaxation, time at the gym, reading history, and sailing.

Vague on his past romantic pursuits, except in one area. "Younger men are too indecisive about their careers and too self-absorbed," he said. Casual attitude toward money. "I've got enough to get by," he said. "Saving is for tomorrow."

Simon had almost finished the last of the wine, and realized he was sliding down in his chair. He moved his feet to brace himself and felt Zach's bare foot against his own.

"I'm glad I'm here," Zach said. "To help."

Zach's foot resting against his own felt comforting and scary. Simon moved his foot away. "I should turn in early," he said.

"Ready to scream?" Zach smiled.

"Something like that," said Simon.

"You're safe with me," Zach added. "If that's what you want."

"T'mrrow," said Simon, his tongue catching on the word, "the Neffs. And Bru-nissh."

As he stood, he felt unsteady on his feet. He hadn't had this much to drink in a long time and, on top of his tiredness, maybe it was too much. Zach was at his side, hands on Simon's shoulders, holding him close. Simon felt the warmth of Zach's large hands through his shirt, felt Zach's breath against his cheek.

"I'm okay," said Simon.

Zach held him a second longer, until Simon moved away, steady enough on his feet now to walk away.

"Good night, sweet prince," Zach said.

Simon went directly to his room, undressed, and got into bed. *That does it,* he thought. *More three-glass dinners.* He promptly fell asleep.

Sometime after midnight, he awoke, his deep sleep colored with troubling dreams. The only image he could remember was of a giant bronze Ayn Rand head being screwed onto the statue in the center of Dickens Square.

His mouth was dry and his nose was stuffed up, a common side effect when he drank wine or hard liquor. *That does it,* he thought. *No more three-glass dinners. Too many pitfalls.*

He pulled on his Egyptian cotton robe, stumbled downstairs to the kitchen, awake but not coordinated, poured a glass of milk, drank it, and returned to the hallway. A light shone behind the partially open doors to Boffin's Bower. He knocked.

"Yes, my dear?" George answered. "Come in."

"You're up late, aren't you?" Simon pushed the door open and entered the suite.

George was sitting in a chaise in the sunroom beyond the sleeping area. Light from the floor lamp behind the chaise reflected against the glass wall in front of him. Miss Tox was curled up at George's feet. Simon sat beside him in a wing chair.

George was reading *Atlas Shrugged.* He placed a bookmark about a hundred pages in and laid the book beside Miss Tox. "To answer your question," George said, "I don't go to bed with the chickens these days. Since Beck died..."

George had lost his partner of nine years, Beck Roland, early in the year, to a sudden heart attack. Simon put his hand on George's. "I'm sorry," he said. "I didn't mean—"

"It's all right," George said. "But what about you? I heard you stumble to bed hours ago, flushed with wine and, no doubt, the blandishments of the silver-tongued Mr. Benjamin."

Simon decided to let that go. "A bad dream," he said.

"About?"

"The future of the Junction."

"We all love your broad manly shoulders," George said, taking said shoulders in his grasp. "But the Junction's fate doesn't rest on them alone, although you've never understood that. This 'investigation' you're doing is dangerous. I wish you'd stop. I don't want to think that there is a doornail out there with your name on it."

Simon chuckled. "I appreciate your concern. I'm glad you're here."

"Are you? With that man just a few feet away from your boudoir? I wonder."

"I met him yesterday," said Simon. He put his feet up on the chaise, not far from George. "You like him, don't you?" This was a risky question; Simon valued George's opinion more than almost anyone else's. No one knew him better.

"I do, dammit," he said. "It doesn't take long to see that he's quite a guy." George gave a sly smile, the corners of his eyes wrinkling. "Of course, so was Ted Bundy."

That Zach might be Roark's murderer had crossed Simon's mind more than once, but he had dismissed the thought each time. Now, he addressed only George's first suggestion. "He's a journalist, and murder is a newsworthy event. There's no evidence that his primary motive for being here is an older owner of a peculiar little bookstore in an even more peculiar small town."

George reached down and began rubbing Simon's feet. "You have your charms."

"Let's just say that they haven't been appreciated in a while." Simon wiggled his toes.

"You think the goods are shopworn by now, my dear?"

Simon pulled his feet back. "This metaphor has grown too thin."

George looked serious now. "Then I shall be more direct: Don't let Zach go because of your coyness, or indifference, or laserlike focus on the Junction. If nothing serious develops, 'no harm, no foul,' they say in sports—although I don't exactly know which sports—and if you do get serious, great. Take the plunge."

"And get hurt?" Simon asked. "I don't want to make the same mistake a third time."

"The only mistake you can make, my dear," George looked at Simon over the tops of his bifocals, "besides getting yourself killed by the madman in our midst, is to hide your lamp under a bushel. As it were." George smiled and ruffled Simon's hair. "Now, go, throw that lamp in the ring and see what happens."

STAVE

THE SECOND OF THE BODIES

Simon was up early the next morning and left the house before George and Zach were awake. He got a good workout at the gym, although he had to fend off questions about finding Roark's body and the future of the Junction. He got to the bookstore before Brock and decided to do a visual scan for inventory gaps that needed filling. Brock was right; the Ayn Rand books were sold out. Simon had read her novels when he was in college. Since he hadn't read her nonfiction, he didn't stock it. He made notes on other books that needed to be reordered. More Flannery O'Connor. A few gaps in the

Nancy Drews. Pippi Longstockings, so popular with the local Scandinavian population. And more Austen, the perennial best seller. At least Dickens was moving, too, although not with the freakish pace of Ms. Rand.

He waited until after nine to call Lowell Brundish. He didn't know Brundish as well as the other property owners in the square; Brundish and his wife had moved to the Junction about five years earlier and bought Nimrod and Reel and the building housing it (and tenants Pickwick Pilates and Finching for Flowers) from the previous owner's widow. The rod and tackle shop had been a labor of love, but it fell victim to a big-box store in Warrenton, across Youngs Bay. Brundish had closed the store six months earlier without notifying any of the other property owners in the square; shortly thereafter, he and his wife divorced and she left the Junction. Simon had seen Brundish only occasionally since that time, most notably the afternoon of Roark's murder.

He looked up Brundish's number on his contact list and dialed. Brundish's voice was gruff even on the voice-mail message: "Leave your number. I'll call back." Simon left a message. Brundish was probably having breakfast at one of the diners on the old highway or in Astoria, or maybe he was screening his calls.

Simon e-mailed Grace that he would see her at the regular time and then started placing his stock orders while waiting for customers. He also left a voice mail with Ariadne Neff, asking her to call at her earliest convenience. Fortunately, he would see her when she arrived at her office next door.

Brock arrived about ten o'clock. He looked tired in his rumpled jeans and unironed shirt, and confirmed that by yawning even before he had put his latte on the counter.

"Late night?" Simon asked.

"Something like that," Brock answered. He yawned again.

"Any chance you saw Lowell Brundish this morning?"

"I came directly here from Bleak House," Brock answered, "except for the coffee. And I didn't see him at the Palace. That's not his usual place, I don't think."

"Ariadne Neff? Or maybe Duncan?"

"Neither one." Brock was starting to look more tired, which Simon hadn't imagined possible.

Ten minutes later, Simon was in the back, dealing with a backorder snafu for *The Mill on the Floss*. When he returned to the front, Brock was asleep at the counter, his head forward, his back rounded. Simon touched his shoulder; Brock jerked awake.

"Are you hung over?" Simon asked.

"You know I don't drink," Brock said. His eyes looked left, right, anywhere but at Simon. "No, I just had a late night last night." He reached in his back pocket, pulled out a folded piece of paper, unfolded it, and handed it to Simon. "You might as well know, too," he said. "Everyone will, sooner or later."

It was a poster advertising: *Anita Distraction's Presents 4 One Nite Only—The Men of Midnight: Male Exotic Dancers.* The poster listed various "names" of dancers—Oblivion, Mysterion,

The Pulse, Rod-Rigo—and showed a grainy black-and-white photo of a man wearing a G-string and an eye mask, posed in a twisted dancelike position, arms above the head, knees slightly bent, crotch pushed forward. Even with all that, Simon recognized Brock's close-cropped hair, round head, thick thighs, and six-pack—he studied them every week after their workout session at the gym.

"Which name is yours?" Simon asked.

"Mysterion. I thought it would be okay—I mean—less obvious—if I wore the mask."

"And not much else."

"I have nothing to be ashamed of," Brock said defensively.

"That is true," Simon said quietly. He hadn't said it to be judgmental. "I wasn't aware that Anita Distraction's had gone so—edgy."

"This was a test," Brock said. "They wanted to see if they could catch the bachelorette crowd on a weeknight." He smiled. "It worked—the place was packed—women of all ages...and a few men in the back."

Simon still held on to the poster. "And how did you do? Any tips?"

"More than two hundred dollars," he said. "I probably could make more if I practice—I'm not a very good dancer."

"My experience—as a patron of male exotic terpsichorean art—informs me that it doesn't much matter in this area," said Simon. "Does Bethany know?"

"Sure," Brock answered. "She and her girlfriends signed me up."

Simon knew Bethany and Ladasha were good friends and would bet this was the girls' night out Ladasha had referred to as a "jazz" night.

"What about your mother?" Simon tried to look absent-minded as he folded the poster and put it in the back pocket of his slacks.

"I decided not to tell her. But here's the weird thing." Brock sat straight up and looked at Simon. "Mom showed up just after midnight, by coincidence, I'm sure, looking for a place to have a drink."

"What made it weird?"

"She came in with Bradford Sturgess," Brock said. "I was backstage waiting to go on, but it looked as if they were, you know, on a date." Brock made a slight pout. "That's what's weird."

In the years Simon had known Mavis, he couldn't recall seeing her with anyone, at least not on a regular basis. Sturgess had been divorced for years. *Well,* Simon thought, *they're single, about the same age*—if they were dating and trying to keep it a secret, that might explain the off-kilter answers they had given him yesterday. If they had been together in Astoria—or were covering for one another—they might have alibis for Roark's murder.

"Your mom's an adult," said Simon. He had a thought, and it made him smile. "You think that your mom on a date is weird, but don't comment on the fact that you stripped in front of her?"

"That would have been weird, too," Brock said, "but they left before I went onstage. I don't think it was Mom's cup of tea.

Or Sturgess's either. But Bethany and her friends had a great time—good tippers, too."

The door to the shop opened; both Brock and Simon looked over. George was standing at the doorway entrance, dressed in fawn pants, a full tweed Inverness cape, and a deerstalker cap. He held an oversize Meerschaum pipe in one hand, an umbrella in the other. "I'm here to solve crimes," he said.

Simon laughed. "I'm thinking you didn't just throw that in your bag when you packed to come here."

"An excellent deduction," George said, attempting to throw a British accent on top of his Georgia drawl. "I got this at Weller's Fictional Characters Costume Shop." With all of the festive events in the Junction, a specialty shop like Weller's was a necessity. "And it seemed like just the thing to cheer you up," George continued. "So much more appropriate than Captain Ahab's peg leg or Hester Prynne's overachievement appliqué."

"I don't think you will be of much assistance to my inquiries if you plan on accompanying me dressed like that."

George took off the cap. "My dear, I have no intention of throwing myself in harm's way along with you. I'm off to do some sketches today."

"Have a good time," Simon told him. "But just be back for the holiday village event at four thirty. I need all the moral support I can get."

The store was busy much of the morning. Brock started to wake up after finishing a second latte, so Simon spent some time in the back room paying invoices and catching up on business mail. Twice more he tried to reach Lowell Brundish, but hung up each time after getting his voice mail.

A stray thought caused Simon to do a search on Marley Enterprises. While he was viewing the material Zach had found yesterday, including the photograph of the elusive Dagny Clack, his cell phone rang.

"Just checking in," Zach said. "Do you have a headache after last night's revels?"

"Fortunately, no," said Simon. "But I'll be wiser next time."

"Darn," Zach said. "I should have taken advantage of you when your defenses were down."

"Who says they'll be up tonight?" Simon couldn't believe he had just said that. "What's on your agenda for today?" he asked, changing the subject.

"More Internet research, and I need to check in with the magazine. Let them know how the article's coming."

"Is it coming?"

"I'm not sure," Zach said. "What I'm doing here with Marley Enterprises, and with you, is a lot more interesting than another 'top ten sites' article."

After Zach agreed to meet him for the holiday village competition, Simon rang off. The sound of Zach's voice had made Simon's heart rate increase. What was that about? Was he, as Brock might have said it, crushing on Zach? Wasn't that for kids, or at least a younger man than himself? Zach's flirtatiousness was flattering, but Simon assumed it was part of his character, not really serious. But what if Zach was serious?

Except for a few casual dates, Simon had not had a relationship since he and David had broken up five years earlier, the city boy going back to the city, leaving Simon alone in Dickens Junction. Zach was another big-city boy. Nothing could come of it, even if he wasn't just flirting. Zach was attractive, intelligent, funny, and even had earned the ultra-finicky George's seal of approval. Simon was capable of returning the flirtation, and more, if it came to that. Maybe George was right—why not see where it would lead? Even if Zach left for Guadeloupe, Palau, Myanmar, Phuket, or wherever his magazine might send him next, why not enjoy his company while he was here?

Simon had picked up his cell phone to try Brundish again when Brock stuck his head in at the door to the back. "Ariadne just unlocked the office door," Brock said.

Simon threw on his sport coat and left the store. Out in the square, the Dickens Carolers were making the rounds, singing "Silent Night." In the day's bright, crisp air, their full-length coats were, no doubt, more than just costumes, and the singer holding the faux-ermine muff must have appreciated it more than usual. Simon smiled at them, and they returned his smile. Then he turned back around and opened the door of Riderhood Realty.

Ariadne stood in the middle of the small office, looking at the four neat desks, two of which were utterly bare. A year earlier, all four desks had been occupied, but Ariadne had let two agents go after the economy started to slide and home sales nearly stopped. Simon knew that the other agent had been dismissed a week earlier. So she was alone now in the office; even the part-time secretary had been let go. Ariadne was handling the few appointments herself with the help of voice mail and a BlackBerry.

"Simon," she said, "what can I do for you?"

Ariadne Neff looked several years younger than her thirty-five years, a combination of excellent genes and skin-care products. She had soft honey-blond hair worn shoulder length, with sharp brown eyes darting constantly, taking everything in. She had high cheekbones, a nose Simon suspected had been shaped by a plastic surgeon, and a narrow jaw that gave her angular face an unapproachable feel, in spite of her beauty. She was always impeccably dressed, today in a navy pencil skirt and white tailored blouse. Her legs were athletic, waxed, and bare. She wore designer heels that lengthened her line and showed off her calves. The skirt's matching navy jacket hung on a padded hanger on the coatrack.

"I hope this isn't a bad time," said Simon. "I wanted to talk with you."

Ariadne looked him up and down, and then gestured with an open palm. Simon thought she was inviting him to sit, but she remained standing. "If you wish," she said. "I'm not going to pretend to be busy. As you can see, I'm not—at the moment." Her voice was cool, almost breathy. She wasn't going to make things easy for Simon.

"I just wanted to ask you a few things about Mervin Roark," he said.

She pursed her thin lips. "I've told everything I know to Detective Boggs," she said.

"Yes," said Simon, "but I'm just trying to understand more about why he was in the Junction, what he wanted."

"You could have asked him yourself," she said. "He called on you, I believe."

"He did," Simon admitted, "but he didn't disclose—at least to me—what he was doing in the village."

"I assume you have found that out by now," she said.

Simon shifted from one foot to the other. "He wanted to buy some property. A lot of it, so it seems."

"What of that?" Ariadne tossed off the line, but with an edge that Simon thought bordered on disrespect.

"He didn't achieve much success with his efforts."

Ariadne checked her nails. "I don't know about that," she said.

Simon took another tack. "I saw you at the tableaux the other night."

She lowered her head for a moment. "I fainted. Yes. It was a horrible sight."

"You had seen Roark before?"

She turned away. "I told Detective Boggs everything I knew about Roark."

"Yes," said Simon, "but I'm trying to understand."

"I met him once or twice," she said. "And spoke to him a few times."

"Were you representing anyone who might have been interested in selling property to Marley Enterprises?"

"That's none of your business," she said. She took her blazer from the coat hanger and put it on, smoothing the front and buttoning the button. *She is as angular as a razor,* Simon thought. *Is she as dangerous?*

"My apologies," he said. "Had you seen him that afternoon before the tableaux?"

"I had not," she said.

"I think I recall seeing him come in here while I was at the Crystal Palace," said Simon.

Ariadne's face flushed. "Oh, yes. He opened the door, but I was on the phone, and he left again without leaving a note."

"And you didn't see him again?"

She checked her nails again. "Not until..."

"Do you mind telling me what you were doing the rest of the afternoon?"

She smirked. "You mean while someone was killing him? I most certainly do mind telling you. But I will. I was meeting with a client." She tugged the cuffs of her blouse past the edges of her blazer. "I have told all of this to Detective Boggs."

"Please," said Simon.

"Everything will come out soon enough, I suppose," she said. "The client was Lowell Brundish."

"Yes," said Simon. "I brushed into him that afternoon. He was leaving your office."

Her eyes widened. "We met again, later. At his house. In private. I was there until I came to the tableaux."

Simon's eyes wandered to the one cluttered desk in the office. On the corner rested a paperback copy of Ayn Rand's *The Virtue of Selfishness.* For obvious reasons, Simon hadn't read that one. He looked at the cover and perfect condition of the thin volume. Neither had Ariadne—at least not yet.

"Now that Roark is dead," Simon started, knowing he was now on shaky ground, "will you be representing Marley Enterprises?"

"Enough questions. You think that everything here belongs to you," Ariadne continued, pushing the words through her teeth. "You're bad for the market. Not everyone has your money—maybe no one in the Junction does. Not now, at least. But because you have enough, you use your influence to keep rents down and keep other owners from maximizing the profit from their investment."

"You've never objected to the modest rent I charge you," he said.

Ariadne tapped her foot. "I've already told you more than I had to, Simon. You'll find out what's going to happen in the Junction soon enough. I can't stop you, but I don't have to help you, either." With a few clipped steps she was in front of the door to the office, opening it. "Now, please excuse me. I have an appointment."

ON HIS WAY TO THE CRYSTAL PALACE TO MEET GRACE, Simon made another call to Lowell Brundish. Voice mail.

When he got to the tearoom, Grace was sitting at their usual table, drinking a cappuccino. Caitlin took Simon's order and returned a few minutes later with his latte in a giant mug.

"I had to get an early start," Grace said, tilting her cup slightly. "I took a sleeping pill last night, went to bed early, and still had trouble getting up this morning. I didn't want any more bad dreams."

"You, too?" Simon asked. "I had a few glasses of wine, but even they didn't stop me from a nightmare or two."

"I hope they catch the murderer soon," she said. "People are starting to get very nervous. Two people backed out of the holiday village competition because of it. Out-of-towners, but still—"

"Have you seen Lowell Brundish?" Simon asked. "I've been trying to reach him all morning."

"I haven't," she said. "He doesn't come into the square much anymore. I hope we won't see more closures after the holidays. Business is down everywhere—Solomon told me yesterday that even his lottery and video-poker receipts are down by twenty percent."

"I thought gambling was recession-proof," said Simon. He had never been happy with video gaming in the square, even though both the Porters and Mr. Dick's had placed their machines in discreet locations inside their establishments.

The tearoom was busier than it had been for the last few days; Simon hoped that, because it was the last full weekend before the holiday, more shoppers would come and give the square its proper holiday feeling. Viola stopped by to say hello. Father Blaise waved to them as he stopped to pick up a coffee drink; Ariadne Neff avoided looking at Simon when she came in later and also picked up something in a go cup. A woman about sixty sat alone eating Miss Havisham's cake and reading a library copy of *The Fountainhead*. Simon wondered, *Why not* Dombey and Son*? Or even* The Da Vinci Code*?*

Grace looked up. A horde of raingear-clad passengers was making its way into the square. One of the tour buses must have arrived for the day's events. "We had better get back to our stores," Grace said. "See you at the judges' table."

THE VILLAGE DISPLAY COMPETITION WAS ONE OF THE newer holiday events. Simon and Grace had judged since the event began eight years ago, and Solomon Dick joined as a third judge when he was elected mayor. Charity Wilkinson had been the volunteer administrator since inception. At her urging, a separate children's competition was established last year.

Grace and Mayor Dick were chatting with Charity near the exhibition entrance at the front of the Wackford Squeers Grade School gymnasium when Simon arrived. Charity handed the preprinted judges' worksheet to Simon, along with a clipboard. A steady stream of individuals lined up to enter the gymnasium. Simon noted at least three different tour-company logos on visitor name badges.

"A good crowd," said Simon. "I was afraid from what Grace had heard about the competitors that we might see similar reluctance on the part of spectators."

"And at least that many are already inside," Charity said.

She straightened the giant green orchid corsage that someone had given her. It looked festive, if somewhat at odds with the pumpkin pantsuit she was wearing. Mayor Dick was wearing his usual too-tight white dress shirt (no undershirt) and bolo tie with gray slacks and houndstooth polyester blazer. Grace had changed into a simple shirtwaist dress a bit small for her, but more suitable than the usual tunic and tights. Simon had stopped by the house to put on a custom-tailored red-and-green windowpane dress shirt, with black slacks and a raw-silk sport coat.

Charity was using Simon's worksheet as her example for all the judges, pointing at various places on the form. "To the Mayor's Award, Most Consistent Theme, and the Grand Prize, we added Best Kinetics this year; for the children, there are Most Humorous and Grand Prize." For each grand-prize winner, the award was a complete set of the works of Dickens, donated by Pip's Pages. Other honorees were awarded gift certificates redeemable at any shop on the square.

"We've got thirty total entrants this year," Charity continued, "ten of those children." Charity looked at each judge in turn. "Don't forget—everything you say will be overheard by some contestant's favorite aunt." Mayor Dick blushed. Last year, a half-unkind remark he had whispered to Simon about an architectural anachronism involving railroad bridges had created a minor melee with the contestant's extended family.

"We'll start with the children," Charity said.

As they entered the gymnasium, Simon heard the garbled sounds of music coming from the various displays that had an accompanying soundtrack. Flashes of light shot through the gym; at the back, a papier-mâché mountain ten feet high towered over all other entrants, including the giant beribboned package housing Elmer Cuttle's complex electronics. A pleasant savory fragrance wafted through the air—sage and onions, perhaps?

"Have you piped in holiday smells," Simon asked, "like one of those mall sweet shops, trying to influence our votes?"

"I don't know where that's coming from," Charity answered. "I noticed it earlier, too. The school kitchen is closed for the holidays, and the concession stand at the far end is only selling hot cider, coffee, and tea."

"Well," said Mayor Dick, "it cheers me up after all this hubbub. I have not had a good day."

Simon enjoyed the innocent creativity of the children's displays, in contrast to the sometimes overenthusiastic productions from the adults. He smiled at nine-year-old Madison Burgee's simple re-creation of Dickens Square, complete with statue, except that the clay head bore an uncanny resemblance to that very popular young-adult zombie novelist whose books Simon didn't finish and, therefore, didn't stock at Pip's Pages.

Grace gestured toward ten-year-old Günter Grub's entry. Günter had built a mantel with carved and painted corbels, on top of which sat various handmade figurines on a bed of spun glass.

"It's called 'First Year,'" said the small boy standing next to the display. Simon recognized a young version of himself—a boy cleaner and better groomed than his classmates, and the only male contestant in the children's division.

Simon looked at his ballot. "That's very clever," he said. "You've attempted to represent someone's first year of collecting."

"These are all my pieces," Günter said, his voice high, clear, and confident beyond his years. "I made the corbels with the router. I wore safety glasses. My mom watched, but she didn't help."

Grace and Mayor Dick had moved on to the next entry. Simon joined them. The smell of sage and onions was making him hungry. Peering over the bonnet of a strolling Dickens Caroler, Simon looked for George and Zach in the various clusters of people inching along the serpentine path through the displays.

Mayor Dick stood in front of twelve-year-old Zanita Albers's entry, a slanted board containing a re-creation of San Francisco's famed Seven Sisters, the hillside Victorian homes featured in virtually every postcard shop in the city. "Very clever," he said. A miniature Transamerica building poked through in the background. The foreground was dotted with springtime trees.

Grace looked around before she spoke. "I suspect her dads helped her," she said, making a negative mark on her ballot.

The three judges continued through the rest of the children's entries until they reached the end. Simon moved them into a corner so that they could mark their worksheets and discuss their findings.

"I need a break before we start the big displays," the mayor said. "I have to eat a cookie or something. I'm starving."

"Five minutes, then," Grace said. "Meet us at the Matterhorn."

Simon walked with Grace toward the papier-mâché monstrosity in the far corner of the gymnasium. Ezekiel Froom had constructed an alpine mountainside with working funicular railway that went to the top and returned on a narrow-gauge track. In addition, he had built a miniature ski lift, complete with skiers and snowboarders. Ski runs with carved-soap moguls wound their way past chalets and, in one case, a miniature hewn-log cabin. A ceramic snowshoer stood near one chalet, tiny shoe prints showing his approach from the bottom of the ski lift. Multiple song snippets played on a loop—Simon recognized "Funiculi, Funicula" and an accordion rendering of "The Happy Wanderer."

"Did you ever get hold of Lowell?" Grace asked.

Simon's eyes followed one ski-lift chair to the top of the mountain and back to the bottom. He shook his head. "I tried three more times after I saw you."

Grace looked around the crowd, as if searching for Brundish. "Look," she said, "here come your friends."

George threaded his way through the crowd; Zach followed behind. As they approached, Simon also noticed others in the crowd. There was Father Blaise, talking with young Günter Grub, while, in another section, Mavis Spurlock chatted with Joelle Creevy. Near them, wearing a chic black ruched cocktail dress and gladiator heels perhaps better suited to a gallery opening than a community contest, Detective Boggs moved among the crowd, watching both the displays and the onlookers. She acknowledged Simon when their eyes met, and started walking toward him.

George and Zach, Detective Boggs, and Mayor Dick, cookie crumbs at the corners of his mouth, were converging at once on Simon and Grace.

"Good afternoon, Detective," said Simon. "I wouldn't have expected this to be your kind of thing."

She smiled again. "I've been pretty busy on the case," she said. "I needed a break."

Grace waited with the mayor while he made notes on the Matterhorn; the others slid over to the next display.

They were standing next to the astounding display of perennial winner Mimsie Tricket. Within a ten-foot square frame, hills gently rolled behind a city grid. The downtown square surrounded an ice skating rink, which, according to the description, was actual ice kept frozen by a hidden compressor. Narrow tracks allowed tiny skaters to perform salchows and axels, while a motorized sleigh circled the perimeter of the rink. Fronting the square, ceramic Edwardian brownstones glowed with tiny interior candles. Working replicas of gas lamps gave each tree-lined street a precious sense of proportion. A small river ran through the center of town, passing a working water wheel and mill. Off the river, Mimsie had built a canal with horse-drawn boat drifting past bucolic taverns, thatched cottages, and a house "on fire," glowing from a flickering red light within. A ceramic fire brigade siphoned water from the canal using a hand-operated pump; a stream of water dribbled through the air into a trough that surrounded the house. The fire hose needed more pressure, Simon thought.

"I'm strangely hungry all of a sudden," George said. "You know, for a Cornish pasty or bubble and squeak. Is that Dickensian enough?"

Mimsie Tricket, a pleasant woman in her early forties who spent the time she wasn't working on her holiday display caring for an invalid mother, was nowhere to be seen. "She's underneath the display," Grace said, when she saw Simon looking for Mimsie. "She has a command post down there to keep track of all of the machinery. She uses floor pedals, like an organ. It looked very complicated when I stopped by yesterday afternoon while she was setting up."

"I like it," the mayor said to Grace. "This may be her best effort yet."

"I'm inclined to agree," Grace said. She made a few notes on her worksheet.

"Have you been busy today?" Zach asked Simon. He stood close. Even through the pall of sage and onions, Simon could smell the wintergreen breath mint Zach had in his mouth, a cool heat on his cheek.

"I didn't reach Lowell Brundish, but I discovered something interesting." He pulled Brock's poster out of his pocket and handed it to Zach.

Zach unfolded the paper. "Too bad we missed this," he said.

"There's more to the story, but not here," said Simon.

"Well, I've been busy," Zach said. "I've spent most of the day on the hunt for the elusive Duncan Neff. Before I knew it, George arrived and it was time to leave. And here we are."

Detective Boggs tapped Simon on the shoulder. "I couldn't help overhearing," she said. "I hope you two aren't doing anything that would interfere with my investigation. This is a murder, you know."

"Just talking to some people," said Simon. "Trying to keep Dickens Junction safe."

"Leave the investigating to me," she said, her voice even, not threatening.

Simon knew he needed to get the detective on his side. He would think about that later. But now, there was a contest to judge.

Simon, Grace, and the mayor finished marking their worksheets, and Detective Boggs walked with them to Elmer Cuttle's holiday village. The smell of sage and onions was now almost overpowering. The mayor pressed his handkerchief to his face, and his usual ruddiness went pale.

Cuttle had chosen a holiday movie theme. In one corner, a porcelain family on a porcelain couch watched a slightly fuzzy version of *It's a Wonderful Life* on an old-fashioned television. In another corner, Dr. Seuss's Grinch, in Santa garb with reindeer-pulled sleigh and suspended from a Calder-like mobile, circled above a village of Dickensian buildings, each containing a lighted holiday tree.

The center of the display was a grand reimagining of an old-time Hollywood movie premiere, the dominant feature a marquee for the Pickwick Theatre. The elaborate theater must have been the expensive piece Charity had mentioned the day before. *Alastair Sim* IS *A Christmas Carol*, the marquee announced in black letters lit from behind. From the edge of a gold-threaded red carpet, three small klieg lights rotated, causing Simon to blink as each light crossed his face. The top of the theater had been cut away, revealing a slice of the interior. Simon peered down on the crescent rows of seats facing the working screen, where Alastair Sim's Scrooge danced silently in his nightgown, giddy as a drunken man.

Elmer Cuttle, a small, rail-thin man in his early forties, slipped into the group, next to Simon. Cuttle was shifting his gaze from the giant box to the silent screen and back. "Must be a loose speaker connection." He scratched his head and then jostled the large gift-wrapped box.

Nothing happened, so Cuttle lifted the lid from the box. A horrendous fist of aromas—sage, onions, and something decaying—hit Simon. Cuttle dropped the lid and crumpled in a faint. Zach caught him just as Detective Boggs positioned herself at Simon's shoulder. Together they peered into the box.

Inside, a loose wire dangled near the stereo speaker, but that was hardly the biggest problem. Lying on top of the speaker was a naked body, sliced open from sternum to belly and eviscerated, the cavity stuffed with mounds of sage and onion dressing, then loosely trussed with twine, like holiday poultry. The face was covered by a lilac sheet of paper, but the air current created by Cuttle's actions lifted the paper, revealing the lifeless, colorless face of Lowell Brundish. The dead man's eyes, even more sunken in death, looked vacantly upward.

Someone gagged.

Simon heard Detective Boggs's strong intake of breath, felt his own heart pounding as the lilac paper descended in gentle switchback arcs to the floor. The elegant script on the paper was bold: *With My Greatest Appreciation.*

Below it, a dramatic flourish in the shape of a dollar sign.

At the bottom of the sheet, the striking and distinct signature: *Dagny Clack.*

ZACH HAD BUILT A FIRE IN SIMON'S LIVING-ROOM fireplace; pungent dry oak logs crackled behind the Asian brass fire screen. George lounged in a wicker chair, drinking monkey-picked oolong; Zach sipped Glenfarclas on one end of the couch. Simon sat opposite Zach, also drinking tea.

The living room had high cove ceilings painted a warm white, with walls in mocha. The bamboo floors were covered with contemporary Tibetan wool area rugs in warm gold, amethyst, and ruby tones. The two couches and the side chairs were upholstered in a nubbly roasted-coffee-bean fabric, accenting caramel wicker shell chairs with taupe cushions. Occasional tables in glass and brushed steel completed the room.

From Grandma Melanie, Simon had learned that even the most elegant house should feel like a home. Favorite paintings from his grandfather's art collection hung from the picture railing that encircled the room. One of George's pieces, a tissue-paper collage from the Mijas Memories series, hung above the fireplace, while a gilt frame held a tiny original Monet watercolor on a tabletop easel. A Dante Marioni vase and ewer in seafoam with cerulean lip wrap held pride of place on a glass stand, illuminated by an overhead puck light.

Simon had designed this room, as he had all the rooms at Gad's Hill Place, to be a refuge from the world, a balance of taste and comfort. But tonight, none of these comforts could fully warm the inner chill he felt from the night's discovery. Even after David had left, he had never felt such a need to hide, hunker down, and shut out the world.

After sitting with George and Zach for some time in peaceful silence, Simon gave himself a moment to think about what had happened. After the gymnasium had been vacated and sealed, all witnesses were required to give statements to Detective Boggs before being released with a request not to leave town. Most locals wouldn't have to be told once to stay in the Junction over the holidays, but Simon suspected that the detective had been wise in issuing her directive.

"How louche it all is," George said, breaking the silence.

"Why Brundish, I wonder?" Simon warmed his hands around his tea bowl.

Zach put his arms over his head and stretched, tightening his black cotton tee shirt across his chest. He had managed during the day to buy some additional clothes; he certainly knew how to accentuate his best features, Simon couldn't help thinking, even in that moment. The murders, as invasive as they were, competed with another, more pleasant development: on the way back from the gymnasium, Zach had walked most of the way with his arm around Simon's shoulder.

"And what had he done," Zach asked, "to earn the 'greatest appreciation' from the CEO of Marley Enterprises?"

"Was the note supposed to be ironic?" Simon asked.

"Maybe it was a forgery," Zach suggested.

"If someone is killed for pleasing Marley Enterprises," George wondered, "what would happen to someone who crosses it?" He turned to Simon. "My dear, I'm not going to say 'I told you so,' but—"

All three men jumped at the sound of a knock at the back door, although that signified a friend, not a stranger. *These days,* Simon thought, *who knows the difference?* He went to the kitchen, turned on the back porch light, and saw Mavis Spurlock's face at the glass, looking serious. He opened the door.

"I'm so sorry to bother you like this, Simon," she said, "but I just needed to get out of Bleak House for a few minutes, and I thought this would be a safe place."

"Of course." Simon was horrified that she had walked anywhere by herself. "We're in the living room."

"No, thank you," she responded, "I wanted to talk with you alone for a minute, if I could." Simon gestured that Mavis should sit at the nook table; he sat beside her. Although Mavis never appeared other than ready for a night at the opera, her face, in spite of impeccable makeup, looked tired.

"Would you like a drink?"

"I'd kill for a Scotch," Mavis said. Simon gave her a look as he stood to pour her one. "That was an ill-timed phrase," she added. Simon poured her a double Glenfarclas and a mineral water for himself.

Mavis sipped from the Waterford old-fashioned glass. "I didn't want to be alone, Simon. Thank you for seeing me."

"Don't you have a full house?"

"The entire tour bus came back from the holiday display and demanded that I check them out immediately. They wanted to go back to Portland, Eugene, wherever they came from. I don't have a single guest tonight at Bleak House. I think that's a first in all the years I've run the place."

"Where's Brock?"

"Staying at Bethany's," she said.

"You're welcome to stay here if you're afraid," said Simon. "I don't have as many guest rooms as you do, but I'm still not full up."

She smiled. "Thank you, but I'm sure I'll be fine. I wanted to talk to you about our discussion yesterday." She paused. Simon placed his hand over hers. "I assume that you've talked with Brock," she said.

Her son's exotic dancing brought Mavis over at this time of night? Simon didn't think so. But he would let Mavis tell her story in her own way.

"He showed me the poster," said Simon. "What's your reaction?"

"Decidedly mixed. On one hand, it's not something I'd ever do myself." She looked at Simon over the edge of the glass, her eyes blue and clear beneath her smoky sapphire eye shadow. "On the other hand, he's got great genes…from his father, I mean."

"I suppose it's a marketable skill like any other."

"You mean, 'strike while the iron is hot?'" Mavis smiled.

"Something like that." Simon released Mavis's hand and stretched his shoulders, realizing that he had been tense for hours.

"I wasn't completely truthful with you yesterday," Mavis said. "About what I was doing when someone was killing Mr. Roark in my storage shed." She paused, as if waiting for Simon to comment. He said nothing. "I did go to Astoria, but I didn't go there alone. I went there with Brad Sturgess."

"That had occurred to me," said Simon.

"It had?" Mavis eyes widened, but then she looked relieved. "Oh, well. Yes. We've been…seeing one another…for a few months, but decided not to broadcast it. The Junction," she said, as she took another sip of Scotch, "I love it, but sometimes it's so small. Everyone knows everything."

"Someone is killing people, and we're all jumping at shadows, even the familiar ones."

"You know what I mean, though. Everyone's talking about you and your new friend already, and he's only been here a couple of days."

Simon's face was warm. "I do know what you mean, Mavis."

"I hadn't even told Brock. Brad and I haven't been 'sneaking around,' if anyone even uses that phrase anymore, but we were being discreet. I don't really have a wholly private place to, umm, entertain a personal guest at Bleak House, and Brad's place—well, let's just say he's lived alone a long time and doesn't seem to understand creature comforts, like fresh towels or clean bathroom grout."

Simon smiled.

"I drove from Bleak House to his place around a quarter to five, and we left from there. We went to Astoria, as I said, had an early dinner at Jinx's, and then rented a room at a hotel near the bridge, where they don't know either of us."

"You don't have to tell me all of this, you know," said Simon, but hoped she would continue anyway.

"I need to clear my conscience with you, and I really have nothing to hide, not any longer." She looked at her nails. "We stayed a little longer than we had planned, and came back to the square somewhere around eight thirty, I think. In our haste to get back here, I forgot to pick up some of the grocery items I had promised Ladasha. Of course, when Brad and I returned to the Square, everything was in chaos because of the murder."

Mavis's mention of Ladasha jogged Simon's memory. "Did Brundish call you?"

"It was the weirdest thing," Mavis said. "He asked if Roark had offered to buy Bleak House. He said people from Marley Enterprises had been calling him for weeks and asking him to sell, each time offering more and more money. He gave me the name Venable—I'm guessing the same man who called to make Roark's reservation."

"Weeks?" Simon asked. "So this has been going on longer than most of us thought. What else did Brundish say?"

"That he was under immense pressure financially, and that selling to Roark would clear up almost all of his debts."

"So what was the problem?"

"He didn't want to sell, he told me, because he had made a promise not to."

Simon arched an eyebrow. "To whom?"

Mavis put down her glass. "I assumed it was to you, frankly, because of your passion for the Junction."

"We weren't that close," said Simon. "It wasn't me."

"I understand the pressure he was describing." Mavis pursed her lips. "I'm on a tight budget, too."

"You are?" Simon had always assumed that Mavis was financially secure: Bleak House and its land had been a gift from his grandfather, and, as far as he could see, the bed and breakfast was a successful business.

Mavis sipped the Scotch, looking pensively at Simon. "Please don't take this the wrong way, but sometimes you forget that most of us don't have the financial independence that you have. Except for you—the smartest one of all of us—virtually everyone I know in the Junction had invested money with Duncan Neff—Brundish, Charity and Viola, Grace, Solomon Dick, Brad. And me. I know how much I lost, but at least Bleak House has good cash flow and no mortgage. I suspect that Brundish's losses, plus the closure of Nimrod and Reel, made Roark's offers incredibly tempting."

Simon was embarrassed. Mavis was right. Although intellectually he knew that his financial independence, along with his ultraconservative investments, kept him immune from most market fluctuations, he occasionally lost sight of the perils that others faced. And now Mavis was the third person to remind Simon of this in as many days.

"I'm sorry," he said.

"I'm sure the Neffs themselves took a financial beating." She sipped the last of her Scotch. "At least I hope so," she added. "I'd hate to think that Neff was too shrewd—or too callous—to take his own financial advice."

"How do you know this?"

"People talk."

Simon thought about his meeting with Ariadne. She was certainly tightly wound, although Simon wasn't sure that was peculiar—he'd known her long enough to consider it a part of her character. He hadn't realized, however, how many Junxonians had been taken in by Duncan's hail-fellow-well-met open face. No-nonsense Viola? Grace? The mayor, whom Simon considered a bit of a schemer himself?

Mavis's cell phone began ringing. She took it from her jacket pocket, looked at the screen, then at Simon. "It's Brad," she said. She pushed the screen. "Yes? Really? Well, I'm at Simon's right now. Okay." She took the phone away from her ear and held it out to Simon. "Brad wants to talk to you," she said.

Simon took the phone. "Yes, Brad?"

Sturgess took no time to get to his point. "Neff is on the warpath," he said. "Alderman Neff, that is," he added emphatically, meaning Duncan, not Ariadne. "He has been on the phone all evening, demanding that the town council immediately cancel the remainder of the holiday festivities."

Simon took a breath. "Surely he can't—"

"Not by himself, of course," Sturgess said. "But he's been pressuring the mayor, and—well, the mayor wants to hold a special council meeting to discuss the options. I said no, of course, but Charity—well, she took a beating from the townspeople as they were herded out of the gym tonight. So, we're having a meeting tomorrow."

"What can I do?" Simon asked. He looked at Mavis; she returned his worried gaze.

"You need to be there. Ten o'clock. In the morning. I'm calling a few other people."

Zach came into the kitchen, holding Simon's cell phone in his outstretched arm. "Sorry to bother you," he said, nodding at Mavis, then looking at Simon. "Your cell phone was on the table and started ringing, so I answered it." Zach introduced himself to Mavis, while handing Simon his cell phone. "It's the mayor."

"I WOULDN'T MISS THIS FOR THE WORLD," GEORGE SAID as he, Zach, and Simon walked the three blocks from Gad's Hill Place to City Hall in a light rain. "Democracy in action, or 'nature, red in tooth and claw,' I can't decide which. Definitely no Angela Lansbury today."

Simon carried a waterproof bag with a manila folder of paper inside.

"What's that?" Zach asked when Simon had run back into the house for it as they were leaving for the meeting that morning.

"Insurance. I'm hoping I won't need it."

Each time Simon was at City Hall, he had to remind himself that it was no longer his childhood home. Every room contained memories. Some parts of the mansion retained the character of Ebbie's and Melanie's original home, right down to the heirloom colors used in the foyer and council chambers (formerly the grand parlor); other areas had been altered structurally to accommodate the needs of the Junction's minuscule municipal bureaucracy.

Although Simon knew the mayor and aldermen well, he had still put on a tie and dress shirt under his best silk sport coat. He sensed a few rocks among the shoals ahead.

The three men sat in the anteroom to the council chambers, the former entrance hall to the mansion. "I used to play tiddlywinks here," Simon told Zach, who sat next to him in a fisherman's pullover and chinos. The sweater made him look even more muscular than usual.

"Not another stroll down memory lane," George said mock-tiredly. "If you let him go on, he'll tell you about the water-department office, which was originally the room where he had his first—"

"Enough," said Simon.

A few other people waited in the hall along with them. Most exchanged quiet hellos and smiles. Ariadne Neff arrived, but stood away from the others in a corner reading her BlackBerry.

Mayor Dick bulldozed his way through the front entrance, stirring up a breeze that rustled the papers tacked to the hall bulletin board. He nodded to Ariadne as he passed her and came up to Simon.

"We'll be with you all in just a minute," he said, pushing through the double doors to the council chamber. The doors closed behind him silently.

Viola entered the hall from the side entrance. She saw Simon and came over. "This is tragic," she said, "and it's not good for business. Charity was up half the night crying."

"I'm sorry to hear that," said Simon. "I suspect it has been a rough night all around."

Viola looked over at Ariadne. "It's her fault," she said.

"Brundish's murder?" Simon asked. Zach moved to stand closer to Simon and Viola. George was pretending to read the bulletin boards.

"I don't know about that," Viola said, pursing her lips, "but I wouldn't be surprised if she cajoled her husband into demanding this meeting this morning."

"Because?"

"I figure he sees it like this: if he has to go down, he might as well take the whole Junction with him. I don't know why those two settled here in the first place."

"Like shooting fish in a barrel?" Zach suggested. "A whole new host of potential investors?"

Viola softened her glance. "Fish? More like rubes. Suckers born every minute."

Charity poked her head through the swinging doors. "We're ready," she said.

Simon and the rest entered the council chambers. Up on the raised platform and behind its long panel desk sat the three aldermen of the Dickens Junction Town Council: Charity Wilkinson, Bradford Sturgess, and Duncan Neff. Mayor Dick sat farther away, on the platform at the mayor's position, which was elevated another few inches off the floor, like a pulpit. Sturgess was scowling. Charity gave Simon a pained look. Neff avoided Simon's eyes.

Simon, George, and Zach sat in the first row of chairs arrayed in a semicircle below the dais. Viola and Ariadne sat in opposite corners of the room. A few other Junxonians, called by Brad or attached to the town grapevine, sat randomly throughout the seating area. Simon nodded at each in recognition as he twisted in his seat; all were customers at the bookstore.

"The meeting will come to order," said the mayor. Dick looked down at the crowd but spoke first to Simon alone. "Thank you for coming, cousin." Simon noted the use of the technically true term. Would he and Dick be on the same side today, or was Dick trying to force Simon to join him? "I knew you would be interested in what the council wanted to discuss this morning." He was speaking in a more theatrical voice than normal. Whatever his feelings were about the Junction, Solomon Dick took his job seriously. "After yesterday's unfortunate occurrence at the holiday village competition"—the room murmured at the understatement—"I have received calls, as have other members of the council, wondering whether the Junction should suspend all future events of the season, for the safety of our citizens."

The doors squeaked and Detective Boggs slipped into the chamber. She was dressed with understated elegance in a black raw-silk pencil skirt and matching peplum jacket over a silk charmeuse winter-white shell. She sat to one side behind Ariadne Neff, who was still reading messages on her phone. Joelle Creevy and Elmer Cuttle had also appeared sometime during the mayor's opening comments.

Duncan Neff appeared to be listening intently while the mayor talked, and he was clearly not happy with the mayor's words. This was the first time Simon had seen Neff since the tableaux. Neff was thirty-two, Simon's height, trim and fit. Simon still saw him regularly at the gym, but the two men spoke only greetings to one another, if that. Simon didn't think Neff was homophobic, just not the cerebral type. The few times he had come into the bookstore, he had appeared frustrated at Simon's peculiar stock; at his last visit, he left with *Shogun*, two early Elizabeth George mysteries, and a pained expression. He was handsome in a suburban way: ash-blond hair that went white in summer, tan skin with freckles, a boy's face on a grown man, and a more easygoing expression than Ariadne's, like that of an aging fraternity boy. Simon was surprised that he had run for alderman in last year's election, and even more surprised that he had won. But that was just before the recession and collapse of Micawber Investments; perhaps if the election had happened later, Neff wouldn't have gotten votes from the many investors who had lost money as a result of his financial advice.

But he wasn't handsome this morning, even in a suburban way; his face grew redder as the mayor talked on.

When the mayor mentioned canceling festivities, Simon took the manila folder out of his case and balanced it on his thighs.

"Ending the holiday events is an extreme measure," Charity said. "No *Frozen Deep* presentation, no Fezziwig Ball?" She looked at Simon. "So many people would be disappointed."

"And you don't think that people are 'disappointed' by the fact that we've had two brutal murders?" Neff shot a look at Charity, then at Simon, for the first time. His eyes were narrow, the pupils black pinpricks. "Do you," he asked, looking at Simon, "or do you"—then at the mayor—"think that the image of this town is more important than citizen safety? I've received so many calls in the last hours that I stopped answering. I took the phone off the hook when my voice mail filled up."

"He's wound up now," George whispered. "Hope he doesn't pop a vein."

"This is your fault," Neff continued, staring Simon down. "You think this town is your personal little kingdom to run. Well, even if it has been in the past, it won't be much longer. The Junction is dangerous. There's a serial murderer on the loose, killing strangers and friends alike. No one is safe, and you don't care."

Simon stood and started to answer, but George pulled him back into the chair.

"That's uncalled for, Neff," Brad Sturgess said, his voice stern and deep. "You don't know anything about how Simon feels—or any of the rest of us, for that matter—about these murders. Except that they're terrible, of course."

Charity nodded. Simon thought she was trying to avoid tears, and felt his own emotions rise in sympathy. The issues at stake reasserted themselves in a visceral way. He willed himself to keep his emotions in check. For now.

"Danger or not," Sturgess continued, "we can't send a message that we should panic, that this town should stop dead in its tracks until the murderer is caught. We don't know that there's a *serial* killer on the loose; we don't know what the motive may be for these killings. I don't want to send a message to the people of Dickens Junction that the holidays are cancelled. I don't like that—at all."

Neff and Sturgess often took opposing sides during council meetings, so the tie-breaking role fell to Charity. She seemed aware of her position when she spoke.

"I have mixed feelings." Her hands fidgeted with her pen. "On one hand, I certainly am not going to be accused by you, Duncan, or anyone else, of being cavalier about the safety of the people of Dickens Junction. I've lived here longer than you, and I care deeply about this place and the people who live and work here. If the killer is still among us, though, how are we protected by staying at home in fear of our lives? Isn't there safety in numbers?" For the first time that morning, it seemed to Simon, the speaker looked elsewhere to make a point. Charity moved her eyes back toward Detective Boggs.

"Detective," she said, "perhaps you'd be willing to tell us what you think?"

Detective Boggs stood. "I'm here this morning as an observer, not as the official spokesperson of the sheriff's office," she said. "And I can't reveal any details about the crimes that either confirm or deny your statements about the safety of Junction citizens. I can tell you, however, that the sheriff issued an order this morning doubling the presence of on-duty troopers until further notice, with an emphasis on public events such as the ones you have named and other large-scale public gatherings here and throughout the county." Boggs looked at Solomon Dick. "I believe the sheriff spoke with the mayor earlier this morning." She sat.

"Why didn't you say anything about this to us?" Neff asked.

"I don't have to tell you everything," the mayor snapped back. "And besides, the sheriff promised me nothing. She said she would have to confer with her commanding officers before taking any action." He looked at Detective Boggs. "Thank you, Detective. I appreciate the news."

"I'm sure," Detective Boggs added from her seat, "that you'll find a copy of the order in your inbox when you check your e-mails."

"Well," the mayor said, "shall we make a motion and vote on whether to cease holiday events?"

"No," said Sturgess, "we should not. There's no decision to make. The sheriff and her officers are protecting our citizens, and that's good enough for me." He stood and started to leave the podium, but Neff stood in his way. "Let me by," Sturgess said, his face inches away from Neff's.

Ariadne Neff stood, her phone beside her on the chair. She appeared to be ready to intervene should her husband—or Sturgess—do something foolish.

Neff waited a second and then stood aside so his fellow alderman could leave the dais. Sturgess nodded at Zach and George as he walked by. "I'll call you later, Simon." Sturgess shoved open the council doors and left the chamber.

Neff stepped down from the platform and stood in front of Simon and Zach. "This isn't over," he growled at Simon. He turned to Zach. "People tell me you've been looking for me. What do you want? I know you're some kind of reporter, but I don't have anything to say to you, or to anyone else." He turned back to Simon. "It's not enough that you put citizens at risk—you take up with someone who will leave here and write about the bad things that have happened? You'll be a laughingstock." He chuckled. "It's no more than you deserve, I suppose."

Zach had stood, and Ariadne was now standing next to him. She took her husband's arm. "Don't do anything you'll regret later. Let's go."

Detective Boggs excused herself from talking with Charity, nearly colliding with the Neffs as they brushed past her toward the exit. "I'd like to see you later," she said to Simon as she left the council chambers.

The mayor stood down and took Simon aside. "I haven't had much chance to talk with you lately," he said, struggling to keep his voice low. "And I didn't want to tell you this over the phone last night. Brundish called me Wednesday night and wanted to meet Thursday morning, but didn't say why. Obviously, we know why he didn't show up for the meeting. Do you think he sold out to Marley Enterprises? Is that what the note meant?"

"I've been puzzled about whether the note was serious or mocking," said Simon. "It could have been either. If serious, it likely confirms Brundish's decision to sell to Dagny Clack. If mocking, I don't know what it means. Have you talked more to Detective Boggs?"

"Not since my statement," the mayor said. "I was on the phone most of the night with the aldermen, and this morning with the sheriff's office—several times."

"Thanks for that," said Simon, putting his hand on his cousin's shoulder. "I appreciate it."

"I did it for the Junction," Mayor Dick said, suddenly gruff again. "Not just for you."

"Of course. I understood that."

"I need to get back to the shop. I hate to say this, but business was booming last night, people coming in to talk, eat, and play the machines after the mess at the school. I sold a mess of Mirrorball tickets. I guess if you don't end up as the Christmas goose, you feel lucky." He attempted a grin, but not even Simon believed that the mayor fully believed in his joke.

Murders or not, Simon had to accept that, for most Junxonians, business was business, and he could not be insensitive to that reality. "And I need to get to Pip's."

Charity replaced the mayor at Simon's side. "I'm so sorry for all of this," she said. "I'm relieved that the sheriff's officers will be out protecting us, but still—" She took in a breath, squeezed his hand, and then, taking nearby Viola's hand, left the room.

George, Zach, and Simon were now the only ones left in the council chambers.

"I don't know what to say," Zach said. He turned to Simon. "Will you defend my honor against Neff's scurrilous accusations?"

George touched Simon's sleeve. "I'd wait a while before answering," he said, smiling. "Until you know whether his intentions are entirely honorable."

ZACH AND GEORGE WENT BACK TO GAD'S HILL PLACE, AND Simon went to the bookstore. Business was, as the mayor had suggested, busier than usual; unfortunately, many of the patrons wanted to ask Simon about the murders, so after fending off several otherwise well-meaning locals, Simon told Brock he would work in the back room unless he was absolutely needed out front.

"No worries, boss," Brock said. "I'm glad I wasn't there yesterday, so nobody wants to ask me what happened."

"Count yourself lucky. I wouldn't wish yesterday's sight on my worst enemy—not even Duncan Neff."

Work had its virtues, Simon considered, as he reviewed reports and decided what stock to order now and what could wait until after the year-end inventory was completed. *For one thing,* he thought, *no more Ayn Rand in the store. Just because I read her novels doesn't mean I have to encourage and support her work by giving it to others. Let the online retailers, superstores, and discount big boxes give Rand to the masses, if they must have it.* He deleted her titles from his reorder list.

He lost track of the time. It could have been hours later when Brock stuck his head in the back room. "Boss," he said. "Detective Boggs to see you."

"Send her back here, please."

Detective Boggs entered while Simon was clearing remaindered books from the spare chair so she could have a seat. "Am I interrupting you?" she asked.

"Not at all," Simon replied. "I've been hoping to talk with you about the case."

Detective Boggs sat and took out a pad and paper. She had notes on some of the pages; she flipped those back to reveal a clean page.

Simon sat in his chair, pushed the laptop aside, and leaned forward. "First, let me say thank you. You made this morning a lot easier for me."

"I had nothing to do with it," she said kindly. "That was between the sheriff and the mayor."

"Duncan Neff is not very happy with us at the moment," he said.

"That, Simon, is obvious." She was smiling.

"Have you had a chance to interview him yet about Roark and Brundish?"

Her smile faded, and her face returned to the impassive expression Simon had come to expect. "Let's not interview me right now. I need to get your official statement on your whereabouts between ten p.m. and midnight the night before last."

"I assume that Brundish was killed during those hours?"

"I'm not going to encourage your amateur detective efforts, Simon." She wasn't frowning, exactly, and she didn't refute his assumption, either. "I have limited ability, as you know, to discuss the case with you. Just details that will be, or have been, released to the press."

"I was at home with my guests, George Bascomb and Zach Benjamin," Simon told her. "At midnight, I think, George and I were sitting on his bed talking about the world's—or maybe just my—problems."

The detective made some notes on her pad. "And they will say the same?" she asked.

"I'm sure they will," he responded. "What else can you tell me about Brundish? Surely he wasn't murdered where we found him?"

"I've warned you, Simon," Detective Boggs said, "not to try to pursue any investigation on your own. Now that there has been a second murder, I'm more serious than ever."

"I haven't done anything that has interfered with you, have I?" He wanted to be careful; he actually believed that the detective was sympathetic to his interest in the case, on a level outside her official capacity. "It's just that it's obvious that the method of the murder couldn't have been carried out without certain—preparations."

"The coroner believes that Brundish was killed somewhere else. After his body had been...*prepared,* as you say, he was transported to the school and placed in the speaker box, sometime between midnight and five in the morning. We found a wheelbarrow outside the gymnasium's back entrance. There's DNA evidence that has been sent for testing. We also found some rubber-tire tracks on the gym floor."

"What about the note from Dagny Clack?" Simon asked. "What does that mean?"

Detective Boggs put down her pen. "We haven't been able to reach her. She has many intermediaries. Interpol is trying to locate her right now. Her attendants can't decide whether she is in Zurich, Montreal, or maybe scuba diving off the island of Gozo, wherever that may be." She looked at Simon with an expression that he read as more amused than angry. "But you probably know as much about her as we do—you have the Internet, too."

"So you don't know what she was thanking him for?"

Detective Boggs shook her head. "We haven't been able to access any sales records, of course, not yet."

Simon told Detective Boggs about Mavis's call to Brundish.

The detective made another note. "A promise?" she asked. "That's very interesting. Mavis didn't disclose that when I talked to her about Roark, and we haven't spoken yet about Brundish's death."

Her call from Brundish wasn't relevant until he was found dead, was it? Simon wasn't so sure about that, but he didn't want to see Mavis in trouble, either. He decided to change the subject. "I've been thinking about something Roark said to me in the shop," he said. "He asked for an Ayn Rand novel, but he didn't know much about her. There must be a connection between Rand and Marley Enterprises, but I'm thinking that Roark either didn't know exactly what it was, or didn't understand it. He said 'I'm new,' which makes me wonder how long he had worked for Marley Enterprises."

Detective Boggs made another note. "You get a gold star for that one," she said. "While Marley Enterprises has been very protective of its CEO, they have released, under some pressure, their records on Mr. Roark. Locals in Kansas City have searched his condo there."

Kansas City, Simon thought. He realized he'd been expecting Roark to have come from somewhere outré or foreign. He could hear George drawling, *Well, Kansas City is certainly both of those.*

Detective Boggs was continuing, "E-mails and such, his laptop and cell phone. He was a very private individual. Apparently either he, or his boss, Dagny Clack, doesn't like electronic or telephone records. They transacted their business—whatever it was—in person. We do know that Roark had worked for Marley Enterprises less than two weeks. His résumé is very clear; he was in sales, pure and simple."

"A closer?" Simon asked.

"Yes." The detective seemed not to have considered the term for Roark before, but liked it. "We think he was given cash, some negotiating authority, and perhaps some information, to encourage people to sell their property to Marley Enterprises."

"Information," Simon repeated. "Does that mean blackmail?"

"As I recall, though," Detective Boggs said, "he didn't make you an offer."

"He did not," said Simon. "And I've been thinking about that, too."

"What have you decided?"

"I think he was waiting until the others—the mayor, Viola, Grace, Brundish, even Mavis Spurlock—caved in. He would then present that to me as a *fait accompli* and I would be forced to sell. What I can't figure out is why Marley Enterprises wants all of the commercial property in the Junction. And is willing to pay more than top dollar."

"So he made no offer—and no threats?"

Simon shook his head. "He didn't. But I don't know how he could have threatened me. I have no secrets."

"Perhaps that's exactly why he didn't make you an offer." Boggs looked earnestly at Simon.

"Does that mean the others have something to hide?"

The detective made another note on her pad. "That's what we're—I mean, I am trying to find out, isn't it?"

"Can we get back to Duncan Neff for a moment?" Simon asked. "Zach had been looking for him for almost two days to talk to him about Roark, even before Brundish's death. What did Neff tell you?"

Detective Boggs again put down her pen. "You are persistent, aren't you?" She paused before continuing. "I will say this—Neff claims that, during the hours in which Brundish was killed, he was in Astoria at the Desdemona Club, having a few drinks. We're checking on that now. After that, he came back to the Junction and went to the storage shed at Bleak House to 'check the inventory' of the tableaux items."

Simon frowned. "That makes no sense whatsoever. He already did that, as soon as the tableaux were taken down."

"We checked the shed after his interview this morning, and we certainly found evidence—which is pending further fingerprint analysis—that someone was there after the crime scene had been photographed and the tableaux inventory returned to the shed."

"What evidence do you have?"

Boggs looked at Simon carefully. "Some props were damaged—Marley's chains, the snuffer cap for the Ghost of Christmas Past. A few of the backdrops had footprints on them."

"Are you saying that Neff vandalized the shed?"

"I am not saying that. He is saying, however, that, maybe after a few drinks, he was unsteady on his feet and tripped over a few things. And maybe damaged them."

"The vindictive son of a bitch," said Simon. He paused a minute. "What about Roark? Where was he when Roark was killed?"

"I've told you more than enough already," Detective Boggs said. "He has given us an alibi that we're checking on. Just like all the others."

"You should arrest him." He stood.

Detective Boggs stood at the same time. "Keep your temper, Simon," she said. "I could do that—maybe for trespassing, maybe for drunk and disorderly, but Neff claims the shed was unlocked. Maybe it was. He can say he got lost on his way home."

"He lives two blocks from Bleak House," said Simon.

"He could say he was confused, maybe had a little too much to drink. Maybe he tripped." Boggs stepped into the front of the shop; Simon followed her across the room, aware of Brock's gaze on them. With her hand on the door to leave, she turned and faced Simon again. "Remember your priorities, Simon. You can replace the damaged items. But we have two humans who are way beyond saving. And I—not you—have a murderer to catch. Before he or she kills again."

AFTER DETECTIVE BOGGS LEFT AND SIMON WAS FREE TO watch the front of the store, Brock stepped out to have a protein shake at Lirriper's Lattes. Simon tried to keep his mind off the murders by rearranging books in the young-adult section. This was a tough job for Simon, since he had not read many of the traditional children's books, and virtually nothing contemporary.

He was adjusting the Nancy Drew titles and returning *The Clue of the Tapping Heels* to where it belonged. Nancy had been his childhood idol—smart, snappy, rich, with good friends, solving crimes and looking great in her roadster, titian hair blowing in the wind. Simon considered his "chums," George and Zach, although George was more like Nancy's Bess Marvin than Bess's hoydenish cousin George Fayne. And did that make Zach the hunky Ned Nickerson, Nancy's boyfriend?

Simon jumped when he felt a hand on his shoulder. Grace. She was holding two to-go coffee cups in her other hand. "I didn't mean to startle you," she said.

"Try calling out, then," Simon teasingly rebuffed, feeling foolish not only to have been startled by a harmless friend such as Grace but also to have been so while daydreaming about his crush, *If that's what he is...*

"Penny for your thoughts."

"Just thinking about my childhood days with Nancy," he said, running his fingertips across the spines of the mystery books. "And trying to keep phrases like *murderer on the loose* and *crazed serial killer* out of my head. Miss Drew never had to deal with those things."

"My treat," Grace said, as she handed one of the cups to Simon. "I thought you could use a break."

"Thank you." His words came out as a sigh. He sipped the double-tall, nonfat, extra-hot latte.

"People all over the square are talking about this morning's 'showdown.'"

"Neff is despicable," said Simon. He shelved *The Password to Larkspur Lane* with an extra tap.

"I'm proud of you for staying out front," Grace said. "I've been hiding in the back room most of the day, avoiding all of the questions about what happened yesterday. Gloria keeps me posted, however, as the gossip filters through. I'm just sorry I didn't hear about the meeting until after it was over," she said. "I turned off my answering machine last night and didn't listen to the mayor's voice mail until late this morning. Otherwise, I would have been there to support you."

"I didn't get the mayor's call until around ten, I think."

"Oh, I was out like a light by then." Grace sipped her coffee and looked at him over the rim. "Sleeping pill again. I have had such dreams."

Simon put his cup down and put a hand on her shoulder. "Don't think about Brundish. I'm trying not to."

"Is it working?"

"No," he said. "By the way, did Brundish say anything to you about promising not to sell his property?"

Grace tilted her head. "No. We used to have coffee from time to time. But he started withdrawing after Nimrod and Reel closed, and after the divorce. I saw so little of him in the last few months."

"The same here," said Simon. "But I wasn't close to him before that, either."

"Where did you hear about a promise?"

"From Mavis," Simon answered. "She talked to Brundish the day Roark was killed. Brundish told Mavis he had made a promise to someone not to sell his property, but that Marley Enterprises had been pressuring him for weeks with phone calls, offering a ton of money. Roark's arrival apparently signified a new level of pressure to sell."

"Roark pressured all of us, that's for sure," Grace said.

"Marley Enterprises must have started with Brundish, though," said Simon. "And was going to end with me, after the rest of you sold."

"I would never sell, Simon," she said. "I told Roark so."

"Viola said the same thing; Mavis, too."

"And Solomon," she said. "Of course he wouldn't sell."

"Wouldn't he?" Simon asked. "I'm not so sure."

Grace reached down and picked up one of Simon's young-adult titles. She lifted the reading glasses from the chain around her neck. "You know," she said, as she examined the title, "you might consider freshening up this section of the store. I'm not sure that many young people are into *Eight Cousins* these days."

Simon chuckled. "Stocking only books that I've read has its limitations. Mr. Roark pointed that out to me the other day."

"What about trying that series with the bitchy teen girls, or those wizards and werewolves, or something with vampires? Maybe some graphic novels. Gloria has one in her hands all the time."

"I read this one," said Simon. He picked up one of the vampire titles. "Just because of the movie. I probably wouldn't get any kids in the store otherwise. I must face the tragic fact that I don't like much contemporary fiction, and I always hope that, when young customers come in, they'll find something worthwhile in a traditional vein."

Grace walked over to the adult literature section and picked *My Antonia* off the shelf. "Good luck with that, Simon," she said drily, wiping imaginary dust from the book's top edge before reshelving it. "Seriously, though, are any of us keeping pace with the times? Viola's tearoom doesn't have an object made in this century, unless it's a reproduction, and I'm carrying pressed-flower greeting cards, handmade soap, and miniature bisque thatched cottages. When was the last time you saw an actual thatched cottage?"

"On the Isle of Skye," Simon answered promptly. "When I was in Scotland last year."

"Wasn't that a museum?" Grace asked. "As I recall from your digital photos—"

"Enough," Simon answered. "But that's what the Junction is all about, Grace. Revering, preserving, celebrating the past and Dickens's values."

"Dickens shunned his wife, alienated her children from her, and kept a mistress for years." Grace was firm, and correct, and smiling as she said it. "We've picked and chosen among the range of available Dickens 'values.' Not that there has to be anything wrong with that."

"Everything else seems so fragile," said Simon. He was thinking of more than just the present. He was thinking of his parents, and of Ebbie and Melanie. Of David. Even of Nancy Drew and *My Antonia.* And of the future... *Does that include Zach?*

"It will be over soon; at least we can hope for that," Grace said. She sipped the last of her latte. "And then let's call a council of the local business owners, see what we can do to preserve the best of the Junction, and bring the rest into the current century. Look at Solomon Dick," she said. "He's doing well enough."

"I'd rather not look at Mr. Dick's as the template for success," said Simon. "Gambling isn't my idea of what's best for the Junction, or for the twenty-first century."

"Bad example," Grace conceded, hands in the air. "All right. Let's make lemonade of these lemons."

Simon crossed to the window as if he would see the first sign of a hopeful future outside. Grace joined him. The reality, however, hit him like a blow to the sternum. A cameraman and reporter from Northwest Cable News stood in the square, interviewing shoppers. The cameraman had set the reporter directly in the line of sight of the Dickens statue. Random Junxonians, including children, jumped and waved to the camera behind the reporter's shoulder. Fortunately, the camera pointed away from Pip's Pages.

"The murderer is destroying the Junction!" *Am I yelling?*

Grace's voice followed Simon's like a whisper. "Maybe he's trying to save it," she said, one hand on the open door.

Simon watched Grace walk away along the perimeter of the square, as far from the reporter as possible.

BETHANY WAS STILL IN THE KITCHEN WHEN SIMON GOT home at six thirty. George was reading *Atlas Shrugged* in the sunroom, and Zach was talking with Bethany as she cooked. He poured Simon a glass of wine—tonight a super Tuscan from Simon's extensive 1997 collection, just now coming into its prime—even before Simon sat.

"To what do we owe the privilege of your culinary talents tonight?" Simon asked.

"I had the energy," Bethany said. "And the need to avoid all of this negativity around town right now—I wanted an outlet."

"And she tells me her kitchen has ramen and a sad rind of brie," Zach said.

"Chicken carbonara?" Bethany was rendering pancetta lardons.

"And Caesar salad, fresh garlic twists, and cranberry granita with shortbread cookies for dessert."

"It'll be nice to eat with you for once." Simon sipped the wine. *Worth every minute of the multiyear wait.*

"I won't be staying," Bethany said, stirring the chicken breast pieces and diced onions into the rendered fat. "Brock is taking me into Astoria for dinner tonight."

"Not Anita Distraction's, I hope."

"No," she said, laughing. "Juicy Sushi. For unagi and uni."

Simon made a face; sushi was one of the few types of food he didn't care for. "I wouldn't think sea urchin would be Brock's cup of tea."

"It's not," Bethany said. "But it's fun to watch him learn."

Zach stood and moved behind Simon's chair to rub his neck. Simon felt his strong hands knead the tight cords of his neck; at first it hurt, and then it didn't.

"Could today have been any worse?" Zach asked.

"Maybe if I had been Lowell Brundish," Simon answered. He looked at Bethany. "Memo for my chef: No sage at Christmas."

"We need to compare notes on the day," Zach said. "I've learned one or two tidbits that might be of interest."

"I have, too," said Simon. "But let's wait until after dinner. I would like to relax."

Zach's knuckles dug lower, deeper, into Simon's shoulder—a pleasant pain. "No worries. I could just stay here and do this if you like." His voice was low, almost a purr.

"Get a room, boys," Bethany said.

"What's that I smell?" George came in from the hall.

"Dinner," said Simon. "And I'm sure it will be fabulous."

"I'll be done in a minute," Bethany said. "Go, sit, and I will serve you in high style."

Bethany had already set the dining room table with the best china, silver, and crystal. Simon's mother's sterling candlesticks held winter-white tapers. George lit them while Zach poured more wine.

"I could easily get used to domestics," George said, intentionally loud enough for Bethany to hear. When, a few minutes later, she served the meal—the carbonara silky with eggs and bright with the pancetta and barely cooked peas, the twists yeasty and sharp with garlic, the Caesar a perfect blend of anchovy, garlic, and lemon—Bethany snapped her dish towel against George's back.

"I had no idea how hungry I was until I saw this food," Zach said, once the laughter and George's mock wails died down. He guided noodles around his fork with his tablespoon.

"I'm off, guys," Bethany said. "I'll be in at six tomorrow. Any requests?"

"How about your artichoke, sun-dried tomato, and feta strata?" Simon suggested.

"Yes, something light like that," George said, between bites of salad. "I want to spend my *whole* day on the treadmill when I'm not eating."

"I'll do a fresh fruit bowl also," she said. "All right, good night."

The three men finished the meal with desultory conversation deliberately focused away from the murders. Several times Simon's eyes met Zach's across the table; Zach would smile each time and keep eating. It was, to Simon, sexy and alarming, bearing more than a passing similarity to the eating seduction scene in *Tom Jones*. And, except for hair color, Zach did look amazingly like the younger Albert Finney. *Where will the evening take us?*

After dinner, George made a pot of Darjeeling, which all three men enjoyed with the cookies.

Simon looked at Zach. "You first."

"What about me?" George said. "Don't I get to contribute?"

"Of course, George." Simon was grinning. "But didn't you spend the entire day in the sunroom reading?"

"I did," he answered, "not that I'm proud of it."

"So, then"—Zach took up the challenge—"what can you offer?"

George left the table and returned a minute later with his novel. He opened the book to a page marked with the business card Roark had given Simon.

"The dollar sign," he said. He held the card by its purple edges. "It's from the book. It's one of the symbols of the sympathetic rich and powerful characters who go on strike against the United States and the world for its socialist ways." He put the book down. "You know...just like what's happening now—as if."

"Excellent," said Simon. "I had forgotten that after all these years. All I can remember about it now is that it was inane... and it had a death-ray machine at the end, I think."

"Don't spoil the ending for me," George said. "I'm only on page five hundred."

"Let's talk suspects," said Simon. "Let me tell you what else Duncan Neff has been doing." He shared what he had learned about the damage at Bleak House storage shed.

"That's despicable," Zach said. "But he could be lying about the time. Maybe he went there after midnight, after he killed Brundish. Maybe the vandalism was done to cover up something he thought might incriminate him regarding Roark's death."

Simon inhaled the layered aromas of the Darjeeling. "We still don't know what he was doing when Roark was killed."

"And you're not likely to learn it now," George said. "At least not directly from Neff."

"True," Simon admitted. "At least we know that Brock, Mavis, and Brad Sturgess were all in Astoria until after midnight."

Zach chuckled. "You should frame that poster of Brock, Simon."

George nodded. "And present it to him on his fortieth birthday. A *memento mori*."

"What about the others?" Zach asked.

"Well," Simon continued, "Grace said she took a sleeping pill, Viola and Charity are unknown, and the mayor was at home alone. We don't know what Ariadne was doing, and we don't believe Neff's story."

"I would add," Zach said, "that, although Brock's whereabouts are certain, or can be verified by Bethany, Ladasha, and any number of people at Anita Distraction's, Mavis and Brad have only each other as alibis for Brundish's death, until Brock saw them at midnight. So they still might have had the opportunity to kill Brundish, and move his body sometime later."

"Tell me," George said to Simon, "how does Mavis make her poultry stuffing? Is she heavy on the sage, like the murderer?"

Simon couldn't help but smile. "I've had several holiday meals with her. Her own favorite is Southwestern cornbread with cumin."

"So many unknowns," George said. "Dead ends." He looked at Zach, then at Simon. "You may need to leave the rest of this in the capable hands of the police. No more Nancy Drew for you, my dear."

"Shall we retire to the greater comfort of the living room?" Simon asked.

"Sounds delightful." George poured a fresh cup of tea and pushed himself away from the chair. "I feel as if I'm *enceinte*," he groaned, a hand on his stomach.

"I'll get the cognac," Zach said, "and be right there."

By the time Zach returned from the wet bar with two crystal snifters, George had settled in the shell chair across from the sofa, and Simon on one of the couches, his legs stretched out on a small ottoman. Zach handed Simon a snifter, sat next to him, and then slouched and put his head in Simon's lap. Simon's breath caught.

"Do you mind?" Zach murmured, teeth flashing in the low light.

"Not if you're comfortable." Simon tugged the thighs of his chinos.

Miss Tox appeared and made herself a pillow of Zach's feet. Simon caught George's bemused stare, brown eyes warm, inviting pools behind his glasses. He stood, cup in one hand, examining the fingernails of his other hand.

"After witnessing this moment of domestic bliss, I feel a sudden urge to mousse my cuticles," he said. "Following which, I shall put in my ear buds, listen to Debussy, and let myself be transported to Ms. Rand's bizarre dystopia. I will hear nothing."

"If you must," said Simon.

"Missing you already," George said. He picked up his novel from the dining room table, crossed again through the living room, and exited through the French doors.

"He is a great friend, isn't he?" Zach asked, looking up into Simon's eyes.

"He is," Simon answered, delighted to notice that he was feeling calmer, not more nervous. "I don't know what I would do without him. We've been through so many things together. Breakups, the death of his partner, the departure of mine... You know—we've carried one another's baggage."

Zach sighed; Simon felt the weight of his exhalation on his own thighs. Zach's hand rubbed Simon's calf under his chinos, a sexy caress. Where was this going to lead? Simon truly didn't know. It had been five years—what were the rules these days? But perhaps Zach did. Instead of feeling relaxed by Zach's hand, Simon tensed.

"This feels nice," Zach said. "You feel nice."

"Thank you." *Thank you?* Fail, *Brock would say.*

Zach's caress stopped, but his hand didn't move. "Am I being too forward?"

"Not *too* forward. Right at the edge."

"Good." Zach resumed the caress.

"I'm hoping for a good day at the store tomorrow." Simon cleared his throat. Best, perhaps, to keep the discussion focused on the murders. "I don't know that I'll have time to do very much investigating. And I don't know how I will learn about the Neffs' alibis anyway."

"Maybe you had better slow down," Zach said. He was kneading the tension from Simon's left calf. "The longer I've been here, the more I understand how complicated, and how dangerous, this all is. Maybe I pushed too hard."

Simon moved his legs and thighs; he felt a sudden urge to stand, a rising anger. He stood.

Zach pulled his neck forward to avoid his head hitting the couch. He was standing now, too. "Whoa," he said. Miss Tox jumped from the sofa and padded through the open French doors toward Boffin's Bower.

"I may not have wanted to get into this," said Simon, feeling the fury coming quickly now, inexplicably, from a place he usually tried to control. "But now that I'm in it, not George, not you, not Boggs nor anyone can keep me from finding out who wants to destroy Dickens Junction. It means too much to me." The two men were standing less than six feet apart. "I hope you're not trying to patronize me. I won't have that."

"Not at all." Zach sounded contrite.

"I've spent years maintaining, nurturing, growing the ideal that my grandfather had about a small, intimate community joyfully celebrating the life and values of a great author, if not always a great man. I haven't traveled as I could have—I haven't been to the Seychelles. I've stayed here, building a life that I, and others, could enjoy. It has cost me. Time, money, relationships." He looked at Zach, his eyes now stinging with held-back tears. "If you can't understand, or have the ability to accept what the Junction has meant—means—to me, then I need to shut everything down, because there won't be any future for us."

Zach's eyes were like sapphires lit from within. "A future?" he asked. "I mean, you're attracted to me?"

Simon turned away and rubbed his hands down the legs of his chinos. "Jesus," he breathed.

"Because"—Zach paused—"I like a man with convictions. I mean, *really* like a man who acts according to beliefs and values. It's just that I don't meet many of them."

"We are a dying breed," said Simon, quietly, waiting for whatever Zach was working up to.

"And when I do meet one," Zach said, taking a step closer to Simon, then another, then placing his hand on Simon's shoulder, the warmth, the weight, of Zach's hand like a blanket coming over Simon, "he's usually not attracted to a rolling stone like me."

Zach stepped closer still; now Simon could feel the warmth of Zach's breath on his face, his lips. Zach kissed Simon softly, carefully, on his upper lip, his lower lip, then both lips.

Simon breathed, his arms still at his side.

"Well," Zach said, after a moment of silence. "That was—"

"Nice."

Zach stepped back; now Simon could see his eyes, nose, lips, see the black stubble that had lightly scratched his face. "Maybe not the highest compliment I've ever received, but I'll accept it as an opener." He moved to close the distance between them again, but Simon held out his arm.

"I need to think," he said. "Let's take our time."

"Fair enough," Zach said, taking Simon's hand and threading their fingers together. "As Mae West almost said once, 'Someone worth doing, is worth doing slowly.'"

SEVERAL HOURS LATER, SIMON AWOKE WITH A START, this time not from a dream about the murders, but one about Zach's kiss. His mind churned the possibilities of love, loss, disappointment. He replayed his breakup with David from five years ago, the similar one with Andrew eight years before that, both times the results of a frustrated big-city boy and the helpless-feeling small-town Simon. He did not want to reprise that role; he didn't want to get hurt.

When he went to get a drink of water, he saw light under the Bower door. He couldn't resist; he knocked.

"Come in, my dear." George was still reading. "I expected you, I think."

Simon sat on the edge of the chair beside him. "Are your cuticles sufficiently moussed and hydrated?"

George fluttered his fingers at Simon, then returned them to the book. "They are, my dear. And are your ashes sufficiently hauled?"

"I shouldn't dignify your question with a response," he said, allowing a note of humor in his voice, "but I will. The fire has kindled but not yet burned."

"Who is the flint? And who the tinder?"

"I've never been the flint. But I'll tell you something—the tinder is dry, very dry. And brittle, if you know what I mean."

"We had better move on quickly," George said, "before we crush another metaphor under the staggering weight of our repartee. But you are troubled," he continued. "By the obvious?"

"I don't want to get hurt," said Simon. "And I'm right on the edge of losing my objectivity. A few days ago, this was just a nice flirtation. The feelings are stronger now."

"Zach probably gets what he wants most of the time."

"Like Dagny Clack," said Simon.

"She is a nightmare best contemplated in the light of day," George said. "Nighttime is for romance." He patted the cushion. "Settle in," he said. He wrapped his arms around Simon. "I feel just like Marmee to your Jo," he said. "Or is it Beth? I forget."

"Beth dies."

"Oh." George shifted his weight so that he was sitting farther back in the chaise and Simon was now also lying back, still folded in his old friend's arms. "Well, here's one literary reference I'm going to get right. And it's from Henry James, so I know you're familiar with it." George's mouth was near Simon's ear, and he spoke slowly and with an intense hush. "'Live all you can; it's a mistake not to.'"

"Lambert Strether in *The Ambassadors*."

"Exactly. An older man to a younger one, if I recall correctly."

"I believe so," said Simon. "I haven't read it in a long time."

"Critics say that James put his fussbudget queeny self into the skin of Strether," George said. "Don't *you* have that kind of regret. It weighs too much."

"Maybe I'm just vulnerable because I'm under such stress over these murders."

"Maybe you're just...tense," George suggested. "But does it matter? You live too much in your head," he continued, stroking Simon's hair. "All of that reading has stunted your emotional growth."

"But I think—"

George tapped his fists on Simon's sternum. "Stop thinking, my dear. Be safe, yes—but why be careful? Start feeling. Jump. I'll catch you if you fall."

Simon was beginning to melt. "And what happens if I don't fall?"

"If you're lucky," George said, "joy."

STAVE

THE LAST OF THE BODIES

The next few days passed with no developments or resolutions, not for the town and not for Simon. Detective Boggs called with several follow-up questions, and the holiday shoppers came in spite of, or possibly because of, continuing newspaper and television coverage that too frequently contained the phrase "killer on the loose."

Simon tried to concentrate on work, but he felt as if he were playing emotional pinball. Physical contact with Zach became more frequent. Zach would take his hand or stroke his shoulder as he walked by, and kisses occasionally occurred in front of Bethany. Zach even gave Simon a peck on the cheek in front of Brock when Zach stopped by the store on Monday on his way to the *Household Words* office for "research," he said, "for a future assignment." The lingering sensation of Zach's lips went from warming Simon's lips with promise to leaving a chill of uncertainty. *The future.*

On December 21, four days after Brundish's murder, Simon met George at the breakfast table. His friend was drinking Prince of Wales tea and reading the *Huffington Post* on Simon's laptop. *Atlas Shrugged* sat beside him, the bookmark buried deep past the middle of the book.

Simon poured a cup of organic Sumatran and sat in the chair next to George as Bethany returned from the pantry and started carving orange and grapefruit supremes and placing them on a serving tray. "Is that limousine still parked in front of Bleak House?" she asked Simon.

Simon looked out the window toward Bleak House, visible on the ridge below Gad's Hill Place. Sure enough, a large, white, stretch limousine was parked in front of the bed-and-breakfast.

"I have a feeling I know who that might be." Simon walked to the mudroom and put on a hooded parka. "I'll be back."

Simon left through the back door and walked down the hill toward Bleak House. He felt the cold mist turn to rain, and pulled the hood over his head. A car passed him on its way up the hill toward the Astoria city waterworks. Not much farther down, a young man in running shorts and a sweatshirt jogged past. Simon didn't recognize him, but assumed he was one of the students at the college. As he passed, Simon turned and saw *Who is John Galt?* emblazoned across the back of his hoodie.

Instead of entering through the front door of Bleak House, Simon cut through the city hall parking lot and knocked at Bleak House's back door, which was near the path to the storage shed. The crime scene police tape was gone. Simon reminded himself to take a look at the damage Duncan Neff had caused, but first he wanted to confirm his suspicions about what was happening inside.

Ladasha opened the door wielding a wooden spoon. "Un-huh," she said, letting him in. She continued stirring batter for blueberry pancakes. "I thought you might be by when you saw that limo." Simon crossed the kitchen toward the swinging door leading to the breakfast room and entry hall. "Her *people* called late last night to confirm the availability of the Summerson Suite. When Mavis explained the unexpected vacancies as a result of the recent events, her *people* booked the entire top floor. Just for the woman herself, 'for privacy,' they said." Ladasha stirred the batter. "Cheeky, if you ask me."

Simon cushioned the doors with his hands so that they would close silently, and made his way along the edge of the breakfast room. He could hear Mavis and another woman's voice, but could not see either woman.

"I must have absolute privacy." The other woman had a sharp, clear voice, and spoke with the authority of someone accustomed to being acquiesced to, or even obeyed. "I shall be conducting meetings in my room and require the utmost discretion."

"Certainly, Miss Clack," Mavis responded. "I will proceed with as much discretion as a stretch limousine parked outside my front door will allow."

"And silence," Miss Clack continued, her voice not betraying that she'd caught Mavis's sarcasm at all. "I must have utter silence. Your domestics will be allowed in the room only when I am out, and only under the supervision of my amanuensis, Mr. Venable."

"Understood," Mavis said.

"I shall breakfast in my room each morning. I will have fruit, multigrain toast with organic butter, organic yogurt, and coffee made from my own beans, served precisely at seven, left outside my suite on a tray."

"That can also be arranged."

"Of course it can. Anything can be 'arranged,' as you say. It just takes time and money. I have both. And I shall require the *Times*."

"Our daily paper is the *Oregonian*," Mavis said.

"The *London Times*," Miss Clack said. "The only paper I read."

"I shall arrange that," said a third voice, a confident male voice. Mr. Venable, apparently.

Simon edged closer; now he could see Dagny Clack and a tall young man standing near her. Miss Clack had a chiseled face with high cheekbones and platinum hair done in a mid-century style. She was very short—Simon guessed five feet tall (in her heels)—and wore a severely tailored charcoal suit and black heels. He saw no jewelry except a diamond brooch in the shape of a dollar sign on her lapel. Her hands were small, with delicate fingers and polished nails. Simon guessed her age was between forty-five and sixty, depending on the skills of her surgical team.

Mr. Venable had that stunning and forgettable male beauty that came from spending every spare moment in the gym and the day spa. He carried a laptop case over his shoulder. Miss Clack, on the other hand, was enveloped in a sea of perfectly matched chocolate alligator luggage in every shape and size.

"How many days were you hoping to stay?" Mavis asked. "I have the suite booked for the New Year's Festival of the Chimes."

"I will stay until I have achieved my objective," Miss Clack said. "Of course you can move those other people elsewhere if I need to be here beyond New Year's."

"The suite was booked six months ago by a loyal customer."

"I will remain here until I am ready to leave. You will make alternate arrangements for the others. Sebastian will help you."

"Money is no object," Mr. Venable said. His voice was like warm oil.

"Goodwill doesn't have a price," Mavis countered.

"Of course it does," Miss Clack snapped. "Everything has a price. Now, I shall wish to see some of these events for which this little village is so dubiously known. What opportunities will I have?"

Simon watched Mavis hold out a Dickens Junction holiday events brochure toward Miss Clack. Mr. Venable's long arm intervened, and he took the brochure from Mavis.

"Unfortunately," Mavis said, clearly trying to recover her mood and put a good face and voice on a trying set of circumstances, "you have missed many things already."

"Which have been bandied about the broadcast media," Miss Clack noted with an edge in her voice. "So I am told."

"Unfortunately, yes," Mavis said. "The biggest event remaining is the premier event of the season, the costumed Fezziwig Ball tomorrow night. *The Frozen Deep* at the Crummles Theatre isn't until Boxing Day."

"If I am still here then," Miss Clack said, "that might be amusing. I enjoy live theater when my presence doesn't cause a scene. Costume ball, you say? I haven't been to one of those since Gstaad, have I, Sebastian?"

"Correct, Miss Clack," Mr. Venable answered. "You were Lady Macbeth."

"Of course." This must have produced some kind of reverie, since, although Miss Clack's expression didn't change, she stood motionless for what seemed a full minute. Simon heard nothing except kitchen sounds. "Well, I have nothing suitable to wear to a costume ball," Miss Clack continued, as though a pause had never occurred. "And there simply isn't time to have my couturier ship something from Milan."

"We have a fine costume shop just outside Dickens Square," Mavis offered.

"It will have to do. Sebastian will have to call them with my measurements, since I left my traveling mannequin in Zurich. Or Arles."

"Dubrovnik," said Mr. Venable.

Mavis cleared her throat and held out a massive decorative fan. "May I offer you this as a suggestion? It was part of my costume many years ago, when I went as Scrooge's younger sister Fan. 'Always a delicate creature, whom a breath might have withered.'"

"I have never been a delicate creature," Miss Clack said to Mavis.

Mavis put her hand to her cheek, possibly to hide her blushing. Although petite, she was still a few inches taller than Dagny Clack. "I meant the character's stature, Miss Clack. Fan is a delicate creature, and you are the right size."

This explanation seemed to placate Miss Clack. She held the fan in her tiny hand, snapped it open, and held it near her face. "It has a...bucolic charm," she said, her voice softening slightly. "I shall consider it."

"And, if you wish," Mavis offered, "perhaps Madame Mantalini would be able to style your hair to go with your gown."

"That won't be necessary," Miss Clack said. "Sebastian is my stylist. He is a man of singular talents." She held out her hand. "Now, I am ready to see my suite. The key, please."

"Of course," Mavis said. She reached out to give the key to Miss Clack, but at the last moment Miss Clack waved her hand away and Mr. Venable took the key.

"If I need something, I will alert you through Mr. Venable," Miss Clack said. "He shall have the room adjoining mine, correct?" Mavis held out another key, which Mr. Venable also took.

"Good day, Mrs. Spurlock." And with that, Miss Clack walked up the main staircase toward the second floor, leaving her luggage still on the floor. Mr. Venable, carrying only the computer laptop, followed.

Mavis turned and walked toward the kitchen. She jumped when she saw Simon standing just inside the breakfast room.

"Have you been here long enough to see any of that?" Mavis said. "What a diva. Who does she think is going to carry all those bags of hers?"

"I heard enough. How long has she been here?"

"Her private jet landed at the Astoria airport less than an hour ago."

Simon rolled his eyes. "And where did she get a stretch limo?"

"The driver, from Portland, was waiting when Miss Clack arrived. Miss Clack does not take 'no' for an answer."

"So I gathered."

"Do you really think she's going to stay four or five days?" Mavis asked. "Or even longer?"

"If what she wants is to gain control of the Junction, she'll be here until hell freezes," said Simon. "Be prepared for a siege."

Sebastian Venable came down the staircase. "I'm sorry," he said, "I didn't mean to interrupt you, Mrs. Spurlock, but Miss Clack will require special water for drinking and for her tea." He handed Mavis a website printout.

"Of course," Mavis said. "I'll run to the market right away." She looked at the paper. "This water is from Finnish Lapland," she said. "I've never heard of it."

"The other on that page would be a suitable substitute," Venable said. "The one collected from Tasmanian raindrops that have never hit the ground."

"I'll get right on this," Mavis said, exasperation in her voice. She turned. "Mr. Venable, this is Simon Alastair. He is a neighbor of mine."

"Mr. Alastair," said Venable, extending his hand. "I am the personal assistant to Miss Dagny Clack, CEO of Marley Enterprises. We—I mean Miss Clack—has heard of you." Venable started up the stairs. "She will be wanting to see you at the conclusion of her business in Dickens Junction," he continued. "You are on her list." He paused. "Yes. Last. You will be the last."

AFTER RETURNING TO GAD'S HILL PLACE AND BRIEFING ZACH and George on the arrival of Dagny Clack, Simon went to Pip's Pages. Now two news crews were filming in the square. Several youths, out of school for the holidays, were only too happy to walk in front of the cameras to provide holiday "color," as Brock, who was already at work, called it. Reporters tried following Simon into the bookstore, but he was refusing both off- and on-camera interviews about the murders.

Brock was rearranging the DVD collection, a small expansion Simon had agreed on after the recent success of the multiple-Emmy-winning BBC production of *Barnaby Rudge*. He had sold a number of copies, in spite of his reservations about certain aspects of the production that, while highly effective, were not quite Dickensian. And he was thrilled that so many people had been excited enough to buy the original text and other Dickens novels. "It's all good, right?" Brock had said.

Brad Sturgess came by in the late morning to report that Fox News had gotten wind of Dagny Clack's visit to the Junction and was storming the gates of Bleak House that very minute. "Some guy named Venable was fending them off. Mavis told me to tell you that he's a lot tougher than he looks." Sturgess looked tired. "She says this Venable guy has been up and down the stairs all morning with 'Miss Clack needs this' and 'Miss Clack must have that.' Mavis is ready to cut and run. What did you think of Clack, Simon?"

"A tough cookie," he answered. "People are just another kind of object to her, something to steer around or storm over." Simon was standing near the corner of the shelves devoted to Ruth Rendell writing as Barbara Vine. He leaned on a stack of copies of *The House of Stairs*. "Brad, I don't mean to be nosy, but where did you and Mavis have dinner the other night before you went to Anita Distraction's?"

Sturgess gave Simon a look over the top of his glasses. "You really are going to attempt to solve this yourself, aren't you? I don't blame you, I suppose. Although I think you're getting yourself in a heap of trouble. But since you ask." He handed Simon a receipt from his wallet. "We had the crab mac and cheese at Cannery Roe. With a bottle of zinfandel and gooseberry buckle for dessert."

Simon looked at the charge slip. Date and time prominently

displayed, confirming two diners at the restaurant inside the time frame of Brundish's murder.

"Then we walked to Anita's. Had we known about the exotic dancers—or about Brock—we would have come back to the Junction straightaway." Simon handed the slip back to Sturgess.

Sturgess was watching out the windows of Pip's Pages. The Dickens Carolers had arrived in the square; reporters and their cameramen were vying to get the carolers into the shot. One caroler used the enormous muff to nudge one camera away from her face. "This is insanity," Sturgess said.

"I couldn't agree more."

George strolled into the shop wearing a lime-green down jacket, brown corduroy pants, and a Scottish tartan muffler wrapped several times around his neck. He greeted Sturgess, who took his entrance as his signal for leaving. "I'll catch up with you later," Sturgess said to Simon.

"If Mavis calls again," said Simon, "keep me posted."

"This is not good," George said to Simon, gesturing to the events in the square. "They accosted me—me! I don't even live here! But I put them in their place."

Simon grinned. "And just how did you do that?"

"I told them—with all of the Savannah charm that I could muster—that I would only deign to be interviewed by Christiane Amanpour."

"Not much chance of that happening—I hope."

"Anyway, the reason I stopped by—I was going out for my morning constitutional," George said, "when I was asked to bear a message—from God, as it were."

Meaning Zach. "And that is?"

"He suggested that we meet for dinner at the Porters, to soak in local color, apparently."

"Not a bad idea," said Simon. "I'll meet you there after I close the store."

"I won't be able to join you, my dear."

"Why not?"

George took off his glasses, rubbed the lenses with his handkerchief, and then put them back on. "While I have had experience proving that three can be an interesting number, it's no longer my style. No, I found a little nugget in the paper that I think is more my speed." He held out a clipping from the *Daily Astorian*. "Not all of the finest holiday events happen in Dickens Junction. Tonight, the Astoria chapter of the Sons of Norway is having an all-you-can-eat lutefisk and meatball dinner, followed by traditional folk dancing with the musical stylings of master accordionists the Dueling Duoos Brothers." George smiled. "Who knows? I could meet the Lars or Ole of my dreams."

"The meatballs are tasty," Brock piped up from his place among the stacks. "Good lefse, too. The lutefisk, not so much." He made a face and went back to organizing DVDs.

"But first, my dear, I'm off to the beach with La Rand. If I have to be with her, I might as well enjoy the scenery of Haystack Rock while I do it. See you later, darling."

THREE TOUR BUSES ARRIVED FROM PORTLAND RIGHT before lunch. The bookstore enjoyed a rush of customers, even if many of them were more hopeful of being on CNN than of expanding their Edith Wharton collections.

Simon thought only of Dagny Clack. Even though he knew Zach was combing the Internet, Simon brought his laptop to the front of the store and surfed for information. Stories had been filed and posted already about Clack's visit to Dickens Junction, some by local bloggers. Buried deep in a local online newsletter was an uncaptioned photograph of Dagny Clack as Lady Macbeth at the costume ball in Gstaad that she had mentioned. "Unsex me here," came to his mind as he reviewed her photo. She had a small but highly toned athletic body, an Amazon in miniature. What plan did she have to take Dickens Junction by storm? And what could he do to stop her?

During the afternoon, he received several messages referring to Miss Clack's presence in the Junction. The mayor sent an e-mail—he was to see Clack that evening at eight in her suite. Because of the tour buses, Simon and Grace had cancelled their morning coffee, but she told him in a voice mail that she had been "summoned to the presence" of Miss Clack when the store closed at six.

Around four o'clock, Charity and Viola came into the bookstore. "We just saw Miss Clack," Viola said to Simon, "and we'd like to talk to you about it...along with other issues."

Simon ushered them into the back room; they sat on the chairs next to Simon's desk. He pulled up his desk chair so the three of them could sit in a small circle. "What happened?"

"She's an awful person," Charity said.

"Not that she wasn't cordial, you understand," Viola said. She took Charity's hand and held it in her lap. "At least, at first."

"Tell me everything," said Simon.

"We've pretty much kept to ourselves since the council meeting on Saturday," Charity said.

"I stayed home from the tearoom for the last two days," Viola said. "I didn't think I was sociable enough to handle the crowds, all the questions."

"Otherwise we would have seen you sooner, Simon."

"But we had to come out because of the call from Miss Clack. She would not be denied when she said she needed to see me today."

"We were greeted downstairs by that Mr. Venable," Charity said. "At first, he wasn't going to allow me to accompany Viola."

"He said that Miss Clack had asked only for me," Viola said. "I explained that we had been together twenty-five years, and I certainly wasn't going to meet with her alone and talk about money, even if the property is listed only in my name."

"So," Charity continued, "we went upstairs. Hadn't seen the suite before. Mavis has done a nice job keeping the furnishings contemporary without being cold."

"Yes," Viola said. "So, Miss Clack was standing when we arrived, speaking in German on her cell phone. Tiny thing, isn't she?" She waited until Simon nodded. "I couldn't understand anything except *Berlin* and *Freitag*. She motioned to us to sit, and ended the call right after that."

"She offered us tea," Charity said. "Mr. Venable brought it up on Mavis's best silver tray. Some kind of special tea made with water from Tasmanian rain."

"Szechuan yellow gold tea buds," Viola said. "The leaves are handpicked and dipped in actual gold. Miss Clack informed us it was the most expensive tea in the world."

"She never travels without it."

"I think she wanted to intimidate us. It didn't work."

"Maybe not for you," Charity said. "Anyway, Clack got down to business right away."

"True," Viola continued. "She said right off she wanted to buy my property, no questions asked. All I needed to do was name my price."

"What did you tell her?" Simon asked.

"I was so proud of her." Charity squeezed Viola's hand.

Viola smoothed her dark slacks. "I said I wouldn't sell to anyone without a written guarantee that the building would be used for purposes consistent with the wishes of the founder of Dickens Junction. And a ninety-nine-year unbreakable lease for the tea shop."

"Miss Clack was *not* amused by that response," Charity said. "She would, she said, 'have no such truck' with that. What kind of phrase is that?"

"In any case," Viola said, "that was my offer. Clack then asked at what price I would sell my property with no conditions at all. I said there was no price."

"That's when it got uncomfortable," Charity said.

"Clack said I was being unreasonable. She handed me this." Viola released her hand from Charity's grasp. She reached into her wool-jacket pocket and handed Simon another Marley Enterprises business card. The purple edge, the dollar-sign logo. *Dagny Clack, President and CEO.* No telephone number, no website.

"Turn it over." Simon did so. The card showed a number. A very, very large number. Simon breathed in through his teeth.

"This was her counteroffer," Viola said.

"The property is worth far less than this. This is unbelievable." He handed the card back to Viola.

She returned it to her jacket pocket. "If Clack offered Brundish this kind of money, he must have sold to her—earning her 'greatest appreciation.'"

"And possibly getting him killed. You could break a promise to your mother at this price." Simon told her about Mavis's call from Brundish. "Did you ask him to promise you not to sell his property?"

"I didn't," Viola answered. "Why would I have done that?"

"He promised someone," said Simon, "unless he was lying to Mavis."

"Or she was lying to you," Viola said. "Someone is lying to someone in this town."

Yes, at least one person, maybe more. Who to believe? "Back to Clack," said Simon. "What did you say about this offer?"

"Have you seen her, Simon?" Viola asked.

"Only from a distance."

"She's got these amazing eyes," Charity said. "They're like emeralds, hard and bright and gleaming with concentration and intelligence. And the most amazing expression—the best poker face I've ever seen."

"I'm thinking Botox," Viola said. "No real emotion crossed her face. Not once. Even her smile was empty. Anyway, I couldn't keep looking at her face. I felt as if she was trying to steal my soul. I told her I'd give her an answer tomorrow."

"At the Fezziwig Ball," Charity said.

"That's the one time she showed a human emotion," Viola said, her own face registering her new understanding as she was talking. "She will be attending the ball, and she actually sounded as if she was looking forward to it."

"How peculiar," said Simon. "Dickens Junction has nothing on Gstaad." He showed them the photograph of her and explained the reference.

"So I'm just postponing my anguish." Viola looked carefully at Simon. "Of course I'll refuse it."

"It's a lot of money."

"Let's talk about the other reason we're here," Charity said. "We want to tell you about the night Brundish was killed. Where we were. And what we told Detective Boggs."

"You've heard about Lavender Ladies?" Viola said.

Of course Simon had. The social group of gay and bisexual women of Oregon's north coast met regularly, hosting potlucks, movie nights, and raising money for the county women's shelter.

"Brundish was killed the night of the Lavender Ladies' holiday white-elephant exchange and dinner," Charity said.

"By the time the regifting had ended," Viola said, "we had the same fondue set we've brought for the last two years."

"We didn't get home until after midnight," Charity said, "in spite of the busy day we knew was coming."

"And so," Viola continued, "we had a bit of difficulty when Detective Boggs asked us for names to confirm our alibis. Not all of the Ladies are out to their families; a few are still in conventional marriages. The Junction may be extremely welcoming, but not every member of the coastal community shares those views. Not yet, at least."

"I understand," said Simon. "From what I've seen so far of Detective Boggs, I believe she will exercise extreme discretion in everything she does."

"When are you seeing Miss Clack?" Viola asked. "As the primary property owner in the square, you have to be in her sights somewhere."

"In her sights," Simon echoed. "What a figure of speech."

"WHERE'S GEORGE?" ZACH ASKED WHEN SIMON ARRIVED at his booth in the back of the Porters. "I know he gave you the message, because you're here."

"He was lured away by the siren song of twin accordionists."

Zach stood and gave Simon a quick kiss before the two men settled in the booth.

"People will talk," said Simon. On his way through the restaurant, he had passed Mayor Dick sitting with a few locals. The Neffs were at a two-top table talking earnestly, maybe even heatedly. Brad Sturgess was having a drink with his interns at one of the booths near the pool table.

"They already are. Shall I stand on the table and shout like a fourteen-year-old girl that I've got a boyfriend?" Zach started to stand again, as if he were actually going to do just that.

Simon blushed and grabbed his sleeve. *My God, the man is gorgeous. Do not look into those eyes—look away, or you'll drown in the puddles of blue, Simon.* "That would be interesting, I guess. If you do. Have a boyfriend. That is."

"Maybe I'm being premature," Zach said. "If I am"—he put his hand on Simon's—"this is the only time I will be, I assure you."

Joelle Creevy came over to take their orders. Simon guessed her to be in her mid-fifties; the dark skin of her cheeks was dotted with black specks that gave her a more youthful look, paired with liquid brown eyes and a wide smile. A slight gray streak ran on the left side of her short, curly, copper hair. She looked at the men's hands and smiled.

"It's good to see a moment of joy in this craziness," she said. "A customer came in today who claimed to have seen a helicopter flying over the Junction—said it was Diane Sawyer circling about, waiting to see whether she was going to get an interview with that Clack woman staying at Bleak House."

"I didn't hear that one," said Simon. "Nor did I see a helicopter."

"I don't know what to believe right now," Joelle continued. "Or whom." She took their orders—fish and chips for Zach, a Cobb salad for Simon, and two Aviation Gin martinis with twists, no vermouth.

She brought the drinks a few minutes later. "Cheers." Zach clinked his glass against Simon's.

"These last few days have been sweet," said Simon. "At least the parts with you. The rest is nerve-racking—the publicity, waiting for something to happen. To find out what Dagny Clack is after."

Zach picked up his messenger bag and removed some papers. "I kept running into dead ends with her—her people keep very close tabs on her, and not much makes it to the Internet. Some interesting blogs mention her in connection with various Ayn Rand sites—the more fanatical ones at least."

"Are there any Ayn Rand sites that aren't fanatical?" Simon asked.

"Now that you mention it, no," Zach said. "She's either the savior of our nation or the Antichrist."

"Where does Clack get her money? Those who say, 'Money is no object,' must have a great deal of it."

Zach thumbed through his papers. "She invented something about twenty-five years ago when she was in college, some little electronic thingy that apparently needs to go in every computer ever made. That's when she encountered Ayn Rand, *Atlas Shrugged* particularly, and imagined herself as a character in the novel, one of John Galt's recruits for his strike against the world."

"That makes sense," said Simon. "But what does she do with the money?"

"Doesn't give it to charity, that's for sure," Zach said. "She's not like so many of the über-rich, sitting on nonprofit boards and such. She doesn't believe in it." He pulled out two sheets of printed material and passed them over to Simon. "Here's the only published interview that I could find for her. She actually granted a telephone interview with the owner of *ILoveAynRand.org* in 2002. You can read it yourself, but it doesn't contain anything about Marley Enterprises. That name wasn't registered until last year."

"So Marley Enterprises is recent?"

Joelle brought their dinners. After seasoning his food with pepper from a mill the size of a baseball bat, Zach nibbled a french fry before answering. "Looks that way."

As Simon scanned the other tables nonchalantly while unfolding his napkin, Mayor Dick looked up and caught Simon's eye. He stood and left his table, headed toward Simon's.

"Are you fortifying yourself for your meeting with Dagny Clack?" Simon asked as Dick approached.

"This?" He held up the drink he was carrying. "Just one Scotch tonight," he said. "I need to keep my head clear. She's a dangerous woman."

"I'm sure she is," said Simon. "Money can do that to a person."

"A lack of it can do the same thing," the mayor observed. "Has she called you?"

"Not yet. I'm waiting for that shoe to drop."

"Grace is there now," the mayor said. "I asked her to meet me here when it was over, so I could get a sense of what to expect."

"And here she comes now," Zach said.

Grace approached, bundled in a parka and knitted wool cap. As she neared the table, she pulled off the cap and started unzipping the parka. Zach moved farther down the bench to make room for her.

"I have been to the mountain," she said. Her cheeks were bright and flushed from the outside chill. "A tiny mountain, for sure, but a mountain just the same."

"How was it?" Simon asked. Mayor Dick leaned in.

"Do you want something to drink?" Zach asked.

"I'm fine," Grace said. "Just rattled."

"Tell us."

Grace's story sounded similar to Charity's and Viola's—Venable's greeting, the tea, getting down to business. "She offered me an extraordinary amount to sell," Grace said. She pulled out the now-familiar business card and turned it over.

Mayor Dick took a step back. "Is she crazy?" he asked. "No one pays this kind of money for property, especially in this economy."

"Of course," Grace continued, "I asked her about leasing the property back, should I actually sell to her. I would want to continue running the store." Grace looked at Simon, then at the mayor. "Do you know what she said? 'Absolutely not, Ms. Beddoes. I have plans for all of the property that I intend to acquire—*singular* plans.'"

"Whatever Clack wants," said Simon, "it's likely to be singular."

"She told you her plans?" Zach asked.

"No," Grace answered. "I asked her point blank. All she would say was, 'Ms. Beddoes, on that question I must be, for now, in the words of your reprehensible Mr. Dickens, "solitary as an oyster."'"

The ominous reference to Scrooge and his miserly loneliness made Simon shiver. Whatever her motives, she knew her Dickens. He moved his hand closer to Zach's, seeking his warmth.

"How did the meeting end?" Mayor Dick asked.

"Up in the air," Grace answered, "deliberately, on my part. I didn't want her to stare me down any longer. I told her I would give her my final answer after the holidays were over. 'I don't have that kind of time,' Clack said. So I finally agreed to tell her at the Fezziwig Ball tomorrow night."

Mayor Dick checked his watch. "I need to leave," he said. "I'm going to walk slowly."

"Call me when you're done," said Simon. "We should be home by then."

On his way out, Mayor Dick stopped to greet Brad Sturgess. He passed by the Neffs' table but didn't stop; they were still talking seriously. Duncan had one empty martini glass in front of him. In the mayor's wake, Joelle stopped by with another martini for him. Ariadne had a drink in front of her, but didn't appear to be drinking it; the ice had melted. Over in the back corner of the restaurant, the Dickens Carolers were taking a break. They had hung their coats, hats, and muff on the coatrack by the back door, near the unused pool table. They were drinking cider; one of the women stirred her steaming cup with a cinnamon stick.

"Should I have been more forceful?" Grace asked. "It seems weak of me not to have just turned her down flat." She turned to Simon. "What would you have done?"

"Probably the same," said Simon. "I hate conflict."

"But why should I be conflicted?" Grace asked. "I have no intention of selling now or later, and especially not to her."

"It's a lot of money." Zach fingered the card. "More money than I'll make in years, let alone all at once."

"What would I do if I didn't have the shop?" Grace asked Simon.

"With this?" Simon touched the card. "Live a life of leisure, I suppose."

"None of us wants to leave the Junction."

"Not you or Viola," said Simon. "I'm not so sure about the mayor."

"Or Brundish," Grace said. "He didn't want to leave, either."

"And look where that got him," Zach said thoughtfully.

"I should go home." Grace's hand was trembling as she took back Dagny Clack's card. "I'm more upset than I thought."

Simon gestured for Joelle to bring the bill. When she did, he gave her his credit card. "Let us walk you home," said Simon.

"That's not necessary," Grace said.

"It will make *us* feel better," said Simon. "You live two

blocks from me. It's not out of our way at all. Pretend we're not doing it for you."

She smiled weakly. "Since you put it that way—"

"Then it's settled." Simon slid out of the booth; Grace and Zach did the same. He turned to Zach. "On second thought, why don't you go back to Gad's Hill Place and start a fire? I doubt George will be back from the Sons of Norway festivities. Who knows—he may meet a hot Norwegian and stay out all night."

"Good for him," Zach said. "Maybe good for us, too." He put a hand around Simon's waist and pulled him in close, gave him a quick kiss.

Simon signed the bill, and then was distracted by the rough scrape of Ariadne Neff pushing her chair away. She stood in front of Duncan. "Fine!" she yelled at Duncan. "See if I care." She pivoted on her heels, brushed by the Dickens Carolers, and was out of the pub by the back door in a few brittle strides, sending a rush of cold air and the smell of cinnamon toward Simon.

Simon, Zach, and Grace left by the front door, talking for a minute or so before going their separate ways. Grace gave Zach a hug before they parted. Zach disappeared.

Simon and Grace turned around to admire Dickens Square. The night was clear and cold; the garland lights shone with a lambent glow. "You're a lucky man, Simon," Grace said. "Zach is wonderful."

"Everyone tells me that," he said, smiling. "I will draw my own conclusion, thank you."

"You already have. It's in your eyes, your smile. Everywhere." She reached up and touched his face, her ungloved hand warm against the cold night. "I'm so happy for you."

The two turned and exited the square, passing the Porters' dumpster. Grace put her arm back through Simon's as they stepped onto the sidewalk and into the neighborhood outside the square.

In the next moment, Grace's arm was violently pulled away from Simon's; she made a muffled cry and sailed through the air, landing several feet away.

A dark form beside Simon knocked him squarely on the back of the neck with a smooth, hard object, forcing him to his knees. A second blow to the face sent him sideways to the ground, his sense of direction lost, his head landing on his outstretched arm.

Grace was screaming.

Simon might have heard the rapid scrapes of approaching feet, but he was disoriented. His last view was of a weird white cloud descending toward his face.

"You're lucky that Father Blaise was struggling with his sermon and took a late-night constitutional," Detective Boggs said. "Otherwise, you might not be here."

Just after midnight, Simon and Zach sat with Detective Boggs in Simon's living room. Father Blaise had just left. The emergency-room staff had cleaned Simon up, determined that he didn't have a concussion, and sent him home. A bruise was forming on his lower lip, and he had a knot at the back of his head, but the blow that struck him hadn't broken the skin, nor had he any loose or broken teeth from the assailant's attempt to suffocate him with the Dickens Caroler's muff. His nose wasn't broken, but it was sore, with a bruise forming at the bridge. After the hospital staff in Astoria had X-rayed and bandaged Grace's arm, also not broken, she insisted on going back to her own place to sleep, despite Simon's pleas that she stay in one of his guest rooms. Detective Boggs had taken her statement while the nurses were working on her; now, the detective turned her attentions to Simon and Zach.

The fire that had blazed earlier was a heap of embers, dark glowing orange bits of heat. The warmth hung in the room like a comforter.

"What do you recall about the attack?" Detective Boggs had her notepad at the ready. Tonight, the detective wore a snappy maroon cocktail dress with leopard three-inch peep-toe heels. The low-cut bodice was mostly covered by an incongruous and ill-fitting man's parka. *Had she been interrupted during a date?* Simon wondered.

"Grace and I were chatting," said Simon.

"About what?"

Simon looked over. "About Zach, I suppose."

"Anything that might have provoked the assailant if he or she had overheard it?"

Simon started to smile, but his lip ached. "Only if he, or she, found Zach repugnant."

"Or too wonderful for you." Zach tried to joke, but no one else smiled.

"I see," Detective Boggs said. She made a note. "But you heard footsteps?"

"Not really. I felt Grace being pulled away, heard her call my name as she fell, and then felt the blows. The next thing I knew, I was gasping in Father's Blaise's arms."

"Did you see the assailant?"

"It was too dark."

"Shape, color, height, anything?" Detective Boggs asked.

"Probably taller than Dagny Clack," said Simon. "But not as tall as George. Other than that, I can't say."

"So you saw the caroler's muff near the back door of the Porters before you left?"

"Is there only one?" Simon asked.

"We've talked with Serena Olive of Seaside"—Detective Boggs consulted her notes—"and she identified the muff as hers, from a tag on the inside. The women only have one muff between them, because it's so bulky."

"Yes," said Simon. "But it was right near the door. Anyone could have taken it without notice, including someone reaching in from outside the restaurant."

"Who was at the Porters when you left?"

Zach spoke. "Duncan Neff, Bradford Sturgess, the three of us, and a handful of people I didn't know."

"The mayor left right before we did," Simon added.

"As did Ariadne Neff," Zach said.

"She and Duncan had an argument."

Detective Boggs made another note. "What time was it—your best estimate?"

"I looked at my watch before we left," Zach said. "It was ten minutes to eight."

Detective Boggs looked at Zach. "And you heard nothing?"

"I didn't," he said. "I was focused on getting back here—and building a fire. I walked pretty quickly; it was cold, and all I had was my bomber jacket. I'm a Southern California boy," he added. "Yes, this is cold for me."

Simon's cell phone buzzed. "It's a text from George." Everyone looked surprised when he laughed. "He says we'll see him in the morning. He's apparently doing a duet of 'Lady of Spain' with a Dueling Duoos."

"Good for him," Zach said. "But shouldn't you text him about what we're doing?"

Simon put the phone back in his pocket. "Let him have his fun playing scales tonight. He can hear about it in the morning."

Detective Boggs stood. "If I think of anything else, I'll call you tomorrow. And you do the same." She stood next to Simon. "I don't need to tell you how lucky you were. If you continue trying to find out who killed Brundish and Roark on your own, I can't promise that you'll always be so lucky—but I would bet you'll find more trouble."

Simon lowered his eyes. "You're right," he said. "I had underestimated the danger to myself before now. I thought this was a puzzle to solve, not a life-and-death situation."

"I wish I could say we were close to a solution," Detective Boggs said, her voice losing the edge it had had a moment earlier. She drew her shoulders away from her ears, as if aware of the tension in her own body. "I've got to tell you, Simon, that I'm under a lot of pressure about these murders. The forensic evidence in both cases has been complicated by the unusual nature of the deaths, and the sheriff wants a suspect in custody fast, before there's another body. You came too close tonight. If something serious had happened to you, I would have lost my job."

"Not to mention what would have happened to me," said Simon. He smiled, however, and moved his hand toward the sleeve of her parka.

She looked down at his hand for several seconds, saying nothing. "Let me help you," said Simon. "You've resisted my efforts up until now. I know you're worried about police procedures and such, but you're still new to the area, and I've lived here all my life. These people are my friends."

Miniature embers flickered in the reflection in her eyes as she looked into Simon's face. "Are you sure? One of your 'friends' tried to kill you tonight."

"I'm not sure of anything," he said. "Except that I have made sacrifices—many sacrifices—on behalf of the Junction, and I will do everything I can to preserve it, even if that means battling murderers and megalomaniacal recluses with peculiar reading tastes. Just let me help."

Detective Boggs's features softened. Even Simon could see that she was a beautiful woman, not just a strangely dressed law enforcement officer. "I hope you will recover soon, Simon," she said, standing. The skirt reflected shimmers of ember glow. "Good night, Zach."

After showing the detective out, Zach returned to the living room, this time sitting next to Simon. "I haven't known you long," he said softly, caressing Simon's cheek with his fingertips, "but, after last night's discussion, I'm betting this episode has made you *more* determined to find the killer, not less."

Simon tried another smile, and then winced. "Am I so obvious?"

"Consistent," Zach said. He leaned forward and carefully kissed Simon's upper lip.

"Ouch," said Simon mockingly.

"That didn't hurt." Zach repeated the move.

"Who do you think did this?" Simon asked. Zach rubbed Simon's neck, his fingers finding the most tender spots and kneading them away.

"It doesn't matter right now," Zach said. "Besides, worry puts extra lines in your face." He kissed a spot near Simon's eye, stopping Simon mid-frown.

"And the mayor," said Simon, although already feeling less urgent. "I should return his voice mail. I need to find out about his meeting with Dagny Clack."

"Tomorrow," Zach said. "For now, just put yourself in my capable hands."

Tomorrow. Although the timing was terrible, Simon had to ask. "What will you do—when this is all over? File your article and then go—where? Aruba? Iceland? Dar es Salaam?"

Zach ran his finger along Simon's hairline, the sensation like a tickle, a kiss. "You're worried about tomorrow? Next week? Next month? Worried about next year? How about the next millennium? The next geological epoch?" He chuckled. "Let's consider something smaller. The next second. The next minute. The next move." He held Simon's head in his hand, gentle and warm.

Simon put his own hand up against Zach's face, feeling the stubble on his chin. "I'm glad George found his Lars—or Ole."

"Me too," Zach said. He kissed Simon lightly again, then reached down and began unbuttoning Simon's shirt. "But George won't be the only one making music tonight."

GEORGE WAS AT THE NOOK WHEN SIMON CAME DOWN TO breakfast. Bethany was removing a platter of thick-sliced applewood-smoked bacon from the warming oven.

"My dear," George said, standing, "what happened to you?" Bethany put down the platter and came around the island. She and George examined Simon's bruised lip, scraped forehead, and bruise. The knot on the back of Simon's head was not visible.

Simon told them the story of the attack. "And then, the attacker shoved a muff in my mouth."

"That's a first on so many levels," George said.

"I'll be fine," said Simon. He sat beside George and sipped from the coffee that Bethany brought him. "I need to be. Tonight's the Fezziwig Ball."

"You're not going, surely," George said. "After your ordeal?"

"Try and stop me," said Simon.

Zach came in, wearing a pair of Simon's sock-monkey pajamas, the bottoms resting just below his navel, the top unbuttoned and showing a wide expanse of his groomed, muscled chest. Miss Tox trotted in behind him, then curled up on the heating vent and went to sleep.

George looked first at Zach, then at Simon, and then back at Zach. "So that's how it is," he said. "How *Pajama Game* of you." Curiously, Simon was not the least embarrassed at George's insight into the most recent events. He liked that it signaled that somewhere, something must be right.

"And what about you?" Simon asked. "Tell us about the Dueling Duooses."

George smiled. "Did you know that the accordion has one hundred twenty buttons?" He paused. "Let's just say I pushed them all."

Zach put a hand on Simon's back. "A red-letter day all around."

"Okay, boys," Bethany said. "Enough frat-house talk. Here's breakfast." She had made potatoes O'Brien, poached eggs, bacon, and homemade crumpets, dripping with butter and salmonberry preserves.

"It's too much," said Simon.

"You'll eat every bite," she said. "It will keep your strength up for tonight."

"Do you think Clack will show at the ball?" Zach asked.

"I'm betting dollars to doughnuts that she does," said Simon. "She won't miss a chance to make a statement."

"What will it be?" George bit into a crumpet; butter ran down his chin. He wiped it off with a napkin.

"You'll have to be there to find out," said Simon. "You have to be present to win."

"I'm not sure those things are for me," George said. "After all, I'm just a houseguest." He took another bite of crumpet. "But I'll think about it."

On his way to the bookstore, Simon passed Bleak House. He could see Mavis framed in the breakfast-room window, talking with guests at a table for four; the other tables were empty. He looked up toward the windows of the Summerson Suite. The heavy curtains were pulled shut. He continued down the hill.

A block farther past Bleak House, steps away from the entrance to the square, Simon stopped at the scene of last night's events. Daytime made everything look so innocent, so impossible. The only place the assailant could have hidden was near the dumpster behind the Porters, not far from the back door that Ariadne Neff had used minutes before

Simon and Grace left from the front. Here was the corridor out of the square and into the neighborhood. He and Grace had passed through, happy, talking, onto Wade Street and toward Gad's Hill. Two blocks later, they would have turned left toward Grace's cottage. But that never happened.

Simon stood on the sidewalk. He could see where he had fallen; the landscaping in the front yard of the small corner house had been stirred up. Grace, unfortunately, had hit pavement, but only with her arm. She had been pushed or pulled, not hit. A tuft of faux ermine from the muff was stuck to a woody azalea bush. Simon shivered as he recalled his first impressions after the attack—the taste of his own blood mixed with polyester fur as Father Blaise removed the muff, followed by the throbbing in his head.

Inside Dickens Square, now, all was quiet; a few people window-shopped and waited for the stores to open. An elderly couple was coming out of the Crystal Palace. Cricket's Hearth was still dark. In front of Pip's Pages, on the streetlamp standing nearest the store, Simon noticed a laminated poster affixed with wire strung through its top and bottom and laced back around the pole. He looked more closely. Anita Distraction's was announcing its *New Year's Party—dinner, champagne, and final performance of the Men of Midnight—absolutely the LAST NIGHT EVER,* all of this printed over a photo of Brock in one of his more provocative poses, hands positioned in the place one would normally expect to see a bathing suit, or at least a Speedo. There was no visible fabric line.

Simon entered the store. Brock was getting ready to open

the register. "Good morning, boss." His eyes met Simon's. "Jesus," he said, "Bethany wasn't kidding. She texted me already. You look awful."

Simon hung his coat in the back, and returned to the front of the store. "I didn't think I looked so bad, today." He touched his sore lower lip; it was still fairly swollen. He checked his watch, then switched the *closed* sign to *open* and turned on the small neon store logo light.

"How do you feel?" Brock asked. He came over to take a closer look.

"Like the day after a leg workout with you," Simon answered. "That bad."

"You could have been killed. Who did it?"

Simon scratched his head, forgetting for a moment about the goose egg. He told Brock the story as he had relayed it to Detective Boggs. When he finished, he nodded toward the poster outside. "I thought that Mysterion retired."

"He did," Brock said. "Until Anita's made me an offer I couldn't refuse. Besides, I'm thinking about asking Bethany to marry me on Christmas. I need some money for a ring."

"I didn't realize you two were that serious," said Simon. "Am I going to lose the best chef ever?"

"I don't know how much longer I can stay here," Brock said.

"As much as I hate to admit it, the Junction isn't for everyone. But Bethany is still in school. Shouldn't you wait?"

Brock frowned. "She wants to transfer to the University of Oregon after she finishes here in June. I could follow her.

Eugene is a fitness-crazy town. I can get twice or more the minimum wage if I work as a full-time trainer."

Although Simon was paying Brock well above the minimum wage (and above the market pay for the work he did), Simon couldn't argue with the financial—let alone emotional—reasons for leaving Dickens Junction. If he hadn't had responsibilities and a sense of duty—and money—would he have stayed behind? Would he have missed the opportunity that a life with Andrew—or David—would have given him in Portland, Seattle, or San Francisco? *Speculating is pointless,* he thought. He had made the choices he made and was living by them.

Simon considered his next words before saying them. "Twenty-two is awfully young to get married. But if you're set on it, I can lend you whatever you need for a ring—as long as you're sensible about it. Then you wouldn't have to dance at Anita's again."

"Thanks, Simon," Brock said. "But I want to do this on my own. I promised Anita I would do it, and I'm a man of my word." His mouth curved into the slyest of smiles. "Besides. Bethany thinks it's hot."

"Too much information...but your secret is safe with me." Simon admired Brock's sense of responsibility and independence. He wanted to think that the years he had known and mentored him had counted for something.

"You know," Brock said, "I checked the storage shed yesterday. The detective was right about something—someone has been in that shed. There's some damage to the backdrops—footprints, a crack in the plywood of one, and a few things have been bashed around. But we can fix them." After a pause, he added, "That Neff's a little prick."

"I won't argue with you." Simon turned away from Brock, only to see Solomon Dick peering in the window. The mayor entered the bookstore a second later.

"Jesus," Dick said, "what happened to you?" The mayor looked more tired than Simon had seen him since his sister had died, two years earlier. His cheeks were sunken, dark circles spread beneath reddened eyes. He had a spot of grease on the collar of his white shirt.

Simon took the mayor into the back room, wondering as he did so how many times today he would repeat his story.

"That at least explains why you weren't home when I called," the mayor said.

"How did your meeting go with Dagny Clack?"

"She is an unpleasant woman, who can be most persuasive," the mayor said. "She is closing the noose. She believes she will win." The bluster in his voice from just a few days earlier was gone, and Solomon appeared uncomfortable as he took out another of Dagny Clack's business cards and handed it to Simon. Simon turned the card over. The amount written there, in purple ink, was higher than the amounts offered Viola or Grace. Granted, the mayor's buildings were the largest of the holdings not owned by Simon, but still, it was a staggering amount.

"Are you going to accept her offer?"

"That's why I'm here, Simon." He looked at the floor, then hitched his thumbs into his waistband and looked Simon directly in the eyes. "My side of the Dick family didn't manage their wealth like yours," he said. "My grandpap made imprudent investments, while yours turned everything he touched into platinum. My property is my retirement, if this economy will ever let me retire. I know you think I'm wealthy, with the video gaming and such, but two things did me in: the economy and Duncan Neff. Gaming receipts are way down; even the regular customers have decreased their visits or stopped coming entirely." He paused, as if teetering on the edge of betraying confidential information. "Let's just say that Duncan Neff's blunders harmed a lot of people. Everyone I talk to—except, apparently, you—had too much money invested with Neff. 'Never trust a good-looking man,' my grandfather always told my sister. I should have listened to him." He paused. "All of us who own property in the Junction and on the square are feeling the pinch, and then comes this Clack woman, throwing money around like a drunken sailor."

Dick shifted his weight from one foot to the other. "Here's the deal, Simon. I'm not going to beg. In the interest of family, I'm willing to put our differences aside, but I need your help. I don't need as much money as Clack has offered, but I need a return on my investment. If you offered me seventy-five percent of what she has offered me for my property, I'd sell to you instead, and be happy to piss on Clack's plans, whatever they are."

Simon started to speak, but Dick put up his hand to stop him. "Allegra got home last evening," he continued. "We stayed up nearly the whole night talking, trying to figure out a way that preserves what I've worked my whole life for.

This is my community, too. But I have to consider my own security." He paused, took a breath. "There. I've said it."

Simon realized this speech had been very difficult for Solomon Dick. He wasn't looking for a handout, but he couldn't afford to do anything else. From the mayor's perspective, Simon considered, his was a very generous proposal, taking far less than he could, in an effort to maintain community. But from Simon's perspective, even seventy-five percent of Clack's offer was a lot more money than Simon had in available funds. To accomplish the mayor's request, he'd have to sell some of his own holdings, no doubt at a loss in this market, so the true cost of keeping the Junction even partially intact was much higher. And if Grace or Viola made similar requests, he couldn't do it. He would be wiped out. Clack would win.

"Solomon," said Simon, "I can't tell you how grateful I am to you for coming to me. I know how hard it must have been. And I want to do what you ask, but I need a few days to talk with my accountant. Will you give me until New Year's?"

"I'd like to, Simon, but Clack wants an answer before Christmas. I don't know what she plans on doing after that."

"That only gives me two days."

"I realize it's short notice, but—"

Simon looked out the window. He was very surprised to see Dagny Clack, a small notepad in hand, like a mini-Colossus striding through the square across the paving stones. She moved so fast that her coat, a full-length black sable, flew out behind her like the train of a royal robe. Simon had never before seen such a shameless display of excess. Ariadne Neff was trying to keep up with her without being hit by the glistening sable hem. Ariadne's face appeared strained, a look of desperation on it as she talked.

Clack did not appear to be listening; she was making sketches with a piece of charcoal on the pad, looking up at the buildings that Lowell Brundish had owned. A television reporter and camerawoman were trying to catch them. And was that the sound of a helicopter? Simon shuddered.

This was a slim chance to save the Junction, provided that Viola and Grace held out in a way Brundish apparently had not. But not trying to come up with the money was the same as admitting defeat, letting this vile woman win.

"I'll do my best," said Simon, extending his hand. Mayor Dick grasped it with both of his meaty hands and shook it vigorously.

AFTER THE MAYOR LEFT, SIMON IMMEDIATELY CALLED his accountant, Nathaniel Pocket, and they had a lengthy discussion of Mayor Dick's offer. Pocket was dubious about Simon's idea. He thought he might be able to make it happen, but needed time to run estimates of the loss of value to Simon's real estate and investment portfolios. He pledged to call Simon with the numbers as soon as possible, and certainly before leaving his office on Christmas Eve. Pocket made Simon pledge that he would talk with Solomon Dick only after he had called him back. Simon reluctantly agreed.

"I'm only keeping your interests in mind, the same as Dick is his own. Go along with me on this, Simon."

Simon decided that, after all of this high-finance talk, he needed a brief break. "I'm going for a latte," he told Brock. He called Grace, but she didn't answer her cell; he saw as he crossed the square that a clutch of elderly women from yet another tour bus had just descended on Cricket's Hearth. He'd catch up with Grace at the ball.

He got his latte to go and was on his way back to the bookstore, dodging cameramen as he walked, when he bumped into George.

"I have savory and delicious news, my dear," George said, holding the copy of *Atlas Shrugged* in one hand as he descended on Simon and gave him a big hug. "I have encountered La Clack herself. We have had words. Words, I'm telling you."

"I'm confused," said Simon. "She summoned you to Bleak House? How could she even know who you are?"

"Not hardly," George answered. "I stalked her on the square and was gratified with a personal—albeit brief—interview and insight into her unique and twisted psyche."

"Do tell."

They entered Pip's Pages. George put the novel on the counter and pointed at it. "You will notice that I was carrying this when you saw me."

"Brandishing is more like it," Simon suggested.

"Whatever. It was *un objet*, as it were, designed to catch the keen eye of Dagny Clack, Ayn Rand worshipper and one crock of crazy." He paused. "Is it true that Anderson Cooper and

Rachel Maddow were seen in an altercation at Krook's Koffee An' Kiosk over which of them would interview Clack first? That would be something to see. I'll e-mail Anderson forthwith to arm himself with a hardback of *The Fountainhead* and wear it on his lapel for all to see. That should get him the interview."

"The media frenzy in this place is driving me nuts," said Simon. "But go on about Clack. Describe your meeting."

"Well," George continued. "I saw her in the company of that very angular Neff woman. They were bouncing around the square from place to place, and Clack was shouting orders to Neff while drawing little sketches."

"Did you see what the sketches were?"

"Later, yes, when Clack and I were *tête-à-tête.* They looked like buildings, but I couldn't be sure. Very strange buildings, Gearylike, or is it Gaudilike—I can never remember."

"Go on."

"Aren't you savoring each detail?" George asked.

"Like a fine Bordeaux."

"All right, then, I'll continue. So, with my book placed thusly"—he held it behind himself like a bouquet of flowers—"I nonchalantly turned my back on the approaching Clack and pretended to window shop at Twist and Ternan's. Before I knew it, she was upon me. 'You are an admirer of Ayn Rand?' she asked. 'Isn't everyone?' I replied. 'Not around here,' Clack said. 'Can't you see it—this place is a shrine to that socialist.' 'I'm a stranger in these parts,' I said, 'but are you referring to the great nineteenth-century novelist of the people, Charles Dickens?' '"Of the people" is right,' she said, spitting out the words. 'All of that giving to the poor and such. The rich have more because they are smarter—and better—than other people. The only smart thing Dickens ever wrote was that people who go around with "Merry Christmas" on their lips should be boiled in a pudding and buried with a stake of holly through their heart.'"

"Then she stopped"—George himself finally took a breath—"realizing that Neff was staring at her, slack-jawed. I must have been so, too. 'And what do you do,' she continued, 'stranger that you are?'"

"'I'm an artist,' I replied. 'Excellent,' she said. 'Artists are creators of intellectual property and should be admired, unless they expect to be paid for their work by government grants and handouts. Are you one of those?' 'I am not,' I replied."

George was basking in every moment of his recitation; he scanned Simon's and Brock's eyes for signs that he still had their rapt attention before he continued. "'Excellent,' La Clack said, validating my existence with a single word from her surgically tightened throat. She has the most amazing bone structure, don't you think, my dear?" he asked Simon. "But then, you are not an artist. Pity. Although she lacks height, she has stature. But such a thin woman, painfully thin. One imagines her standing in front of a floodlight and giving anatomy lessons from within, as it were."

"Is there more?" Simon asked.

"That's about it," George said. His chest deflated as he completed his performance. "After that, she consulted her BlackBerry, returned it to her coat pocket, and wafted out of the square, Mrs. Neff in tow." He bowed. "By the way, that coat must have cost more than the gross national product of the one of the smaller Balkan countries. It glowed like diamonds in the sun—or like one of those new vampires, perhaps. I'm surprised she hasn't been paintballed by a PETA fanatic."

"Or worse," said Simon.

George sighed. "Well, this brush with greatness has exhausted my meager resources for the day. I've decided to skip the Fezziwig Ball after all."

"No," Simon urged, "you must go."

"I'm too tired," George said, "and you and Zach don't need the fifth wheel, or third eye, or whatever extra dangling appendage I might represent. Take pictures on your iPhone, and then you can regale me with slightly exaggerated tales of it all afterward." He moved toward the door. "Besides," he said, "I've got to finish this book. I suspect a preposterous conclusion."

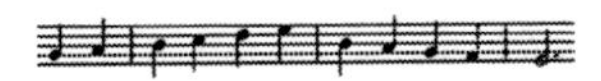

SIMON AND ZACH PREPARED TO ENTER THE HIGH SCHOOL gymnasium where the annual Fezziwig Ball was held (not long after their homecoming dance, to which it bore many similarities, Simon had to admit). They were dressed in white-tie formal dress as Eugene Wrayburn and Mortimer Lightwood, the young lawyers from *Our Mutual Friend*. They wore black beaver top hats. Simon sported a black cane; Zach carried a pair of dress white gloves. Both had draped raincoats over their shoulders to protect their clothes against the drizzle.

They met Father Blaise outside. He was wearing his usual clerical garb with collar. "And what character are you?" Zach asked.

"Minor Canon Septimus Crisparkle from *The Mystery of Edwin Drood*. And you?" He looked at Zach.

"I'm someone named Eugene from a book I haven't read," Zach answered. "Yet. But he and his 'roommate' apparently have a very strong 'affection' for one another." Zach put his arm around Simon's waist.

"Where is your other friend—the Southern gentleman?" Father Blaise asked. "He makes me laugh."

"George is under the weather," said Simon. "He is exhausted from an intellectual *contretemps* he had today with Dagny Clack." Father Blaise looked suitably horrified on George's behalf.

The three men went through the single entrance to the ball. After handing over their tickets, Simon led Zach toward the cloakroom while Father Blaise, coatless, went directly to the gymnasium door. "I'll see you inside," he called.

The cloakroom was a temporary one, a large space usually used for storing sports equipment. Six long coatracks had been installed between the front and back doors, the latter of which led directly into the gymnasium and the ball. Ladasha Creevy sat at the front of the cloakroom. A sign on the desk beside her said, *Absolutely NO Photography Inside.*

"You make a lovely Tattycoram," said Simon, admiring Ladasha's deliberately faded Victorian gown.

"Thanks, Simon." She gave them tokens that corresponded with tokens on the hangers for the self-service racks. "It's unfortunate that Dickens created so few black characters."

"Short-sighted," Simon agreed. "He was great, but not perfect. Race was one of his blind spots. Is your mom here?"

"No," Ladasha answered. "She's holding down the fort at the Porters. She figures the pub will be extra busy tonight with all of the people who aren't party people." She paused, her eyes scanning Simon's face. "We heard you were attacked last night...is everything okay?"

"Just a bit of bruising," said Simon, pleased that he must be looking a little better. "And a knot on my head that's still sore."

"There's a crazy person out there," Ladasha said. "You're lucky you weren't badly hurt—or killed."

"I'm confident that Detective Boggs will capture whoever is doing all of this."

"I hope you don't spend the whole evening here," said Zach to Ladasha.

"I get a break later. Caitlin Lodge from the Crystal Palace is going to take the second shift, after nine, so I can enjoy the ball then."

"Excellent," said Simon. "We shall see you later."

The two men threaded through the racks, found their empty hangers, and hung up their raincoats.

"A lot of people are here already," Zach said. The coats blocked the view of Ladasha in front and the doors to the ball at the back.

"Well," said Simon, "we had better get inside to see and be seen."

Simon was always impressed at what could be done with lights, crepe paper, ribbons, and artificial foliage to turn a high school gymnasium into a festive venue. "'Oh, Mary, it takes a fairy to make something pretty,'" said Simon half under his breath.

The string quartet in one corner could barely be heard over the din of partygoers in their elaborate costumes and gowns. Opposite the quartet was the no-host bar, and beside that, tables of hors d'oeuvres, punch, coffee, and sodas. Nearby, a table garlanded with holly displayed *petits fours*, éclairs, and several plum puddings to entice guests. Simon saw Duncan Neff upending a cocktail and tossing the plastic cup into a recycle bin. He was, Simon thought, unimaginatively dressed in his tableau Bob Cratchit costume. Neff threw the muffler around his neck before stepping up to the bar and ordering another drink, and then stepping away into the crowd.

One thing different about this year's ball was something that Simon couldn't help notice, in spite of efforts made to downplay it. Several law enforcement officers stood in strategic locations around the gymnasium perimeter. Someone had found them nineteenth-century police outfits, and the officers had been good-natured enough to wear them, but Simon was sure that the nightsticks and holstered guns were fully functional.

Simon scanned the crowd. It was hectic, but not as bustling as in prior years. There were Sam Wellers, the usual clutch of Artful Dodgers and Nancys, Aunt Betseys and several Mr. Dicks. A Scrooge here and there, several men affecting their best Dickens poses (usually in his later years), with young women favoring Amy Dorrit, Lucie Manette, and Kate Nickleby. Another thing that was different—almost as if by silent agreement: no Ghosts of Christmas Yet to Come, a perennial favorite, since the costume was relatively simple. There must have been a number of last-minute costume substitutions. No need to bring reminders of Roark's death to the party.

Mavis Spurlock touched Simon's arm; he turned to see her and Brad Sturgess. Sturgess was perfectly costumed as Mr. Pickwick, complete with extended belly, white trousers, and gaiters. Mavis's elaborate costume, full Victorian dress with elaborate shawl and huge hat, stumped Simon for a moment.

"You can't guess?" she asked. "Maybe if I tell you that 'the gravy alone, is enough to add twenty years to one's age'?"

"Mrs. Todgers!" said Simon. "I should have known."

She fluttered her eyelashes just like the aging lodging-house proprietress from *Martin Chuzzlewit.* Then, Mavis spoke again: "Is she here yet?"

"She means Clack," Sturgess said.

"We just arrived ourselves," said Zach. "I'm sure we'll know it when she shows up."

"May I talk with you a minute?" Sturgess asked Simon.

"Sure."

"I think that's our cue," Zach said, taking Mavis's arm, "to retire to the bar for a drink." He led her away.

"What's up, Brad?" Simon asked.

"First of all—how are you? I can't believe you and Grace were attacked just last night. You seem remarkably well."

"Unfortunately, it's true, to that first part," said Simon, "and thank you, to the second part. I *am* better."

"Do you think whoever did it was at the Porters the same time we were?"

"Had to be. At least nearby, and inside long enough to steal the caroler's muff from the coatrack."

"The interns and I didn't leave until after eleven."

"It's good to have an alibi, isn't it?" Simon gave a small smile. *Still…*

"And the Neffs were there, although didn't Ariadne leave before you?"

"Just before."

"I don't remember seeing Duncan leave. He wasn't there when the kids and I left. And the mayor," Sturgess added. "He left before you did, didn't he?"

Someone else appears to be catching the Sherlock bug. "Yes. To meet with Clack at eight o'clock. The attack took place a few minutes before that." Simon paused. "But anyone could have come in from outside and stolen the muff," he said.

"That's true." Sturgess placed his hands on his Pickwick belly. "I've been thinking about Brundish's death. I just don't get it," he said. "So I went to the county recording office. I found some very interesting things." Sturgess more than had the detecting bug—he was downright feverish with it. "Did you know that my landlord—I mean, the owner of the *Household Words* building—is Marley Enterprises? They own it and subcontract administration out to the Taggart Group, a holding company that does building maintenance. I pay Taggart, not knowing that Marley Enterprises has owned the building for almost a year. You might own the Crummles Theatre, Simon, but Marley Enterprises—that means Dagny Clack—owns the rest of that block."

Simon's mouth dropped open.

Sturgess took out a map he had made of the square and showed it to Simon. "That means, if Brundish really sold to Clack, she has put a wedge between the remaining three property owners—Grace on one side, and Solomon and Viola on the other. Of course, Clack has been after Mavis, too." One ink-smudged fingertip gestured beyond the edge of the page. "Marley Enterprises also purchased property near City Hall," Sturgess continued. "Two residences and an adjoining commercial space. Those sales took place within the last four months. I suspect they may be involved in another two properties that appear to have sold but not closed. If Clack manages to make those sales, she'll own more than half of the square and big chunks of the Junction itself."

"More than I own," said Simon. "Now I'm frightened." Instinctively, needing a hand to hold, he looked for Zach. He and Mavis were still at the bar across the gym. Mavis was attempting to greet Ariadne Neff, who was dressed in an enormously full-skirted black bombazine pleated dress, apparently as Lady Dedlock in flight from London near the climax of *Bleak House*. Ariadne brushed by Mavis, her head turning, scanning the room, searching frantically.

Grace, handsomely dressed as Mrs. Cratchit, was now at Simon's side. "You two look so serious," she said. "Has the tiny terror arrived yet?"

"Not that we've seen," said Simon. He examined Grace's face and arms. "Are you better now?"

"I got tired today at the shop," she answered. "Things were busier than I expected. But, except for my arm being sore and my face still being scuffed up, I'm fine."

Viola and Charity joined the group. Charity was padded to look heavier underneath her frowsy petticoats and black skirt, with a stained apron and tattered lace ruffled cap on top. An empty whiskey bottle completed the ensemble.

"A perfect Mrs. Gamp," said Simon.

"'I takes a little drink,'" Charity said in a London slum accent, hoisting the bottle, "'when I am so dispoged.'"

"But I'm having trouble with yours," Simon admitted to Viola. She was dressed austerely in a mid-nineteenth-century gown without expansive petticoats, her fawn dress simply accented by a white collar fixed with a small brooch. A simple shawl draped around her arms.

"I knew you should have gone more flamboyant," Charity said. "No one will guess Miss Wade from *Little Dorrit*."

"I think not," Viola said. "If Simon couldn't get it, no one will."

"Maybe I have trouble seeing you as the woman so scorned she turns to other women for comfort—if you believe the revisionist critics," Simon said, scowling. "I'm still not convinced of that one."

"I tried to dress out of character," Viola said, "so I'll take that as a compliment, Simon. I've also had other things on my mind, of course."

"Haven't we all?" Grace added.

"How are both of you after last night's attack?" Viola looked at Simon and Grace from head to toe.

"Fair," Grace said. "Shaken more than anything else. The worst thing was hearing the sound of Simon getting struck by the murderer. He could have been killed. And the screaming. I hated that I started screaming."

"It's natural, I'm sure," Viola said. "I would have done the same."

"We've been so afraid to leave the house," Charity said. "Of course, we wouldn't miss this, but we didn't do our Bunco for Girls night last night because of all that's been going on."

From across the room, Simon noticed the two holiday village competition rivals, Mimsie Tricket and Elmer Cuttle, standing together at the punch table. They appeared to be enjoying themselves. Mimsie had managed a decent Flora Finching look, and Elmer once again wore his perennial costume, a navy greatcoat and tricornered hat, making him an undernourished Mr. Bumble. Since Cuttle spent so much energy on the village competition, he must, Simon assumed, have had nothing creative left to give to the Fezziwig Ball.

Brock and Bethany approached. Brock was an unbelievably mature and hearty Tiny Tim, biceps bulging under the tattered sleeves of the tunic straining across his chest; muscular hairy calves twitched beneath the short pants. The crutch he carried would have been suitable for a real child. Bethany looked lovely in a broad brocaded gown and a huge curly wig.

"Fanny Dorrit, I presume?" Simon asked.

"You're amazing, Simon," Bethany said. She turned to Brock. "I told you he would guess."

"I'm so glad the council didn't vote to cancel the ball," Charity said, sounding almost like her old content self. Still, none of them could resist looking about, each one's gaze stopping to rest on a police officer.

"Simon." A voice came from behind him; Simon turned to see Detective Boggs. Unlike the rest of the attendees, she was in modern-day clothes. Nevertheless, she looked stunning in an orchid-purple silk shantung gown cut on the bias. A fitted bodice forced the full skirt out in shimmering draped folds. She carried a silver clutch. For the first time, Simon wondered whether the detective carried a gun. Brock eyed her with appreciation.

"Good evening, Detective," Simon replied.

"I'm glad to see that you're sufficiently recovered to be here."

Simon touched the edge of his lower lip where George had carefully applied concealer before Simon and Zach had left for the ball. "I believe I will live."

"We discovered something interesting this afternoon," she said. "We have the weapon used in your attack. Joelle Creevy mentioned in her interview this morning that she was missing a pepper mill from one of the pub tables."

"I'm familiar with them," said Simon.

"So we went back to the crime scene and began a careful search of the bushes and houses nearby. We found the missing pepper mill beneath a juniper bush about two hundred yards from where you and Grace were attacked."

"Any fingerprints?"

"Unfortunately, no," Detective Boggs said. "The assailant must have worn gloves."

"Have you made any progress at identifying suspects?"

"We've been doing exhaustive background checks on everyone of interest in the case. But it's slow going."

"Have you found anything?"

Detective Boggs gave Simon the tiniest of smiles. "You know I can't tell you that." She gestured toward one of the officers standing near the string quartet. "We're doing everything we can to protect you, Simon. Don't throw yourself in harm's way anymore. Next time, the attacker might try harder."

Simon was distracted from the detective's words by voices buzzing behind him. He turned to see a very large woman enter through the cloakroom. She was hunched over, her face lined and dotted with warts and moles, her nose crooked, her grizzled hair spilling out the sides of a lace cap. She had a dirty bundle over one crooked shoulder. But the extraordinary detail was the huge muslin skirt, its bottom hem heavy with evenly spaced wooden rings that clacked as the woman slowly crossed toward Simon and the group.

"Who—or what—is that?" Grace asked.

"I have no idea," Simon answered.

The woman started to speak as she approached. "'Why wasn't he natural in his lifetime?'" the voice cackled in a strangely recognizable way. "'If he had been, he'd have had somebody to look after him when he was struck with Death, instead of lying gasping out his last there, alone by himself.'" The last words disintegrated from the weird Cockney accent into a Georgia drawl as the woman stood tall and George's distinct features emerged through the stage makeup and warts.

Everyone in the group began to laugh. "You are sure to win Best Costume with this one," Viola said. Sturgess shook George's hand.

"I agree," said Simon. "I don't think anyone has come as the laundress who steals Scrooge's bed-curtains, let alone designed a dress from them." He reached down and shook a fold of fabric, setting the curtain rings to clattering again.

"I'm very proud of this, I admit." George bared his stained brown teeth. "I argued with the woman at the costume shop for almost an hour about the proper number of wens." He pointed to a large stick-on wart at the end of his nose. "But, in the end, I prevailed."

"What caused you to change your mind?" Simon asked.

"It was never my intention to stay away," George said, putting his peasant-blouse-clad arm around Simon. "You need all of the protection you can get from Clack."

The quartet made a flourish that signaled the arrival of Mayor Dick and his wife Allegra as Mr. and Mrs. Fezziwig. The crowd applauded Solomon's bright-blue waistcoat, white vest, tight black trousers, striped gaiters, and black buckled shoes. A short, dark-brown wig with side knots adorned his head, not quite perfectly spirit-gummed in place. Allegra Dick wore a full, deep-yellow flower-printed skirt with a lacy apron, a white tucker shielding a portion of the open bodice. They looked extraordinarily Dickensian and jolly. Someone had rouged the mayor's cheeks, Simon thought, unless he had been drinking beforehand.

"Sir Roger de Coverley!" the head violinist announced. Not everyone knew how to do the Virginia reel–style dance, but the mayor and his wife had practiced; Simon had, too. He took Grace's hand and led her toward the center of the gymnasium. The mayor, making every effort to dance like Mr. Fezziwig with his "winking" calves, was nearly out of breath when, as top couple, he and his Mrs. Fezziwig returned to their position at the end of the song.

"I can't do that again," he panted to Simon, who, though not winded, was wiping perspiration from his own forehead. Together with Grace and Allegra, Simon and the mayor walked back to the larger group, which Zach and Mavis had rejoined.

"I brought you a drink," Zach said, handing Simon a Scotch.

"Look!" said Allegra, grasping Simon's arm and pointing at a brilliant light beyond where the Dickens Carolers stood. "She's here."

Standing just inside the gymnasium, Dagny Clack had made her entrance.

"I don't think she got the memo," George said. Grace and Viola emitted small gasps.

Dagny Clack wore Mavis's open fan in her hair, but it was the only concession she had made to Dickens. She was wearing a full-skirted heavily brocaded and beaded gown in dazzling white over multiple layers of stiff petticoats. The sleeveless bodice was low-cut, framing a lavaliere with a single gem-cut diamond the size of a quail egg. As she moved, the dress swished audibly; its weight gave it a complex architectural drape that caught the crowd's full attention. She reflected as much light as a mirrorball; pinpoints of light danced across the crowd and walls of the gym. In one hand, she held a tiny, topaz-encrusted nautilus clutch.

"She's the Virgin Queen," George said. "What Dickens book is that from?"

"Hush," said Simon.

"How does she walk in that?" Charity asked. "I'll bet that gown weighs forty pounds."

From across the gymnasium, Ariadne and Duncan Neff made a beeline toward Miss Clack. She appeared startled at their appearance. Simon was too far away and the crowd noise too loud for him to hear their words; after what looked like a clipped greeting, Clack waved both of them off with her clutch and they moved away. Simon thought Duncan stumbled twice as he headed toward the bar, while Ariadne moved over into a corner and began furiously working her BlackBerry.

The string quartet took a break; recorded music, contemporary tunes age-appropriate to the young boomers and old Xers, replaced the Dickensian carols and classics. Even so, the first song was a waltz.

"Dance with me," Zach said, taking Simon's uninjured arm. "I may not know how to do the Roger de-whatever, but I can do a mean waltz." He carefully removed Simon's top hat and his own and placed them on a nearby chair.

"Yes, let's dance," Charity said to Viola.

Viola took a deep breath. "Later, sweetie." She gave Charity a peck on the cheek. "I need to go see Clack and give her our final answer." She looked at Simon. "If I'm not back in ten minutes, call for assistance." Viola moved toward Clack.

Zach led Simon to the center of the gym and held him close. "Lead or follow?" he asked.

"Let's trade off," said Simon. "But why don't you lead now?"

"Happy to."

Zach was a fluid, confident dancer, and clearly comfortable being in charge. Simon's feet glided across the floor. He hadn't danced in a long time, and certainly not in front of such a large, mixed crowd. But nobody was paying attention.

As Zach stepped Simon through a sweeping promenade diagonally across the floor, Simon saw Viola and Clack disappear into the cloakroom.

"I could get used to this," Zach said.

"What?" Simon asked. "The dance, holding me, or the Fezziwig Ball?"

"All of the above." Without losing his steps, Zach kissed Simon. "Wait until I get you home."

Simon let himself go with the music, trying to slough off Roark, Brundish, last night's attack. Except for an occasional throb at the back of his head, he was able to, at least as long as the music played. He had a few pangs about Solomon Dick's offer, but was pretty sure he knew what his answer would be, although he had promised he would wait for Nathaniel Pocket's opinion before sharing his answer with the mayor.

He focused on Zach's muscularity, palpable through his stiff morning coat; the pressure of Zach's hand at the small of Simon's back; the swell of Zach's shoulder under Simon's right hand. Yes, a man could get used to this kind of treatment...all of it.

As the music played and the seventies chanteuse's husky voice seeped into Simon's skin, he decided. *I will give in. I will risk everything for this man, for his humor, his strength, his tenderness. I've held back too long, kept myself from getting hurt, so I wouldn't have to deal with loss. But, in doing that, I haven't given myself a chance to feel joy, either. But enough. Lead with the heart this time, not the head. Risk. Feel. Love.*

When the music stopped, Simon hugged Zach close. "Thank you," he said. "That was the best thing I've done in a long time."

"Don't give up," Zach said. "I'm hoping it's not even the best thing you do tonight." His arm still around Simon, Zach led him back to the group.

Charity was drinking tea. "I'm like water on a griddle," she said. She was only partly looking at Simon; her head was turned toward the cloakroom door. It remained shut.

"Because you don't know what Viola will say?" Simon asked.

Charity shook her head. "I'm not worried about Viola at all," she said. "We've been together twenty-five years; I know her. It's Clack. She's a wild card. Ruthless. She has no heart."

The cloakroom door opened, and Viola emerged. A few seconds later, Dagny Clack re-entered the gymnasium. She looked confused, somehow smaller than she had been moments before.

When she arrived where the group stood, Viola was laughing. "What's funny?" Charity asked.

"That little woman," Viola said. "She has no idea of the meaning of words like community, family, support. She offered even more money for my property. When I told her that 'no' was my final answer, she tried something else."

"What was that?" Zach asked.

"She said she would 'go public with the nature of the relationship between you and Miss Wilkinson.' I said, 'Honey, *The Children's Hour* was generations ago. Times have changed.' I laughed in her face and sent her packing. What a stupid, stupid cow." Viola took Charity's hand. "Now, let's dance," she said, and led her away.

"I'm going to get a drink," Grace said.

George looked around. "I'm sitting it out for a while. I'm tired of having these rings hitting my calves with every step I take. An idea better in its conception than its execution, I fear." He moved away toward a row of chairs set up against one wall.

"And I need to use the restroom," said Simon.

Brock and Bethany had already wandered off to join a group of younger people by the bar; the mayor and his wife were talking to a small group of their friends in another corner, although to Simon the mayor appeared distracted and uncomfortable. As Simon walked toward the men's restroom (actually the boys' locker room), he saw Ariadne Neff watching Dagny Clack move regally along the edge of the gymnasium, trying to avoid a print journalist (the pad and pencil in his hand were the clues) who had gained entrance to the ball dressed as Uriah Heep.

Simon ducked into the locker room. The quiet pushed against his ears after the din outside. It felt good.

As Simon was standing at the urinal, Mayor Dick entered the locker room. "We need to talk," the mayor said. "Now."

SIMON RETURNED TO THE GYMNASIUM. HIS GROUP HAD scattered. As he scanned the floor, looking for any of his friends, he felt a presence beside him and heard a rustle; when he turned, he was looking directly into Mavis's open multicolored fan, nestled in the platinum chignon of Dagny Clack.

"Mr. Simon Alastair," she said, her voice cutting clearly through the surrounding din. "Dagny Clack." She pronounced her name in the Norwegian fashion, *Dahg-nee.* "We finally meet...somewhat sooner than I had planned," she added. She did not extend a hand in greeting. She looked like a wax figure, her skin eerily smooth and tight over her cheekbones, no hint of aging in the neck or the smooth brow. Her eyes were crystal-green, that especially light color, almost like no color at all.

"I am last," said Simon. "As I understood from Mr. Venable yesterday," he added, his voice as formal and distant as he could make it.

"I am not finding my visit to this part of the world as productive as I had hoped," she continued. "Although I have known it since my people began calling here, the citizens of this place are a truculent lot, full of obsolete values and outdated philosophies."

"That is one opinion only," Simon replied. "Many of us find those 'obsolete' values fresh and useful, and our 'philosophies,' as you put it, comforting." He took a breath. "I don't see any need to be diplomatic with you, Miss Clack," he continued. "Why exactly did you send Mervin Roark here to buy land in the Junction? What was your business with Lowell Brundish, and why are you here now yourself?"

She took a step back from Simon so she could take in his full figure, since he was almost a head taller than she, even in her rhinestone heels. "You come from entrepreneurial stock, don't you?"

"My grandfather and his brother were timber barons, I suppose you would call them," he answered. "They came to Oregon after World War I and earned their fortunes in the logging industry and land acquisition."

"But you choose not to follow in their footsteps and create new wealth. You merely live off the wealth created by others."

He pushed away his increasing irritation. "My grandfather created wealth, but he also understood the responsibility that comes with it, and instilled that responsibility in my father and, later, me. I have tried to live according to those principles."

"You believe in charity," she said, pronouncing the last word as if it caused her pain to say it. "Such as this around you. All of these *happy people.*"

"I feel honored and privileged to be in this community," he said, "among these happy people, who are not happy right now because your actions have directly, or indirectly, caused two people to die."

"I am not responsible for that," said Miss Clack, "as I have told your pesky policeperson woman." She appeared to attempt a frown, but did not, or could not, furrow her brow. "I know nothing of these—unfortunate—crimes. I met Mervin Roark on only two occasions before he came here on my assignment. And this Brundish person—I only spoke to him on the telephone. He called my people."

"How dare you come here and stir up trouble," said Simon. "You will not gain what you desire, whatever it is. This is a decent community of proud people."

"I may be temporarily thwarted by such small-minded folks as you, that Viola Mintun, the ninny Miss Beddoes, and your silly mayor," Miss Clack said, "but I will prevail. The true Dickens humbug—the Carol philosophy and its humanist ilk—such cant is doomed and outdated. The only workable philosophy in these times is self-centered. This Victorian love of socialism and its contemporary forms must be crushed."

"You are appalling," said Simon.

"I am right," Clack responded. "Since you ask me what I wish, Mr. Alastair, I will tell you outright. I am going to acquire enough land to create a community of my own making—Galtopia, built upon the foundations of the greatest human achievement in the history of the world, *Atlas Shrugged*, by Ayn Rand, and her other philosophical novels and writings. Ms. Rand, by virtue of her genius, is the supreme arbiter in any issue pertaining to what is rational, moral, or appropriate to man's life on earth."

Simon was incredulous. This was beyond his imagining. "Ms. Rand is a bad philosopher and a worse novelist," he said. "You're joking."

Miss Clack stared at him with her strange green eyes. "I most certainly am not. I will acquire all the land I need until all that remains of the place now called Dickens Square will be the little L"—she paused at the unintentional sound of the phrase, *Simon's little hell,* which clearly pleased her—"yes, the little L of it that you own. Your land will become worthless when I have built Galtopia. There will be no room for you. People will come here from all over the civilized world to study, review, and revere the work of Rand and to learn how to practice Objectivism. I myself will teach master classes on the virtue of selfishness."

"I'm sure you could do that," said Simon. He could barely contain his anger and realized that he actually had the desire to slap her face, hurt her physically. He couldn't believe how such strong emotion had risen, almost broken through to the commission of an irredeemable act.

"Make no mistake, Mr. Alastair," Clack said, her words acting as a shield against Simon striking her, as if, he realized, she sensed it herself. "Money hard-won through individual achievement, as mine is, always prevails. Pity that your grandfather didn't know how to use it properly. You will see." She checked her watch, then looked over toward the cloakroom. "I have an appointment," she said. "Unlike your mayor," she added, "I keep my appointments timely. Even ten minutes of my time is too much to waste." She turned to step away from him, and then turned back. "Watch me, Mr. Alastair," Clack added. "There will be bulldozers in your beloved square by Easter. That ridiculous statue of Dickens will topple as surely as did the one of Saddam Hussein."

Clack went one direction, and Simon headed the opposite way, seeking Zach, or George, or anyone to whom he could reveal Dagny Clack's shocking motive for being in the Junction.

Duncan Neff stumbled past Simon and into the cloakroom. He was followed by Dagny Clack, whose white gown glimmered with a demanding, almost overpowering light. Ariadne Neff followed in Clack's wake. Ariadne was speaking, gesticulating, but Clack seemed implacable, even dismissive, as she stayed focused on Duncan. Ariadne, in frustration, Simon thought, exited the gymnasium through one of the emergency exit fire doors along the side wall. The mayor and Grace watched the action from near the dessert table.

Simon finally spotted George across the gym floor and started crossing toward him, but he moved too quickly and jostled a woman's arm, causing her to spill her drink on the floor.

"I'm so sorry," said Simon. The woman was Mimsie Trick-et. Elmer Cuttle was standing next to her, very close, Simon noticed.

"It's all right," Mimsie said in her high thin voice, as Cuttle reached down and wiped the floor clean with his canapé nap-kin. "It's a lovely party," she said, "considering everything."

Simon stopped to catch his breath. He looked from Mimsie to Elmer. "I just realized I haven't apologized for not award-ing a winning entry this year in the adult category. Under the circumstances—"

"It's all right," Elmer said. He was a thin willowy man not too much older than Mimsie. "It's more than all right. We've been talking about next year's competition."

"That's right," Mimsie said. "We're thinking of joining forces and working together instead of at cross-purposes."

"You would be unstoppable," said Simon. He looked into the crowd again. George had moved, but there was Zach, talking to Father Blaise. "Excuse me," he said, but Mimsie continued talking.

"I just don't have the stamina I used to," she said. "This year's work took nearly everything out of me. I barely got ev-erything done in time. I didn't even unpack my pedals until after nine o'clock." She touched Simon's hand. "If they hadn't kicked Elmer and me out at ten, I might even have seen the murder—or been murdered myself!"

"That wouldn't have done at all," Cuttle said.

Zach and Father Blaise started strolling together, about to disappear into the crowd again. "No, that wouldn't have done at all," said Simon absentmindedly, patting Mimsie's hand. "Now, please excuse me."

Before Simon could connect with Zach and Father Blaise, his cell phone rang. He checked the screen. It was Nathaniel Pocket.

"Nat? Nat?" Simon pushed open one of the one-way fire doors that led from the gymnasium directly outside. "Now I can hear you—"

But before Simon let the door close behind him, he heard a sound from across the gymnasium that caused him to drop his phone and turn back. A scream.

Simon rushed across the gymnasium, past Brock and Bethany on the dance floor, past Allegra Dick, past other faces, all turned toward the screaming Ladasha, who had collapsed in Mavis's arms outside the cloakroom. Simon dashed past them into the cloakroom. Behind him, a phalanx of the costumed law enforcement officers had formed around the cloakroom entrance. Simon noted a subtle aroma of alcohol, like cognac. He felt the presence of, then saw, Detective Boggs beside him. They quickly pushed aside the full coatracks to get a clear view of where Ladasha had been stationed. They gazed silently on what lay before them.

The body of Dagny Clack, clad in its draped, white, beaded gown, was slumped in Ladasha's chair, the head tilted backward at an impossible angle. The still partially unfurled fan that once decorated her now-tousled locks had been shoved down her throat to an unnatural depth. But more horrifying, a stake had been driven through her chest, its outer end wrapped with a garland of bright green holly and winking red berries. A trickle of blood ran down the front of the ballooned gown and petticoats spread between Clack's akimbo legs. Resting in Clack's weirdly outstretched hands, a small plum pudding on a silver tray still flickered with orange and blue flames from the alcohol that ignited it.

STAVE

THE END OF IT

Simon had taken a sleeping pill—the easy way out—and awoke the next morning groggy, frightened, and angry. He called Brock to say he wouldn't be in to work, and Brock could keep the store closed if he wished. Brock didn't mind leaving it open, he said; the square, except for reporters and cameras, was nearly deserted of locals. The daily tours had all been canceled at the request of the sheriff's office, pending further investigation into Dagny Clack's murder.

The interviews by Detective Boggs had lasted until well past midnight, when Simon, Zach, and George arrived back home. Simon had pieced together a few facts from what he had been asked about and what he'd overheard. When Caitlin failed to show on time to replace her, Ladasha had taken an urgent restroom break and left the cloakroom unattended for a few minutes. She returned just as Caitlin was arriving. The two women chatted for a few minutes, during which time no one left the cloakroom. Ladasha went through the cloakroom on her way to the ball, and discovered Clack's body. According to ticket takers out front, no one but Caitlin had entered the school by the main door, although Duncan Neff had left by that same door a few minutes earlier, where he had vomited on the front lawn within sight of the ticket takers. Simon reported that he had seen Ariadne Neff exit through the door next to the one he had used. Everyone else had remained inside the gymnasium.

"Something is very, very wrong," said Simon, pushing away Bethany's scones and poached eggs as he stood. "I'm going to go for a walk."

Zach rose too. "Do you want company?"

"No." Simon stopped, thinking his voice had been too sharp. He touched Zach's shoulder. "I just want to clear my head and think about things."

He put on his winter jacket and muffler and walked uphill, away from Gad's Hill Place toward where the street deadended in forest. The wind was broken here by tree cover, but Simon was still cold. His hands thrust in his pockets, he walked onto the path, threading his way past the fallen dead leaves, broken branches, and rotting stumps, across to the parallel path that led back into the Junction along the street that fronted St. Ina's.

As he neared the church, he heard through a partially open upper window the organist practicing for tomorrow's Christmas Eve midnight service. Simon pushed against the front entrance to the church; it was open. He stepped inside.

It was warmer than outside, and the air was moist with the sounds coming from the organ loft. Simon took a seat in a back pew and rested his chin on his hands.

Three people murdered, two assaulted. An unbelievable series of tragedies, all seemingly connected. What had Simon done or learned that would make someone want to injure, maybe kill him, too?

The organist, probably Cornelius Yancey from Astoria, finished the song he was playing. The church was still. Simon could hear himself breathe. The altar was decorated simply for the remaining days of Advent. Although he had never said as much to Father Blaise, out of kindness and friendship, Simon was not a believer, but he still admired the pageantry and honored the ethics that stood aside and away from the dogma. He loved this town; he loved what Dickens stood for. Maybe, even, he loved Zach. Was a week too soon to tell?

Atlas Shrugged versus *A Christmas Carol.* Rand versus Dickens. Buyers versus sellers. Community versus selfishness. Three people dead, two injured. It had to stop.

The organist started the familiar strains of "Jesu, Joy of Man's Desiring." First, Simon heard the melody line in the higher notes, their overtones reminding him of bagpipes, then the deep rumble as the bass pedals pushed the air and notes into his ears and off the rafters. The highest notes and the lowest notes almost dissonant, yet coming together in a way that signaled union and fulfillment, the true joy of man's desiring.

And, in that moment, Simon understood everything that had happened, who had committed the crimes. Not why, at least not completely, but a wave of guilt washed over him, and a physical pain, like a blow to the stomach. He could have prevented it—if not all of it, at least Clack's death—if he had only known, if he had only acted...He was at once angry, sad, anxious, and tingling with energy.

In his haste to exit the church, he stumbled, catching the attention of the organist in the loft, but didn't answer the question, "Is there someone there?" because by then he was outside the church, punching Detective Boggs's number into his cell phone.

"I know who did it," he said, almost out of breath. "I know almost everything. But I would need a few things from you."

"Not a chance," Detective Boggs said. "We've got a killer on the loose. Don't you listen to the news?"

"There won't be more murders," he said. "Listen." He told her what he thought and why.

When he finished, Detective Boggs didn't speak right away; Simon anticipated each of the slow breaths she took. "We haven't ruled out what you say," Detective Boggs said. "And I'll be honest, no one yet has posed the scenario exactly as you describe it."

"I know I'm right," said Simon. "And I know my way will work."

"But it may not be enough for an arrest. The sheriff is doubtful, and she's ready to crucify me over the messiness of the evidence. There were thousands of fingerprints in that gymnasium."

"This isn't about fingerprints, Detective," said Simon. "It's about trust, and letting down your guard, and carelessness, and maybe just a little desire to have it all come to an end." He could hear her breathing, but she hadn't interrupted him yet. "I'm talking about you, here, not the murderer."

"Very funny, Simon," she said, but her words sounded carefully chosen, based on what he had already revealed. "Keep talking."

"I can help you," he said; "But you have to trust me. I promise I won't compromise whatever evidence you have, but you'll never get the evidence I already know."

"What do you want to do?"

He could hear in her voice the frustration, the readiness he needed. "Invite all of the suspects to the bookstore tomorrow," he said. "That will give us time to get the facts that I don't yet know, but am sure are true. You can do that. Let's start with the Neffs."

THE SIGN ON THE DOOR OF PIP'S PAGES SAID, *Closed for the holidays. Back on Boxing Day.* Inside, Simon had arranged folding chairs in rows of five, just as he would have for an author reading. As people arrived in small groups, Bethany unlocked the door to let people in, while Zach escorted each to a seat, according to a chart Simon had given him. Simon had not revealed his thoughts to Zach, despite a strong desire to share the burden of his suspicions. If he were wrong, he would only have himself to blame.

Detective Boggs had confirmed less than two hours earlier that she had the information he needed; after they discussed it, she agreed to have her deputies call the people on Simon's list to appear at the bookstore at two o'clock on Christmas Eve afternoon. It was a minor miracle that no one on the list had made plans to travel, but almost all made their livelihoods from the holiday commerce of Dickens Junction, so perhaps it wasn't so surprising after all. And everyone wanted to know what the mystery was. Almost everyone.

Mavis and Brock arrived first. As instructed, Zach sat Mavis in the front row on the end, Brock in the second row on the opposite end. Solomon and Allegra Dick arrived next. Rather than seating them together, however, Zach placed the mayor next to Mavis and Allegra in the fourth row. The mayor and Mavis began talking together in low tones; Allegra Dick sat quietly with her hands in her lap.

Simon stood behind the counter, trying not to look at people's faces as they arrived. If someone managed to make eye contact, he nodded politely but did not smile. This was serious business, not time for holiday greetings.

Grace arrived next, immediately followed by Brad Sturgess. Zach seated Grace next to the mayor in front, Sturgess in the second row next to Brock.

Father Blaise arrived shortly thereafter; Zach seated him in the second row, next to Sturgess and behind Grace.

The Neffs arrived, looking uncomfortable and holding hands. Zach, however, separated them, putting Ariadne in the front row on the opposite end as Mavis, with Duncan in the second row, directly behind Mavis.

Ladasha Creevy, looking confused and shaken, was next to arrive. Zach seated her in the fourth row next to Allegra Dick.

Viola and Charity were next. "Are we late?" Viola asked Zach. Without answering, he guided her to the empty chair in the front row next to Ariadne, while placing Charity in the last empty chair in the second row between Duncan Neff and Father Blaise.

A minute or two later, Mimsie Tricket showed herself at the door, her mouth a perfect O of surprise, confusion, and worry when she saw the other people who were assembled. Zach led her to the back row, next to Ladasha.

At another signal from Simon, Bethany checked the door lock one more time, then pulled the almost-never-used shade down over the glass. George lowered the louvered blinds on each of the plate-glass windows. The bookstore was fully dark until Simon turned on all of the overhead lights to full capacity. When he came back into the main area of the store, Detective Boggs accompanied him. Zach, too, crossed the store and stood next to her.

George and Bethany took the remaining seats in the fourth row of chairs, leaving the third row empty.

"And now," George said, leaning slightly toward Mimsie Tricket, "the ratiocination. Buckle up." She looked back at him, mortified and confused.

Simon stepped into the place where he would have set a lectern for a visiting author. He had been rehearsing his remarks all night, pending the confirmation by Detective Boggs of several suspicions for which he could not establish certain proof. The Junction would either stand—or fall—on what was about to happen. His high school debating experience paled in comparison with this. He was risking everything—including the possibility of slander. To be wrong might ruin his reputation. To be right would ruin one—or more—lives.

He moved back and forth, until he stood in front of Viola Mintun. "Detective Boggs graciously requested that each of you appear today to discuss the recent events in Dickens Junction." He took a breath. "We have had three tragic deaths within a week in this community, and another attack that left two more injured. Why did this happen to us? And what can we do about it? Today, I think I know those answers. These crimes happened because of ego, greed, and fear. We must discover who committed these crimes, and why."

Viola craned her neck to look at Charity; Mayor Dick did the same to his wife. Duncan and Ariadne Neff looked straight ahead at Simon, heads unmoving.

"Let's start," Simon continued, "with a theory that all the crimes—the murders of Mervin Roark, Lowell Brundish, and Dagny Clack, plus the assault on Grace Beddoes and me—are connected. By doing that, we can simplify the process of determining who might—and who might not—have committed the crimes. Someone with a provable alibi for one crime might not then need an unassailable alibi for another.

"Everything seemingly began with the appearance of Mervin Roark. One minute he was not here; the next he was everywhere at once in Dickens Junction, leaving cards and offers to buy property on behalf of Marley Enterprises in his wake. Why did that matter? Well, each of you in the front row—Mavis, Solomon, Grace, Viola, and Ariadne—had something to gain from the sale of real property in Dickens Junction, either directly or"—here his gaze hesitated on Ariadne—"indirectly." Ariadne stiffened, apparently about to object, but then relaxed her torso and sat back in her chair. She smoothed her skirt with a shaking hand.

"As his day went on, it became more apparent that Roark was on a mission from Marley Enterprises to buy certain pieces of land—most here on the square—and that, as the cliché goes, money was no object. He made offers to Grace, Solomon, Viola, and Mavis for sure; let's assume that he also made an offer to Lowell Brundish at or before that same time. We will return to Brundish in a minute.

"Detective Boggs has determined through the interviews she conducted, supplemented with information I collected, that Roark was killed between four fifteen, the time I last saw him in the square, and six thirty, when Brock loaded Roark's corpse onto his truck to bring to the square for the tableaux. So, what do we know about the suspects' whereabouts during that time? Two people have numerous eyewitnesses for that period of time: Father Blaise, who was judging the Tiny Tim costume contest at Squeers Grade School, and Viola, who was sharing a reformer with several others at Pickwick Pilates starting at four and lasting until six, after which she has Joelle as an alibi until the tableaux started. Where were the others? Ariadne Neff claims to have been meeting with Lowell Brundish, who unfortunately cannot confirm her statement. Grace went for a walk alone; Mavis and Brad were driving to Astoria to a location where they would not likely be seen"—despite his nerves, presenting in front of the group, Simon noticed both Mavis and Brad swallowed hard—"Mayor Dick, angry at allegedly being stood up by Roark for a meeting, was home alone; and Charity claimed to be at school, although without a corroborating witness. Duncan's whereabouts could not be immediately confirmed; he was hard to locate right after the crime had been committed. Brock, of course, claims not to have noticed that he was wheeling a corpse instead of a dummy. He could have murdered Roark in the shed, prepared the body, and wheeled it nonchalantly into place beside me on the square."

Mavis put her hands to her face, as if the thought Simon had just expressed had never occurred to her. She dropped her hands and opened her mouth to speak, then closed it again and shook her head.

"Your whereabouts were also uncorroborated, Simon," Detective Boggs broke in.

"That's correct," said Simon. "I claimed to be here in the store alone, preparing to take part in the tableau. But why was

Roark killed?" he continued. "This requires some speculation. What works for me right now is simple blackmail. Clack had been planning this attack on Dickens Junction for months, possibly longer. Roark was just a pawn. He was acting on Clack's orders; he barely knew what Marley Enterprises did, or who Clack's muse, Ayn Rand, was. Marley Enterprises had researched each and every one of us—Roark claimed to know information about me—and perhaps threatened to go public with this information unless the owners sold out. The handsome above-market prices could do much to soothe the sting of giving in to a blackmailer. Maybe yes, maybe no.

"Let's move on to Brundish," said Simon. "But before we talk about who might have killed him, we need to talk about why. This area involves more speculation. We know that Brundish received a note signed by Dagny Clack, expressing her 'great appreciation' for an unknown task; let's assume that he had finally agreed to sell his property to Marley Enterprises. Furthermore, we know from Brundish's frantic call to Mavis on the day of Roark's death that he didn't want to sell, at least in part because of a 'promise' he had made, yet no one appears to know to whom this promise was made. Let's assume, then, that he made the promise to the murderer, and when the murderer found out, probably from Brundish himself, that he had broken the promise, the murderer killed Brundish, an act of uncharacteristic, unimaginable, and yet premeditated rage, given the savage treatment of the body."

He stopped a moment to drink from a bottle of water he had been holding. "Detective Boggs tells us that Brundish was killed somewhere other than the school, then transported there. But not before ten, because that's when Mimsie Tricket and Elmer Cuttle were asked to leave for the night and the gymnasium was closed. The coroner's evidence establishes the outside time for the murder at midnight. So where were the suspects when Brundish was killed?

"Brock was at Anita Distraction's by ten at the latest, and we have numerous eyewitnesses for his whereabouts until well after midnight." Simon couldn't suppress a small smile at this point. He made eye contact with Zach, but quickly realized that would cause a loss of focus, not a mustering of the concentration he required, so he looked away. "What do we know about Brad and Mavis? We know where they were at midnight, but before that, we must rely on corroboration of witnesses at the restaurant and hotel they visited. Today, Detective Boggs informs me that such corroboration exists for the hotel; I have seen confirmation of the restaurant alibi myself. So Mavis and Brad were not in Dickens Junction at the time Brundish was killed, stuffed, trussed, and dumped into Elmer Cuttle's holiday village display. Viola and Charity were also away from the Junction, enjoying the company of friends in Astoria at a potluck dinner that lasted beyond both of the limits established for the time of Brundish's death.

"Unfortunately, others are not so lucky. Mayor Dick claims to have been home alone, at least part of that time, on the telephone with Brundish, but, once again, Brundish is not here to supply an alibi. In statements made to Detective Boggs, Ariadne and Grace also claimed to be home alone; neither story can be confirmed. Duncan Neff, after finally being located, offered a most incriminating alibi—he says that at the time of Brundish's murder, he was in the Bleak House storage shed, vandalizing the holiday tableaux display." Ariadne shot Simon a look of genuine surprise. "While we can confirm the damage, we cannot confirm the time it occurred." Neff crossed his arms and made a harrumphing sound; Simon ignored it.

Detective Boggs cleared her throat. "Let me just add that proof of your whereabouts, Simon, during those hours, relies solely on the reports of your two friends, Zach Benjamin and George Bascomb."

"True," Simon admitted. "There is the possibility of a conspiracy among us. So let's hold on to the recognition that I still could be a suspect in Brundish's murder." Detective Boggs nodded.

Simon paced; his heart was racing, hurting with certainty, but he knew he had to finish what he'd started. "On to Dagny Clack. Everyone in the Western world, it seems, must have been surprised when the seldom-seen CEO of Marley Enterprises turned up in Dickens Junction. From my personal interaction with her, I can assert that she believed she was on the cusp of achieving her goal—the real and symbolic destruction of Dickens Junction as we know it, and its replacement with an educational shrine dedicated to Ayn Rand and her cult of Objectivism.

"But Clack's mission, which had already proved fatal to two, also ended her life. She had meetings—*audiences* might be a better term—and made increasingly outrageous offers to purchase properties on the square as well as Bleak House itself. From what she said to me, I believe that she was going to present these sales as a *fait accompli* to me, then demand that I sell to her or risk a total loss in the value of my property when she began bulldozing the square and the Inimitable Boz to make room for her Galtopia."

He took another breath. "But before Clack was murdered, Grace and I were attacked walking home from the Porters after spending the evening with Zach, George, and the mayor, debriefing offers Clack had made to them earlier that day. At the Porters at the same time were Ariadne and Duncan Neff and Brad Sturgess. The mayor left before we did, ostensibly to keep his appointment with Miss Clack, but he was late."

Mayor Dick gasped. "I lost my nerve," he said. "I got sick in the street from stress."

"Maybe so," said Simon, "but you were not at Bleak House a few minutes before eight, when the attack occurred, so you could have been the person who attacked Grace and me minutes earlier. That would explain why you were late for your meeting with Miss Clack."

"Simon—" Mayor Dick started, but Simon interrupted him.

"Brad Sturgess remained behind at the Porters," he went on, "in full view of his interns during the time of the attack, but any of the others I just named could have pushed Grace aside, bludgeoned me with a pepper mill, and then attempted to suffocate me with the Caroler's muff," Simon continued. "Ariadne was seen leaving before my group did, but easily could have put the pepper mill in her purse, exited the pub, dashed in the back door to grab the muff, and then attacked us." Ariadne remained looking forward, but did not look at Simon.

"Why was Dagny Clack killed? We all can think of reasons. Each of us who dealt with her might have wanted to see it happen and might not have mourned her once she was dead. I believe that the person who killed Dagny Clack did so out of desperation. Some premeditation was obvious—the holly and the plum pudding weren't handy, nor were they necessary beyond making some horrific artistic statement—but the murderer of Miss Clack, and Roark, and Brundish was trying to salvage something of value and beauty in the world—Dickens Junction. Let's talk about the rest of the suspects and see whether that motive fits their world.

"Duncan Neff? Hardly a model guardian of this community, since he admits that he attempted to vandalize part of our celebration decorations, and his behavior at the council, wanting to shut down the festivities, represented at its best a backhanded desire to protect the citizens of the Junction. While he expressed concern for citizen safety, I suspect that was also a sham. The cancellation of holiday events would more likely have increased citizen panic and therefore increased the likelihood that the reluctant property owners would sell out to Clack. Luckily for Duncan, he was sick on the front lawn of the high school during the minuscule window of opportunity for killing Dagny Clack in the cloakroom. Furthermore, Detective Boggs has showed Neff's picture around several bars in and around Astoria and has been able to establish positive identification of

Neff on the afternoon of Roark's murder, and around the time of Brundish's. So, perhaps after downing one too many drinks, Neff did go to the Bleak House storage shed and vandalize the tableaux backdrops, but that may be the worst of his crimes.

"And Ariadne? Although she may possess many convictions, compassion for the welfare of Junxonians isn't among them. I can speculate that Clack originally offered Ariadne a nice finder's fee for sales of the Dickens Junctions properties, but lost interest when Ariadne couldn't deliver anything to her, with the possible exception of Lowell Brundish. Therefore, dissatisfied with Ariadne's performance, Clack double-crossed her and told her so in no uncertain terms at the Fezziwig Ball. While this might be reason enough to kill Clack, Ariadne took that unexpectedly fortunate moment to exit the gymnasium by way of the fire door. She could not have reentered, except by the front door, where the ticket takers would, and did not, see her."

People in the room, Simon had no doubt, were ticking off the suspects along with him. Heads started to turn as the remaining possibilities dwindled; people looked at one another and, upon making eye contact, looked away quickly. Mimsie Tricket bit her nails to the quick; Allegra Dick was weeping into an embroidered handkerchief. Ariadne was trying to stifle her own tears.

Simon took another drink of water. He looked at George, and got in return that look that only a friend as old as George could give—a look of total support and a nod. George knew, Simon realized. He understood it all now, too. Including how hard the next part would be.

A uniformed sheriff's deputy stepped from the back room into the bookstore and stood between Zach and Detective Boggs.

Simon walked along the front row of chairs. Mavis's eyes followed him, Mayor Dick's eyes were red and brimful, and Grace looked confused, Viola puzzled, and Ariadne defiant behind her mascara-smeared eyes.

"Solomon," said Simon, "you had no real alibis for the first two murders, and no one has come forth regarding your position in the gymnasium at the time Dagny Clack was murdered. We have already discussed you as a suspect in the assault on Grace and me, no matter what you might offer as an excuse."

"Simon, you know—" the mayor began. His voice cracked.

Simon put his hand on his cousin's shoulder. "I know that, before Dagny Clack was killed, your motive for killing her disappeared completely. Because"—Simon looked across the faces of the crowd—"moments before Clack was killed, I made an offer to buy Solomon's property at a price not equal to, but reasonably close to, what Clack was offering. Solomon's gracious acceptance of my offer—and the other agreements we reached—make me believe that he had no need to kill Dagny Clack in order to preserve Dickens Junction, because he had already done everything he could by selling his property to me, knowing that I would never succumb to her pressure." Allegra Dick burst into sobs. George, sitting next to her, took her hand.

Viola started to stand, but the uniformed deputy took a step forward; she slumped back into her chair. "I don't understand," she said. "By my count, you've exonerated us all. No one in this room could have committed all of these crimes."

"Correct." Simon moved away from Mayor Dick. "That is because I said at the beginning that our assumption would be that all of the crimes were connected. *But they aren't.* One of them is not like the others, and the murderer hoped that the police would not discover it. But we have two criminals."

Simon stopped walking. He was standing in the middle of the front row. "Don't we, Grace?" he said softly.

Grace said nothing.

"You were the only one who had the motive, means, and opportunity to commit three murders. I think that you, not Brundish, were the first person Dagny Clack targeted. You started getting offers from Marley Enterprises several months ago and confided in your friend Lowell Brundish, who admitted that he, too, had received some offers. Each of you pledged to the other that you would stick together. I don't know what his reasons were, possibly loyalty to the community—I believe that's what yours was. Accepting an offer from Marley Enterprises would have made your life easier." Simon knelt next to his old, old friend. "I know about the gambling, Grace." She pulled her hand away, and, strangely, that's when Simon's heart hurt. He stood. "You hoped that, in time, you would be able to pay down your massive credit card debt, recoup your losses from your investments with Neff, and that the upside-down mortgages would right themselves in time.

"But Mervin Roark came to town, and he wasn't very nice. He threatened to expose your gambling addiction and notify the credit card companies, who would then cut off your credit, even limit your existing cards, forcing you into bankruptcy and ruin. I don't know why you didn't confide in me, or whether I could have helped you if you did, but you killed Roark. And hoped it would end there."

Grace had her head partially in her hands. She was still, however, watching Simon, tears rolling silently down her face.

As much as this hurt Simon and his old friend, he knew he had to go on. "But Brundish told you that he had broken the promise he made to you. Maybe he showed you Miss Clack's note. After holding on so long, and now feeling that Brundish betrayed your trust, you killed him, probably in a fit of anger, your rage expressing itself in such a savage, dehumanizing way. And you hoped it would be over."

Another breath, another sip of water. He was almost done. "Then Dagny Clack came to the Junction to finish the work Roark had started, and you found out the true nature of her selfishness and lack of concern for anyone, for this town. I think she recognized your vulnerability, and told you her complete, disgusting plans for the elimination of the Junction, its values, its way of life. She played on your weaknesses because she only cared about her own goals. In her eyes, you weren't a value creator, but merely another mouth at the trough, another Bob Cratchit with too little money and too many debts. Maybe she told you so? I hope you had second thoughts about killing her, but I suspect that she was unfeeling toward, perhaps even contemptuous of, you spending money that you would never earn. She had no concept of charity, of generosity of spirit, of compassion. If she had ever possessed any in life, her discipline long ago wrung that out of her. I think she shamed you beyond caring. And so you killed her."

Grace opened her mouth, but Detective Boggs stepped forth. "Ms. Beddoes," she began, "you have the right to remain silent…"

Grace listened to the Miranda rights in silence. When she was through, Grace spoke. "I understand," she said, her voice breathy. "The attack—" she offered weakly.

"Was fortuitous and unexpected," Simon continued, "and provided you a shield that I think you hoped would be enough. After all, a number of people had no alibis for either Roark's or Clack's murder. But you were the only person who could have murdered Brundish, because only you had been at the school after the gymnasium closed for the night."

"How can you say that?" Charity asked. She was shaking.

Simon looked to the back row. "Mimsie Tricket was the key. If only I had talked to her earlier at the ball, I might have saved Miss Clack."

"What did I do?" Mimsie said, standing.

"The pedals," said Simon. "I realized as I was listening to the organist play the pedals at St. Ina's. You told me at the ball that you hadn't unpacked the pedals that operated your display until after nine that night, but Grace told the mayor and me while we were judging that she had seen underneath your display, *in the afternoon*, how your village worked."

"She *did*," Mayor Dick said, aghast. "My God." Mimsie sat down, her body a deflated balloon.

Simon looked at Grace. "And when I knew that, I understood the rest. I think you brought in Brundish's body, tried to find a place for it, and saw that, if you put it underneath Mimsie's display, the body would be discovered earlier than you wished; therefore, you found Elmer's roomy wrapped package as a better—even more ghoulish—alternative."

The uniformed deputy joined Detective Boggs near Grace's chair. She stood. "Everything you say is true, Simon. I got so careless a few years ago. At first, just a few lottery tickets, then an hour at the video machines, then a day at the casinos. Everybody did it, you know, more or less. Apparently less. Finally the online opportunities. The money—I don't know where it went. Before I knew it, the rest of my inheritance was gone, between gambling and my losses to Micawber Investments. That stopped me for a while, but not long. At that time, it was so easy to get a new credit card and use it for cash, so easy to refinance one, two, then three mortgages. I knew I was in trouble before I started getting calls from Marley Enterprises to sell. I talked to Lowell. Nimrod and Reel was still open, but he was struggling, too, and Marley Enterprises was on the phone. We confided in each other, and pledged to do the right thing for ourselves and the Junction, not to give in."

Grace rubbed her eyes with her wrists. "But then Roark showed up," she continued. "He wasn't like that Mr. Venable and the others who called. He was here in the Junction, in my face, in everyone's face. He was so nasty to me. He knew everything, somehow—bank statements, credit card balances. I lied. I told him I would meet him at the storage shed because I had to help load up props for the tableaux. I was pretty sure I knew how long Brock would take between trips. I found the nail gun and—I intended to leave the body there, but somehow I wanted to humiliate Roark in death, the way he had tried to humiliate me. And it felt good to see him like that.

"Lowell promised—he promised"—she broke down momentarily—"but when he gave in, he didn't seem to feel any remorse for me, only relief for himself. We met at Nimrod and Reel. I killed him there and decided, once again, that he needed to suffer. I think, though, that I blanked out for a while—even I was shocked when I saw his body in Elmer's display. Please forgive me. It wasn't me. It's true about Mimsie's display—I had no idea when I said to you that I had seen underneath her display that I had given myself away."

Detective Boggs removed a pair of handcuffs from her belt.

"You don't need those," Grace said. "I won't cause any trouble."

"I'm required," was all Detective Boggs said. Grace stood passively as Detective Boggs cuffed Grace's wrists at her back.

"Dagny Clack was an evil woman," Grace added. "You're right, Simon. She had no generosity of spirit. She was a squeezing, wrenching, grasping, scraping, clutching, covetous, old sinner. In the cloakroom, she finally revealed the purpose behind her buying spree, and I hated it. I couldn't let the Junction be destroyed because I had been foolish with my own money. I had no idea that my actions could jeopardize others. She was mean-spirited, like Scrooge, and deserved to die the death he most despised. The holly and the nearby pudding were too tempting to pass up, never mind the danger of being caught. It was easy to kill her. By that time, I had nothing left to lose. I felt such relief when it was over."

Charity was crying, Viola was stifling her own tears, and Allegra Dick was weeping into George's shoulder. Simon felt his throat constrict as he looked into Grace's warm, tired eyes. Zach moved toward Simon and put his arm on Simon's shoulder.

"I'm so sorry, Grace," he said. "I wish it had been some other way. Old friends," he said, "tell old friends their secrets."

"It was too late," she said. "I was too embarrassed, and then too desperate. I didn't see any other way out." Tears fell on her cheeks and the lenses of the glasses around her neck. "At least the Junction is safe," she said. "Good-bye, Simon. I'll miss you."

Detective Boggs and the deputy led Grace toward the back room. Beyond that, just outside the rear entrance to the store, a sheriff's patrol car waited.

After the officers and Grace left the bookstore, the group remaining sat silent in their seats. Simon had followed Detective Boggs to the back, and when he returned to the main room, all eyes were on him, except for those of Duncan Neff, who looked at the floor.

"Since Grace didn't assault you," Viola said, "then who did?"

Simon stood near the second row of chairs, right next to Duncan, but was looking at Ariadne across the row and in front. She had a startled, frightened look in her eyes.

"While there may be sufficient evidence to get an indictment, I have decided, and Detective Boggs has agreed, that we won't press criminal or civil charges if the person who most likely assaulted me will agree to receive treatment for his illness." Simon stood away so he could look Duncan in the face. Neff, as if feeling Simon's eyes on him, looked up. He was angry, ashamed, defeated. "You have had trouble before," said Simon to Neff. "A previous driving while intoxicated conviction ten years ago before you and Ariadne came to the Junction. It's a public record in that county. Too much alcohol caused you to make bad choices. You were remembered at the Desdemona Club in Astoria the night of Brundish's death because of your disorderly conduct, you were obviously drunk at the Fezziwig Ball, and you had had at least a few cocktails at the Porters before you decided to get even with me for what happened at the council meeting the day before."

"You can't prove anything," Neff said, teeth clenched.

Ariadne got up from her chair and came over to the two men. "But if he doesn't agree—" she said.

"Just think about the defense costs," said Simon quietly. "I'm not trying to make trouble here—I'm trying to prevent more harm."

"I had no idea about the damage at the storage shed," Ariadne said. She put her hand on Duncan's forearm. Her voice was low and firm. "If we want to save anything," she said, "you'll do this." She stood again and looked at Simon directly. "Just not here, not in the Junction," she said. "I don't think we'll be staying here much longer."

She reached forward again and took her husband's arm. As he stood, Bethany rose and unlocked the front door, then went over and picked up Ariadne's purse and yellow raincoat from the floor beside her chair. She handed them to Ariadne as the Neffs moved through the door and out into the square.

Detective Boggs came back into the store from the back room. The individuals began rising from their chairs and moving awkwardly about, talking in small groups. Several thanked Simon, some smiling, some tearful. Brock held Bethany tenderly, Viola and Charity huddled together, and Mavis cried quietly on Brad's shoulder.

Solomon and Allegra Dick came over to where George, Zach, and Simon were standing. Zach had his arm around Simon's waist.

"We can't thank you enough," Allegra said to Simon, taking his hand in hers. Her hands were warm. "How you must feel, knowing it was Grace—"

"When it could have been me," the mayor said. "Or any one of us."

"That was the hardest thing," said Simon. "When I knew it was a friend."

The mayor and his wife moved away and made room for Detective Boggs. "Thank you, Detective," said Simon. He shook her hand. "I know this would never have happened without your help and encouragement."

"Don't say encouragement," she said, a hint of smile at the edge of her lips. "We never encourage citizens to risk their own lives to solve a crime. Let's say that you offered a unique opportunity to have evidence presented in a way that would not have been available with typical procedures. I'm sure it won't happen again."

"We shall hope for that," Zach said, pulling Simon closer.

"Yes," Simon agreed. "Let's go home."

ON CHRISTMAS DAY, THE MOOD AT BLEAK HOUSE WAS subdued. A fire burned in the fireplace of the breakfast room, which Mavis had transformed for the occasion into a dining room. She had decided to host a community meal. Ladasha and Bethany offered to cook, as long as the menu didn't include any stuffed fowl.

Savory aromas wafted into the living room, where the guests sat drinking cocktails and munching on chipotle black-bean cakes and goat-butter shortbread crisps while waiting for the call to dine. Simon and Zach sat on one end of the couch holding hands; Mavis and Brad Sturgess did the same at the opposite end. George, Viola, Charity, Solomon and Allegra Dick, and Joelle Creevy sat on the stuffed chairs and settees that lined the room and formed a rough circle. Brock sat on the floor beside George, the Tiny Tim crutch beside him. Father Blaise stood holding a Scotch tasting glass, his back to the fire. Mimsie Tricket and Elmer Cuttle had declined Mavis's invitation; they were going to visit Mimsie's aging mother.

"By the way," Mavis said, "when we returned home last night, Mr. Venable had paid, packed, and left without a note."

"I suspect we've seen the last of Marley Enterprises around these parts," said Simon.

A short silence followed.

"I don't think I stopped crying until after midnight," Charity said. The redness of her eyes supported what she said.

"Poor Grace," Viola said. "If she had said something, perhaps we could have helped her."

"I don't know," said Simon. "She had managed to accumulate more than half a million in debt over five years."

"Shocking," Solomon said. He looked at Simon. "I'm so glad we—"

"Let's wait until after dinner," said Simon.

Mavis looked around the room. "Let's decide right now. No more talking about the murders. At least for today. It's a holiday."

Everyone in the room nodded in agreement.

Bethany and Ladasha stood at the hall entryway. "Dinner," they said in unison, "is served."

The group filed into the makeshift dining room and took their places at the table. The highlight of the table was a medium-rare salt-crusted prime rib, pink and oozing with juice, along with horseradish sauce, Yorkshire pudding, whipped potatoes (Yukon gold and sweet), curried onions, roasted Brussels sprouts, bacon cornbread, and Waldorf salad.

"A magnificent spread, ladies," Mavis said to Bethany and Ladasha.

The group ate mostly in silence except for the sounds of forks against plates and crystal clinking as Washington cabernet flowed into the wine glasses, and later, the sound of pie servers scooping pumpkin and gooseberry pie onto dessert plates and stirring spoons hitting the sides of hot cups of coffee with cream.

"I think we have a few announcements," said Simon, as the coffee pot went around the table a second time.

"Yes, announcements," said Zach.

Simon gave him a puzzled look.

"Let's start with ours," Solomon Dick said, looking at Simon. "As you know," the mayor said, "Simon agreed to purchase my property. I accepted that offer, but since yesterday, we have renegotiated the price. I accepted market value only." Allegra bent forward and kissed her husband's cheek. "But I did exact from Simon a significant concession—he will allow me to continue operating Mr. Dick's, rent free." Several at the table exchanged glances. "With some changes," the mayor continued. "Mr. Dick's will no longer contain gaming devices of any kind. We're reinventing the shop as a gourmet lunch counter with a new, cutting-edge menu, featuring the latest food craze—"

"Sandwiches by Ladasha," Ladasha chimed in. "I will be the executive chef for Solomon and design and execute a new menu for Mr. Dick's." She looked at Mavis. "You knew I was leaving sometime," she said, smiling, since she wasn't going far.

"It's wonderful, Solomon," Mavis said. "She's been great for business here—I'm sure she'll do the same for Mr. Dick's."

"I'm going to open my own place one of these days," Ladasha said, taking her mother's hand, "but how can you turn down an offer where someone else covers the research, development, and overhead?" She cocked her wine glass in Simon's direction.

"I hope you don't mind the competition," Solomon said to Viola and Joelle across the table.

"Not at all," Joelle said. "Simon and I talked yesterday, and I also will be removing all of the gaming devices from the Porters. The Junction doesn't need them, and neither do I. I have a feeling that business will be booming in the new year. I just have to feel that way." She turned to her daughter. "And I don't think your haute cuisine will interfere at all with my fish-and-chips crowd. Besides, I'm thinking of bringing some new recipes in myself, from your grandmother's recipe box." She smiled at Simon. "Did Dickens ever eat shrimp and grits?"

"And I'll have more time to manage Mr. Dick's," the mayor added. "I will not be seeking reelection next year." Brad Sturgess, a bemused look on his face, leaned across the table with outstretched hand. Mayor Dick hesitated a moment until Allegra brushed his elbow and he reached out and gave Sturgess's hand a hearty shake. Then Dick looked around the room. "The job will be vacant. Any takers?"

No one answered right away.

"I might be interested," Charity said finally.

Simon looked at Zach. "Other announcements?"

Zach put down his wine glass and patted Simon's hand. "Yes, as a matter of fact. I have been in touch with my sometime employer, *Rainbows* magazine, and notified them—two days ago, actually—that I would only accept contract work from them in the future. Regarding the original reason for my visit, I have told the magazine that I can't do the article on Dickens Junction because I have a conflict of interest—I just accepted a new full-time job with *Household Words*."

Simon wasn't sure he had heard Zach correctly.

"The Junction's own Oscar Wilde," George said, "more or less."

"Zach made a compelling case, is all I can say," Brad Sturgess said. "I'm losing all of my interns after New Year's, anyway. Zach will be the primary news correspondent, with one investigative piece each month, one regional travel article, and a regular news beat. It's time to give the magazine a more modern edge." He looked at Simon. "We'll still keep all of the Dickens pastiche work, but the rest will be new. Fresh. Current."

"So I start right on January first," Zach added.

"Where will you live?" Allegra Dick asked.

Zach looked at Simon. "That remains to be seen."

"I'm excited for you," Bethany said. She looked at Simon. "I have to tell you, dearest Simon, that I won't be able to cook for you much longer."

"Because?" Simon asked.

Brock finished swallowing his last bite of pie. "Mom, everybody—Bethany and I are getting married." After a squeal, Mavis started crying.

Bethany held out her hand, proudly displaying the modest diamond she apparently had been wearing all day in the kitchen but that no one had noticed, due to all the amazing food before them.

"Oh my God," Mavis said, catching her breath. "When?"

"Sometime next year," Bethany said. "Brock and I need to work out a few details about my education and where we'll live."

"I'll do the cake," Ladasha said, glancing at Viola. "I promise I won't set it on fire."

"Would you marry us?" Bethany asked Father Blaise, her eyes moist.

"I'd be delighted," he said. He gave Brock a congratulatory pat on the shoulder.

"I knew I might have to look for a new employee sometime soon," said Simon.

Zach and Brad stood and started to clear the table. As he leaned down to remove Simon's plates, Zach kissed Simon on the cheek; Brad did the same to Mavis as he passed by.

"Where's the smoking bishop?" George asked. "Isn't that what Scrooge and Bob Cratchit drink at the end of the book?"

Simon smiled. "George, your literary erudition amazes me. In this visit alone, you've demonstrated knowledge of Ayn Rand, Henry James, Louisa May Alcott, and Dickens."

Ladasha left the room. Simon looked around the table. Despite everything horrible that had happened, small bursts of other things, good things, were happening, too. Zach's surprise brought opportunities, fun, and, Simon knew, the risk of hurt. He would give in to his feelings for Zach, let them fall where they may.

Simon remembered George's use of the word *joy* when he was encouraging Simon to be open to love again. Was joy in Simon's future? In Ladasha's? Brock's and Bethany's? Solomon's? And the others'? He could only hope.

Ladasha returned to the dining room, wearing oversize oven mitts and cradling a huge copper punchbowl topped with a heavy lid. "Smoking bishop, as ordered," she said, glancing at George. She placed the punchbowl in the middle of the dining room table. Bethany handed cups around.

Mavis walked over to the nearby sideboard, removed a ladle, and handed it to Simon. "The founder of our feast," she said.

Simon took the ladle and leaned in over the punchbowl as Ladasha removed the lid. Fragrant aromas of cloves, oranges, and port wine, plus the sting of warm vaporized cognac (Mavis's special added ingredient), forced Simon to close his eyes. When he opened them again, his vision was temporarily impaired by the heavy cloud of steam rising from the punchbowl and creating a moment of hallucinatory impressions—a hotel...a precious document...a brilliant jewel...exotic beauty, both male and female...blood? He could not know at that moment that, within months, these visions would recur, when he and Zach faced the challenges of *The Edwin Drood Murders.*

He pulled his face away from the cloud, slightly dazed until he felt Zach's hand slipping around his shoulder and restoring his sense of calm, comfort, and safety.

"I thought I'd lost you," Zach said. He pulled Simon closer and kissed him.

"Not that easily, mister," said Simon. "And not for a long, long, time." He leaned into Zach, enjoying the pressure and warmth.

Ladasha took the ladle from Simon and finished filling everyone's cups. George and Brock drank sparkling water.

With Simon in the lead, all raised their cups and glasses. The scene made his heart leap. On this day, of all days, he would enjoy the goodwill of his friends and, in a nod to Solomon and Allegra, his family. Simon hoped that it could be said of him that he knew how to keep Christmas well, if anyone possessed the knowledge.

"Happy holidays," he said.

"Happy holidays," sounded around the table.

Brock held his glass in one hand, his Tiny Tim crutch in the other. "God bless us," he said. "God bless us, every one."

ACKNOWLEDGMENTS

The curtains of his bed were drawn aside, I tell you, by a hand...and Scrooge, starting up into a half-recumbent attitude, found himself face to face with the unearthly visitor who drew them: as close to it as I am now to you, and I am standing in the spirit at your elbow.

-From *A Christmas Carol*, Stave Two:
"The First of the Spirits."

Many stood at my elbow to make *The Christmas Carol Murders* possible:

Critical readers: Elbert J. Boone, Rebecca Clemons, Candace Haines. Special thanks to Carol Frischmann.

Technical advice: Adam Roberts, Emily Way.

Inspiration from professionals: Rhys Bowen, Chelsea Cain, Margaret Coel. Thank you for everything.

My dream team: Kristin Thiel, Laura Meehan, Alan Dubinsky, Tina Granzo. Each of you found something in my vision and aligned it with your own great talents. The book is tighter, funnier, and more beautiful because of your work. Special thanks to Vinnie Kinsella and Jessica Glenn for making the book happen and for finding these wonderful Portlanders to work with.

To Mark Sanford for his November 2, 2009, *Newsweek* review of *Ayn Rand and the World She Made* by Anne Heller. Without his review and quotes I would not have been able to give voice to some of Dagny Clack's vision for Galtopia. And to Ms. Heller, whose book I read much later. She also grasps the special clash between the worlds of Rand and Boz.

Endless gratitude to Nancy Boutin. For keeping me honest. And at the computer for all these years.

The teachers: Eric Witchey, James N. Frey, Tom Spanbauer, Alan Cheuse.

Unique thanks to Carl Wilson, for being who he is.

To Charles Dickens, Wilkie Collins, Agatha Christie, and Carolyn Keene (among many others), whose books give Simon something to put on his shelves besides *The Fountainhead*. And who have given me a nearly infinite number of ideas.

And Evan: the next book, like everything else I have, is for you.

ABOUT THE AUTHOR

Christopher Lord was born in Astoria, Oregon, near the very heart of Dickens Junction.

His short stories have appeared in *Men on Men 7*, *His 3*, *Everything I Have is Blue*, *Confrontaiion*, *Harrington Quarterly*, *The James White Review*, *Blithe House Quarterly*, and *Lodestar Quarterly*. He has been a recipient of an Oregon Literary Fellowship from Literary Arts, Inc.

He and Simon have read almost all of the same books.

He lives in Portland, Oregon, with his partner Evan (who is not a writer).

The Christmas Carol Murders is his first published novel.

Please visit the website at *dickensjunction.com* for more news about Simon, Zach, and their adventures.

A NOTE ABOUT THE TYPE

Having been an early admirer of the beauty of letters, I became insensibly desirous of contributing to the perfection of them. I formed to myself ideas of greater accuracy than had yet appeared, and had endeavoured to produce a set of types according to what I conceived to be their true proportion.

—John Baskerville, *Anatomy of a Typeface*

The Christmas Carol Murders is set in **Baskerville** from Monotype, Ltd. This modern interpretation is based on John Baskerville's mid-17th century typeface. Baskerville produced a high contrast, humanized type that differed from the sterile, balanced fonts of his contemporaries. The Baskerville typeface is considered a transitional work bridging classical and modern typefaces.

The title treatment also incorporates Adobe's 2005 **Univers Lt Std**, originally designed by Adrian Frutiger and released in 1957 by the Deberny & Peignot foundry. A student at the time he worked on Univers, Frutiger based his typeface on Aksidenz-Grotesk, placing it among other neo-grotesque sanserif type (two others were also released in 1957: Folio and Neue Haas Grotesk, the latter later renamed Helvetica).

CPSIA information can be obtained at www.ICGtesting.com
Printed in the USA
LVOW10s1909310813

350413LV00003B/6/P